WHO KILLED
THE RABBI'S WIFE?

WHO KILLED
THE RABBI'S WIFE?

SAUL GOLUBCOW

WILDSIDE PRESS

With love, for my grandchildren:
Nathan, Ilan, Zachary, and Noa

ACKNOWLEDGMENTS

I had intended to write "a" story about an elderly Holocaust survivor named Frank Wolf who becomes a private detective in Brooklyn and solves "a" case. But after publishing the short story version of *The Cost of Living*, I discovered how much I enjoyed spending time with Frank and his family. So I continued writing about how he, with his grandson Joel, solves additional mysteries in the 1970s New York Jewish communities. The result was a compilation of three novella length stories in *The Cost of Living and Other Mysteries* released in 2022.

Many kind readers have asked over the last two years when Frank will next appear. With the publication of *Who Killed the Rabbi's Wife?*, Frank and Joel are back (along with Joel's wife Aliya) in a novel-length mystery that (hopefully) challenges the reader to pay attention to the details of the crime and figure out *who dun it,* while wrestling with questions of what is meant by being complicit in a murder.

Desire, energy and this thing called creativity can take you through many months of writing and re-writing—but then, you have your off-spring—the completed draft. While the writer may view it and feel satisfied that it is well done, one does not write for oneself. What will others, the readers, think? Trepidation aside, one must let go and allow the offspring to be exposed to the greater world.

Here is where I have been fortunate in multiple ways. For whatever I have written during my adult life, my wife, Hedy Teglasi, has been my first reader and, thus, my first line of defense against overdone prose, tin-eared dialogue, and self-indulgent insights. I love you for many reasons, but your honesty and clarity have very much guided my writing. Thank you, Hedy.

Then there is the *Doomers* writers group who welcomed me into their midst and read my draft from beginning to end. Barry, Carla, John, Karen, Meg, and Sandi, I would have had to pay thousands of dollars and spent years in a creative writing program to garner what I learned from you in a few months. My book's perspective is sharper, action moves more fluidly, "showing" replaces "telling," and various "how did I not see that inconsistency" are eliminated. Thank you, Doomers.

Susan Cavanaugh, your copy reading was extraordinary. I may have jestingly called you "eagle eyes," but based on your reviews of two drafts, you certainly deserve that attribution. And let's not forget about your clarifying questions which often made me consider that what's so important in my head may not be so obvious to a reader. The poems, your own writings, are so well crafted. Keep writing, and thank you, Susan.

There may never have been public exposure of Frank Wolf if not for John Betancourt, my editor and publisher at Wildside Press. John is a talented publishing professional with great ears and eyes for dialogue, syntax, consistency, flow, and perspective. John appreciated Frank Wolf for the character I intended him to be within the classic crime detective framework. "For the next one, try making it novel length," John suggested. I listened. A paraphrased 2000-year-old Jewish maxim states: one needs to acquire a teacher, and, in doing so, acquires a friend. With John, I believe I have both. Thank you, John.

—Saul Golubcow
Potomac, Maryland

WHO KILLED
THE RABBI'S WIFE?

All these years later, the picture of Batya Flaum's battered face still haunts Aliya. I also have my moments.

THURSDAY, JULY 3, 1975

I came home that afternoon to our apartment in Manhattan's Stuyvesant Town and found my wife, Aliya, at our small kitchen table with Shoshannah Marcus, her best friend. I stopped short, taking in how closely they sat near each other, the moistness in Shoshi's eyes, and the fright on both faces. Aliya's right hand pressed down on Shoshi's left, their fingers entwined.

Aliya and Shoshi, both 25, had gone from kindergarten through high school to the same Jewish, Modern Orthodox academy that I also had attended a year ahead. Both went on to Brooklyn College. Upon graduation, Aliya continued to graduate school in clinical psychology at NYU, while Shoshi, not yet 22, the daughter of Rabbi David Flaum, spiritual leader of Congregation P'nai Hesed in Brooklyn, married Ben Marcus. He was three years her senior and an accountant in the City with Arthur Young.

Shoshi now had two boys, Uri, three and Tzvi, ten months. Though they lived in an apartment off of Avenue M in the Midwood section of Brooklyn, a 45-minute train ride away, we saw Shoshi and Ben at least once a week. Ben and I played stickball on many Sunday mornings. I liked both of them.

Tragedy had struck Shoshi's family back on February 21, 1975, when someone bludgeoned Shoshi's mother, Batya Flaum, to death in the family home on East 10th Street in Brooklyn. Police never found the murder weapon and made no arrests. The newspapers indicated robbery as the motive since the assailant stole money intended for a bank deposit that day.

My gaze left their plaited fingers, and I looked from Shoshi to Aliya. "Oh, hi Shoshi, how are you?" I asked. But then I added, "What's going on? Are you two okay? And where are the kids?"

I came closer to the table. Neither Shoshi nor Aliya answered my questions. Instead, Aliya said, "Look," while she pointed with her free hand to an open copy of *The Daily News*.

Why would they have a copy of *The Daily News*? We and our friends read *The New York Times*. I peered down at a double-page spread across the fold that included pictures of the Flaum family and others.

After a few seconds and before I could say anything, Aliya closed the paper to the front page where the headline screamed: **SHOCKING DISCOVERY IN FLAUM MURDER CASE: RABBI HAD A MISTRESS**. Under the headline, I scanned crime scene pictures of Batya Flaum lying dead, a photo of Rabbi Flaum looking back at the camera from afar, and a shot of a fierce-eyed, attractive woman whom I did not recognize. Aliya flipped back to the middle section, and I saw that Martha Brennan wrote the piece. Brennan was known for her exposé articles. She also made frequent appearances on local TV news shows. Was she pointing the finger at Rabbi Flaum as his wife's murderer?

Shoshi unwound her fingers and stood. She was trying her best to withhold tears. "Joel, the kids are with my mother-in-law, and I need to hurry back to them." After leaning down and throwing her arms around Aliya, she said: "Please call me tomorrow after your meeting with Mr. Wolf."

Then turning to me, she added, "Aliya will explain."

Shoshi grabbed her bag and rushed out. I looked at Aliya.

"Tomorrow, at my grandfather's office? But our vacation starts tomorrow morning. What's going on?"

* * * *

Ninety minutes earlier, around 2:00, the phone had rung in my 43rd floor law office at Prentice, Walters, & Reis on Lexington Avenue near 54th Street. Larry Seidman, my mentor at PWR, congratulated me on having completed one year at the firm and indicated that with Independence Day tomorrow, I could leave early to start my two-week vacation. I thanked him profusely as any junior associate with one year under his belt would, ran out, and caught the #6 Train toward 14th Street.

After spending a year working long hours, often six days a week, I planned to enjoy a few days of doing absolutely nothing followed by renting a car and driving with Aliya around upstate New York and on to Montreal. Having never been more than 100 miles out of the New York City area in my 26 years—except for a high school excursion to Washington, D.C.—I pictured visiting towns and sites such as Corning, Seneca Falls, Saratoga, and Lake George with the same allure as if I were contemplating travels to Machu Pichu, Angkor Wat, or Victoria Falls.

* * * *

With Shoshi gone, Aliya arose and gave me a glancing hug. "I'm as disappointed as you are, but we won't be able to do our vacation plans this year. Shoshi and her family need our help desperately."

"But," I retorted, "we've been looking forward to our vacation for weeks now. What does this article have to do with our not going?"

Aliya picked up the paper and flung it down to the table. "Martha Brennan is implying that Rabbi Flaum is somehow implicated in the murder of his wife. Do you understand? Shoshi is dazed, angry, afraid. She doesn't know if she can hold it together in front of the children. Joel, you know she's like a sister to me, and we need to help her and the family."

"But how?"

Aliya took in a breath. "Okay, now listen. Shoshi came not only to cry on her oldest friend's shoulder, but also because her father knows that our being family might induce your grandfather into taking this case. Rabbi Flaum wants to hire Zaida to clear his name."

I tried hard to put brakes on my incredulity. "But I know my grandfather. He won't take a case on the basis of clearing somebody's name. I...."

Aliya put up a hand. "I'm not sure on what basis, but he's agreed to consider it. I already called him, and we're to see him in his office tomorrow morning. And Zaida instructed me to let Shoshi's father know that he is expected on Sunday at 1:00 in Zaida's office."

"You called my grandfather?"

"Yes, I have his number. Are you upset I called Zaida?"

"No, no, but tomorrow is July 4th!"

"And your point? Will his key not open his office tomorrow morning? Will the subway not be running for us to get to the Boro Hall stop? Look Joel, I know you're upset about missing our vacation, and I can understand to a point, but not to the degree of your grouching and not comprehending that we must help Shoshi."

With that, she turned and headed to our bedroom, closing the door behind her.

I sagged onto the couch and read the Brennan piece slowly. Then I knocked on the bedroom door to ask what I might put together for dinner.

FRIDAY, JULY 4, 1975

We walked the four avenue blocks to the Lexington Avenue #4 Train that took Aliya and me from 14th Street to Brooklyn's Boro Hall stop. The train was half full. It may have been Independence Day, but in New York, if only a fraction of the seven million people had to get somewhere, that meant a lot of traffic. Aliya and I exchanged everyday comments, and I hoped we had put our tiff behind us. But earlier, during a quick breakfast, she had said firmly:

"I'd like not to discuss the Flaum case until we get to Zaida's office, okay?"

I did not object. I did take note of Aliya's use of the word "case." After moonlighting with my grandfather for short periods of time on three previous cases, I had gotten used to his sleuthing ways and enjoyed, under his guidance, the challenge and—yes—the excitement of solving these crimes. I might have said that to Aliya, but for some reason I didn't. Instead, as we quickly walked the two blocks and up three flights of stairs to his office, my mind battled the disappointment of losing my vacation and wondered how a case so close to home would affect us.

Aliya quickly opened the door, but I had enough time to see the smoked glass door's painted sign that read **FRANK WOLF DETECTIVE AGENCY** was no longer flecked and faded as it was back in October when we worked the dorm murder case. It now gleamed with sharp, black letters. I had suggested to Grandfather that a badly tended sign at his place of business did not reflect well professionally, particularly after his successes and the recognition he had received. He had thought for a moment and smiled:

"Yoeli, I find your assessment reasonable. While the sign by itself will not affect my ability to execute my work, a well-maintained designation should signify the presence of orderliness on the door's inside. And it will be a good reminder to my own self."

The office contained a single window that looked out to the next building's red brick façade. In addition to the door's refurbishment, my mother and I had convinced Grandfather to install a top-of-the-line window air conditioner unit. The cool air blew well.

Grandfather came out from behind his desk. A spinal stoop reduced a thin 5'10" frame. Following his European custom even during the heat of summer daytime, he dressed in a white shirt, brown suit, a vest, and a tie with a gold-plated tie clasp that I knew had come from my mother's jewelry store.

A kippah covered wispy, silver hair that had been receding each year. He sported a silvery, pencil thin mustache which he tended with daily care. Sparkly eyes shone through glasses.

He hugged us and took Aliya's hand and mine in each of his own hands, forming a circle.

"Good morning, my children, I am very pleased to see you. Unfortunately, we have some troubling business before us, do we not?"

Grandfather returned to the swivel chair behind his desk. The only guest chair in the middle of the office faced my grandfather. I indicated to Aliya to take it, and I moved toward the desk to stand near Grandfather, the way I often had positioned myself during the previous cases. But now I stopped and awkwardly turned back toward Aliya, who had seated herself. I planted myself to her right, with my left hand on the chair back.

"Thank you Zaida," Aliya said quickly. "Just terrible for the family! Someone murdered Mrs. Flaum five months ago, and the murderer is still on the loose. Now all of New York suspects that Rabbi Flaum had something to do with it. You have met my friend Shoshi. She is furious at her father about the affair, but she's also furious about the article's implication that he had something to do with the murder. So she came to me to see if Joel and I could persuade you to take the case, to clear her father."

I watched Aliya as she spoke. Based on her appearance, people often underestimated her. She rarely wore makeup, especially during the summer. She usually wore her long hair pulled back into a ponytail, looking not much older than a teenager. But no one underestimated Aliya when she spoke in her firm voice. I had fallen in love with that contradiction.

Grandfather said softly. "My child, you do not have to convince me. I am eager to take the case. But I wish to be certain. It was Rabbi Flaum's notion to ask for my involvement?"

Aliya looked at me and then back at Grandfather. "Yes Zaida, it was Rabbi Flaum's own idea to ask for your assistance to clear him."

Grandfather leaned toward Aliya. "Then please understand that we would not begin our work with any assumption of Rabbi Flaum's innocence, yes?"

Was I vindicated to some degree about the terms for my grandfather taking the case? Aliya hesitated before saying, "Yes," and I nodded.

"Good then, my children, because if we are able to establish Rabbi Flaum's innocence, clearing his name also means that we must find the real killer. There is no other way, as otherwise he will always remain under suspicion. Do you understand the task before us? Are you willing to dedicate your efforts to assist me?"

"Certainly," Aliya answered, "whatever it takes. As you know, Joel and I were to be on vacation anyway for the next two weeks. I wasn't going to spend a minute looking at my dissertation. We can dedicate all of that time to working with you, Zaida. Right Joel?"

"Of course," I said. But then I added, "I'm used to working with Zaida, but I'm not sure what you would be doing, Aliya."

Aliya flinched. I quickly added: "What I mean is, we have to establish our game plan so we maximize our working together as a team."

Aliya said nothing, and we sat silent for a few seconds until Grandfather said: "Very well, my children, I see we are all agreed on the necessity of effort and time given to this case."

Grandfather picked up copies of *The Daily News* that were lying on his desk and handed one each to Aliya and me. They were yesterday's edition with the Flaum murder headline.

"I am sure we all read carefully the story published in yesterday's paper. Let us take a few moments to review again its contents and establish an overview of its allegations and incriminations."

Aliya folded her arms. "It's all sensational nonsense. She doesn't say it directly, but Brennan strongly ties this affair and one person's hearsay to Rabbi Flaum's having a motive for his wife's killing. There's no way Rabbi Flaum is connected to the murder!"

I put my hand on Aliya's shoulder as Grandfather responded. "Aliya, sha, sha, sha. I understand the emotions behind your words. For almost all of your life, you have been close with the Flaum family. But for now, let us try to put emotions aside and digest as objectively as possible the information in this article as an introduction to the case. Then through our own review of the police report, interviews, background investigations, examination of the crime scene, and perambulations of the neighborhood, we will utilize our critical analyses skills to build and enter the world in which Batya Flaum lived and was murdered. For our construction project, we will be interested in processing the emotions of others, with awareness of, but not imposition of our own feelings. Yes?"

We both nodded. I assumed that Grandfather would want me to start the article's review. But Grandfather said, "Aliya, might you begin anew?"

"Okay," she agreed. One year into our marriage, I knew Aliya's calmed and re-focused voice.

"The bombshell information is an interview that Martha Brennan had with Barbara Burns, a CPH congregant, who claims that she and Rabbi Flaum had been having an affair just previous to the murder. Burns is a television personality of sorts, a weather woman at WPIX. She's a divorcee, previously married to a Burton Horowitz but uses her maiden name, if it is her maiden name, for professional purposes.

"But here's the big deal. Burns claims that the affair had gone on for several months." Aliya stopped to thumb through the article. "Barbara Burns is quoted: 'He always told me that his wife was a real drag on his life, quarrelsome, not interested in his career, but he couldn't divorce her and retain his position and the important work he was doing for his congregation and his community. But after his wife's death, he still wouldn't commit to marrying me. He claimed it was much too soon, and his congregation wouldn't understand. So two months ago, I told him I had had enough. Since then, I felt freer and further away from the relationship, so I started thinking that he may have had something to do with his wife's death. I'm going public to prod the police to look again into Rabbi Flaum's possible involvement.'"

"And Rabbi Flaum, what have been his pronouncements?" Grandfather asked.

"In the article, the reporter indicates that Rabbi Flaum refused to talk with her when she appeared at the synagogue or at his home and that he has not returned her calls."

Aliya's muscles knotted under my hand on her shoulder. She continued. "After the article hit the streets yesterday morning, the rabbi called Shoshi and her brother, Jonathan, around 7:00 and told them to come as quickly as possible to the house on East 10th. Shoshi was surprised that her father wasn't at morning prayers at the synagogue. She and her brother rushed over. Shoshi said her father looked distraught. He acknowledged the affair with Barbara Burns, but he swore to them that he had nothing to do with their mother's murder."

"And the rabbi's children, what was their reaction?"

"Shoshi said she was stunned and angry about her father's affair." Aliya looked up at me. "You know how much she adores her father. I think she's put the affair part in the background to deal with it later. Her focus now is defending her father against complicity in the murder, which she insists is impossible."

"And the brother?" Grandfather asked. "What was his reaction?"

"Shoshi doesn't know for sure. She says Jonathan got up and left without a word to them after a few minutes of not saying much."

"And it was at the house that the rabbi suggested seeking my assistance?"

"Not quite. Shoshi returned to her apartment around 9:00 so Ben could go to work. At 10:00, her father called sounding much stronger and asked if Shoshi could request through me and Joel your help to clear his name. Shoshi didn't think twice, made arrangements for her mother-in-law to watch the kids, called me, and asked if she could come to our apartment. I, of course, agreed."

Aliya's muscles were still taut. I wanted to relieve some of the pressure and said: "Zaida, I'm glad we will be working on the case. How do we proceed?"

Grandfather shot me a quick smile. "Just a few moments more, Yoeli. Before we discuss our next steps, could you please continue to review who else is mentioned in the article and what information is provided about them?"

"Yes, of course." That Grandfather had turned to me pleased me. "There's also a flattering picture of Mrs. Flaum, perhaps from I'd guess several years ago. Mrs. Flaum is described as exemplary, devout, generous, family centered, and community oriented. She is lauded for having opened, with her partner Marcia Gelb, Bezalel Judaica Gifts, an arts and crafts store on Avenue J, as a service to the Jewish community."

"Please tell me," Grandfather asked, "did the reporter try to contact Shoshannah or her brother for the story? How are they mentioned?"

Aliya took this question. "After the murder and the bombardment of reporters' questions, Shoshi and Ben changed to an unlisted number. So Shoshi didn't get any calls, but she does remember a woman fitting Brennan's description coming to the apartment door. Shoshi suspected her of being a reporter and did not open. So she never spoke to Brennan before the story broke. And Jonathan, I don't know. He moved out of their family home a month after his mother's death, to a basement apartment somewhere off Prospect Park."

Grandfather followed up. "And let us review further. How are Shoshannah and her brother depicted in the story?"

I answered. "Brennan writes that Shoshi did not respond to her request for information. There's nothing else about her. Now Jonathan, well, Brennan reports that CPH congregants told her that he works with computers and that 'he has been employed on and off since graduating from college a year ago.' Zaida, I don't think you ever met Jonathan, but even though he may not be the best-looking guy in the world, that picture of him in the story makes him appear like a wild-eyed escapee from a lunatic asylum."

Grandfather threw me a look. While I may have gotten across my impression of how Brennan chose to paint Jonathan for her readers, I could have been more professionally descriptive.

Grandfather asked: "And the partner, Marcia Gelb?"

I wanted to reestablish my probity and hurried to answer. "She was interviewed by Brennan at the Avenue J store that Gelb has kept running. The story contains a picture of her. She's the smallish, heavyset woman standing behind a counter. Brennan includes Gelb talking about still being traumatized after finding the body, the wonderful relationship she and Mrs. Flaum had as business partners, and a slew of other compliments about what Mrs. Flaum meant to her, the congregation, and community."

Grandfather stopped talking and raised his eyes toward the ceiling. I imagined his sorting information into various mental folders to be retrieved when needed. Finally, Grandfather said, "And there is a photo of another individual in the story, do I remember correctly?"

Aliya relaxed somewhat. I took my hand off her shoulder and hoped she would reply. After a moment, she did.

"You mean besides a flattering picture of Barbara Burns, there's a terrible picture, this one of Burton Horowitz, her ex-husband. He is standing with his fist raised, snarling something at the photographer and perhaps Brennan herself. Brennan writes that he shouted 'no comment' to all of her questions.

"I imagine he was dragged into Brennan's story to further sensationalize it. Horowitz is a real estate developer, quite wealthy, and a major contributor to the synagogue. While they were still married, he and Barbara Burns used to live in Brooklyn before they moved to Jamaica Estates in Queens."

Aliya blushed. "I know all this from Shoshi and our gossip sessions growing up. He and Barbara would drive to services on Shabbat, as do several other CPH members."

Grandfather shrugged. "Yes, driving on the Sabbath is not permitted in the Orthodox tradition, but I do not judge them in any way, my child."

"So Zaida," I remarked, "that pretty much completes our review of who is pictured in *The Daily News* story and what's written about them. Brennan gives very little information about the murder itself, as if she takes for granted her readers know the background and are only interested in the sensational news about the affair and its contrived implications."

"Yes, Yoeli, the journalism profession, and the tabloid journalism profession even more so, must examine its role in how it contributes to providing information ethically and factually in our open society. Since Gutenberg changed the world over 500 years ago, we have been presented with this challenge, yes?"

Grandfather picked up his copy of *The Daily News*. "But we have the means to clarify what is presented in the story, do we not? We shall ask Martha Brennan to come to this office to discuss what she has uncovered."

Aliya and I looked at each other.

"We will?" I gasped. "She's going to agree?"

Grandfather opened his hands toward us. "And why would she not? Is it not to her benefit to do so? Are we not, as investigators called in by Rabbi Flaum to assist, now part of her story? Joel, you will please call her and let her know you are part of a team at the Frank Wolf Detective Agency working with police on the case based on the new information her story has provided."

"I will, but we're working with the police?"

Grandfather chuckled. "Is it possible, my children, that I have not yet informed you that once again, our friend Sergeant Max Fink of the 90th Precinct in Williamsburg, who helped us immensely with the Yosele Rosenstock case, has contacted Detective Anthony Carlucci in the 61st Precinct who is leading this murder investigation? Detective Carlucci welcomes our involvement and has made copies of the police report for us to review."

Looking from me to Aliya, Grandfather then asked: "Might you pick up the report at the 61st Precinct on Avenue U and the East 15th Street before the Sabbath descends on us tonight? It is perhaps not a too far distance from our house?"

"We will," Aliya answered, rising and reaching for my hand.

"Wait, wait, wait." Grandfather motioned for Aliya to sit. "There is more for us to discuss and plan. We will review the police report Sunday morning at 10:00 with Detective Carlucci, who has agreed to meet with us in his office before Rabbi Flaum joins us here at 1:00. It will be beneficial to ask the detective questions about the report prior to the rabbi's arrival. The Flaum house is no longer a crime scene, but I believe it is incumbent on us to visit it to gain any additional knowledge and form our own impressions of where the murder occurred. We must make arrangements when we speak to Rabbi Flaum. Following our interview with the rabbi, we will determine the other individuals to interview and in what sequence."

"Yes," both Aliya and I uttered at the same time. Then I said, "So we'll pick up the police report, do a read, and drop it off at the house for you to look at before the Sabbath begins. Then we'll come by Sunday morning to go together to see Detective Carlucci."

Grandfather replied. "Not fully, Yoeli. You and Aliya also need to return to your apartment to bring appropriate clothes for staying overnight at the house and going to services tomorrow morning at Congregation P'nai Hesed."

"We're going to services at P'nai Hesed tomorrow?" I exclaimed.

"Yoeli, if you had not been taken by surprise, I think you yourself know the answer. The shocking news has just been released. How will Rabbi Flaum deal with it in front of his congregation, which will certainly fill the sanctuary? We will benefit from observing him, the congregation, and perhaps the various people mentioned in the story."

It's not that I was opposed to attending services the next day, but something just didn't sit right with me. Would we be violating some ethical or religious principle if we used a prayer service for a business purpose?

"But Zaida, I've never seen you work on the Sabbath. Wouldn't we be doing so if we go to CPH tomorrow?"

"You are correct to wonder, Yoeli. I also questioned my motives and ultimate rationalization. In the end, I believe I will pray no differently than if I went to my usual synagogue. We are never capable of shuttering our eyes from what we see when we are at services, so we will absorb what we absorb. We will not discuss the case per se during the Sabbath, and we will not process what each of us observes until evening descends. But I will not be disingenuous. What we see, what we absorb will stay with us and influence our analyses and subsequent conversations."

Before I could respond, Aliya said. "We will all go to services together. No question about it."

"Very good," Grandfather replied, looking more at me than at Aliya. "I have already spoken to your mother, who as usual on Fridays will be home by 3:00 from the jewelry store. She is eager to prepare a Sabbath meal for us. And if you arrive early, you might help your dear mother with the preparations, yes?"

* * * *

Aliya and I left Grandfather's office at 11:30. We walked for ten minutes to the DeKalb Avenue station to pick up the Q Train to the 61st Precinct station. When we came to Willoughby Street to head down to Flatbush Avenue and DeKalb, Aliya stopped us at a phone booth.

"I should have called Shoshi from Zaida's office to confirm that Grandfather agreed to take the case and that Rabbi Flaum should come to Grandfather's office on Sunday at 1:00."

Aliya was not on the phone for long. The three-minute timer clinked, and Aliya ended her conversation. We resumed walking, and she linked her arm with mine. For the few minutes until we reached the station, we discussed the case, with Aliya vehemently insisting that Rabbi Flaum could not have been involved in the murder. As we were about to descend the steps into the station, she stopped and gave me a kiss on my cheek.

"What's that for?" I asked with a grin.

"To thank you for being you. I know sometimes you pout, but I can count on you to catch yourself and regain an equilibrium for what's needed. That's not something guys your age do easily or well, so again thank you. And I appreciate the battle you're waging against yourself to not be a male chauvinist, like when you wondered what I, a woman of all beings, could do to be helpful on the case."

I blushed and could only say "You're welcome. And I'm trying."

* * * *

After a 25-minute train ride, we came down to the sidewalk from the Avenue U Station platform. We could see the limestone-yellow 61st Precinct just ahead. But we also noticed a kosher falafel restaurant on Avenue U, and we were suddenly hungry. It made sense to eat before picking up the police report.

"We close at 3:00 today," the raspy voice of a man, partially visible from behind a glass partition, called out.

I understood that a kosher restaurant closed early on Fridays so as not to violate the Sabbath, but did he really think we would hang around for three hours?

The man had a dark complexion with a white goatee and a maroon embroidered kippah that covered a mound of white hair. He spoke with a Middle Eastern accent.

"You serve yourself," he pointed toward a glass buffet station lined with chafing pans and bowls filled with falafel, pita bread, hummus, tahini, baba ghanoush, olives, pickles, Israeli salad, red cabbage, and assorted sauces. "Sit where you like, eat as much as you want, and when you are finished, come here and pay me. Everything is $2.99 a person, tax included, with a soda in that case against the wall 50 cents, tax included, extra. If you don't want soda, there is a water fountain and cups next to the sodas. No cards, just cash, and if you want to tip, leave tip on the table."

Aliya and I filled our plates. The falafel shop had a back window with an air conditioner that kept the room bearable. The soda case that proclaimed **COKE—IT'S THE REAL THING** wept moisture along its glass front that hid the selections inside. I slid the case open and took a mostly-cold bottle of Coke. Aliya helped herself to water in a paper cup.

We found a wobbly, paint-chipped red steel table for two with plastic utensils on paper doilies and a napkin holder in the center. Diners took up five or six other tables, two with police officers, probably from the 61st Precinct.

"I'd like to talk about your grandfather and his approach to solving cases," Aliya said as soon as we sat. "I think I get it when he talks about 'critical analyses,' but I want to make sure. You've already worked cases with him, so you must have a good feel for how he operates. I want to fit in and, as soon as possible, contribute to this case. So go ahead, tell me your grandfather's definition of 'critical analyses.'"

I took my first food bite. "Okay," I answered after swallowing hastily. "Some of what I'm going to tell you is almost verbatim from what I've heard him say and some my own understanding."

"Good enough, go on."

"To start, it's classic detective stuff. And Grandfather already mentioned some of it back in his office. Examine the crime scene, look at the official police report, determine and then study evidence, and interview everyone known to be connected to what occurred. Then Grandfather says we may allow our critical analyses engine to start shaping our conclusions."

Aliya ate slowly, her eyes narrowed. When she ate during a discussion, mastication and deliberation were synchronous gears.

"So, Joel, if we are good detectives, we observe and listen to the stories each individual weaves from the events surrounding the crime and built-in assumptions and emotions by which the person understands life. Concurrently, we try as much as possible to set aside our own built-in assumptions and emotions as we make our way into the minds and the hearts of the others, right?"

Before I could respond, Aliya laughed heartily. "Hah, it's a good deal like what I'm being trained to do in my clinical psychology program. But does Zaida think we're like robots, that we can get away from our emotions?"

"Not at all. I think Zaida would say that when the detective is confident that the crime's environment is well established, that there is sufficient confidence in the 'facts,' and that contradictions in the facts are exposed and filed for further examination, then the detective's gut is allowed to express itself, such as with a hunch."

"And our emotions, Joel?"

"Well, I'll just answer with how I've observed my grandfather dealing with emotions as he works a case. After completing the cerebral part of the investigation, he carries both the facts, the main actors' emotions, and to a limited extent his own emotions into the world of the crime scene, all the way to that 'emotional' instance when the crime occurs. For instance, Zaida's own personal emotions as a parent and a Holocaust survivor led him to figure out who killed Joe Stein in the murder of the Boro Park butcher, the first case I worked with my grandfather."

"Joel, what about motive? I haven't heard you say a word about it. We watch TV police and detective shows, and they're always bringing up motive. Seems to me that in the three cases you worked with your grandfather, motive had little to do with the crime, right?"

Aliya caught on quickly. Did it threaten me? A bit. But as the saying goes, "love conquers all."

"Yes, you're on the right track. I think Zaida would say that 'motive' should certainly be pursued when solving crimes. But he often has said that so much harm and evil are perpetrated on the individual and societies without tangible premeditation that comprehending the near motiveless nature of some crimes is essential. And so with Joe Stein's death, Yosele Rosenstock's kidnapping, and Ori Gold's murder."

I had mopped my plate clean minutes before. Aliya finished, stood, and said: "I think I'll fit in just fine. Let's get the police report and start solving this case with your grandfather."

I put a dollar bill on the table and gave the white-haired man a five and two singles. He rang it up and slid change back to me.

* * * *

I didn't say it out loud, but back at the falafel shop I felt like cautioning Aliya with "patience, my love, patience." The irony, I thought, is that while Grandfather had shushed me to have patience, he had solved each of our three cases in just a few days.

The desk sergeant at the 61st had three copies of the Batya Flaum murder report ready for us, and we were in and out within a few minutes. Despite the heat, we walked briskly to the Avenue U station, where we hopped on a Q Train just as we hit the platform. We both had the same idea — read the report while we rode, since we didn't have to switch trains to 14th Street.

* * * *

Around an hour later, we were back in our apartment eager to shower. Aliya, who had grown subdued, went first. I didn't have to ask why. On the subway, when I came to the graphic pictures of Batya Flaum's body lying on the foyer floor of her house, I looked over toward Aliya. She was pale, with terrified eyes frozen on the worst of the pictures showing Mrs. Flaum's battered face. I turned away when Aliya finally went on to the next document, but short of patronizingly suggesting that she stop looking at the report, I couldn't do anything. When we exited the 14th Street station, Aliya stopped and took my hand.

"Joel, do you mind if we don't discuss the report just now?"

"Of course, I don't think my grandfather will bring it up until Sunday morning when we meet with Detective Carlucci."

We finished our showers and since the Sabbath didn't start until candle lighting at 8:20, I wasn't in a hurry to get to Flatbush.

"We've already had a long day," I suggested. "How about if we nap for an hour or so?"

"Thirty minutes," Aliya countered, "and we take a cab since we need to bring dress clothes for services tomorrow. More importantly, it's the end of the week, and your mother is probably tired from working in the store. Your grandfather's right. How about we help her with dinner?"

"Sure," I said. I had forgotten Grandfather's suggestion of helping my mother prepare. Growing up, except for taking out garbage, I didn't do domestic activities such as cooking or cleaning. My mother never asked, and it never struck me to volunteer. After I got married, things changed. Aliya made it clear that I had two hands and a brain and could put together a meal as well as she could.

The cab let us off at the house on East 7th Street off Avenue P at 5:00. My mother was busy preparing a traditional Friday evening feast of salad, noodle kugel, chicken soup, brisket, and string beans, with mandel bread and compote for dessert. Grandfather sat at the kitchen table keeping her company. My mother rushed over to welcome us. After hugging her, Aliya and I went and kissed Grandfather. He smiled broadly.

We dropped our stuff in my former bedroom and returned to the kitchen. I gave one of the police reports to Grandfather, while Aliya went straight to a drawer and took out two aprons. Grandfather opened the folder, thumbed through quickly, and closed it. He then stood.

"If it is acceptable to you, Malkeh," he said addressing my mother and then Aliya and me, "and to you, my children, I would like to take this police report to my room for a careful perusal. Only two hours remain before it is the time to go for the Sabbath eve service. And I see here I can offer little assistance."

I shrugged, and Aliya nodded. But my mother, using the Yiddish word for father, said: "Fotter, of course it's alright. But might you instead just rest and put off reading the report until tomorrow evening when you will have renewed strength?"

"Malkeh, I understand your concern," Grandfather answered, "but I feel I have the strength at this moment to review clearly the report so that my mind might digest information for storage before the Sabbath is upon us, and I separate from work."

She didn't press further. Perhaps because my mother survived the Holocaust in hiding as a child, she constantly feared for the safety of those she loved. One day as a thoughtless teenager, I had watched my mother nag Grandfather about dressing more warmly as he prepared to go out on a cold winter's day.

"C'mon Mom," I had chided, "he's a grown man and can take care of himself." After all, I had reasoned, he had taken care of me all my life, especially after my father died when I was 14.

My mother responded evenly. She spoke with a slightly accented, clipped tone. Her cadence was similar to Grandfather's, though with a much lesser accent. "Ever since the War and the time in the cellar, particularly after your Bubbe Rivkah's death, your Zaida and I have been taking care of each other and worrying about each other. I might be obsessive, but please understand."

I made an effort to understand back then but more so during the cases Grandfather and I worked together. I noticed there were times when I felt energetic, and Grandfather might show fatigue. When I charged ahead walking to the subway, he would be a few steps behind. When climbing steps, he would be out of breath. So I, too, wished he would relax for the two hours, but I was certain he would not. Instead, he would fine-tooth-comb the report word for word, picture by picture, forensic result by result in preparation for our discussion with Detective Carlucci on Sunday.

In the kitchen, I accepted my sous chef tools and precise instructions on how to prepare the salad. I joined in now and then while my mother and Aliya spoke about the cooking, current events, what they would wear to services the next day, whether Ashe or Connors would win Wimbledon, and the mediocre seasons the Mets and Yankees were both experiencing.

Having been ardent Dodgers fans before the Dodgers moved to Los Angeles, my family couldn't possibly replace them in our hearts by rooting for the Yankees. So in 1962, in their first year of play, we became ardent Mets fans. Aliya's father grew up in the Bronx and strongly favored the Yankees. When Aliya and I married, our friends kidded that we were having an interfaith wedding.

My mother and Aliya had become very close. Right after our marriage, Aliya's parents moved to Florida. We saw them twice during the last year, and while Aliya spoke to them over the phone once a week, the dreaded long-distance charges hung over each conversation until one of her parents ended the call saying, "This is getting expensive. We'll talk again soon."

Her sister Brenda, six years older, lived with her husband and three children across the river in Fort Lee, New Jersey. In the year Aliya and I had been married, they had not come to us once. A few times, when Aliya and I were not overwhelmed with our work, we visited them for a few hours on a Sunday.

Often when Aliya and I spent the night at my childhood home, I would yawn and coax Aliya into coming to bed. But if she were in the midst of a conversation with my mother, Aliya would say, "Joel, you go ahead. I'll come in a few minutes."

If I were still awake when she came into the bedroom, I'd ask her what she and my mother discussed. "Oh, this and that," Aliya would answer, assigning general categories such as food, fashion, or gossip. There were times Aliya would say, "Your mom just wanted to get something off her chest," or "Your mom wanted to process something that was troubling her."

At first, I would ask somewhat peevishly, "Is she okay? What exactly did she want to discuss?" But then Aliya would draw me toward her and answer soothingly, "She really is okay. If there were something really wrong, she would tell you. But you know how a confidante can't tell someone else what was confided? I'd like to respect your mother's trust."

"But she never has confided in me in that way!"

Aliya pulled me even closer. "I think if you let go of your only child preoccupation and think about your mother's history, you'd understand."

After a few similar discussions, I stopped pressing. During those moments I started my "letting go" journey that culminated years later, shortly before my mother's death. Then, with her overall memory failing, she recounted precise portraits of fear—the six years she and my grandfather hid in the country house cellar during the Holocaust; her mother dying from a fever in that cellar with nothing besides a cold cloth to her burning forehead; she and Grandfather scraping out a grave in the dark of night in nearby woods to bury her mother; coming to America at 21, speaking little English, and dealing with the tumult of Brooklyn after six years in isolation; frozen to our home's front window when I was five and my father took me out on East 7th Street to teach me how to ride a bike; watching my father smoking on our back porch, nagging but to no avail until he passed away from cancer when I was fourteen.

At 7:15, Grandfather emerged from his bedroom with his suit jacket on and carefully placed his fedora on his head. He looked toward me. In anticipation, a few minutes before, I had changed into a dress shirt and slacks with my Sabbath kippah bobby-pinned to my hair. I knew he would appreciate my accompanying him to services at the Oseh Shalom *shtiebel*, literally "little house synagogue of making peace," on Quentin Road, just a few minutes walk. Grandfather had attended services there since moving to the East 7th Street house with my parents a year before I was born.

Even after my mother and father became members of the Modern Orthodox Young Israel of Ocean Parkway Synagogue, my father and I would join my grandfather for Sabbath eve services at the *shtiebel*. It took up the ground floor of a large duplex, an unadorned, one large room synagogue with a wooden ark that housed two Torahs. Prayer books and prayer shawls piled tables, and around 50 metal folding chairs faced the ark. A strung red velvet divider separated the Men's from the Women's section.

But at these Friday evening services, I never saw any women. They remained home preparing the Sabbath meal. The men all seemed to be elderly like Grandfather, all Holocaust survivors, mostly from Hungary or Austria, speaking Yiddish or Hungarian. I remember the dim light of the room, the men holding the prayer books close to their eyes, no one minding my roaming at will between the aisles and all around the room. The men would look up when I passed, smiles on their faces as hands gently reached out to pat my head.

At the end of services, as everyone greeted each other with "a gutten Shabbos," out would come an assortment of candies from camphor or cedar smelling suit pockets, handed to me and the other young boys. As hard as I tried, I couldn't avoid the men's pinches to my cheeks.

When I arrived home, I would tell my mother: "I like the candy Zaida's friends give me, but why do they pinch my face?"

My mother would enfold me in her arms. "First of all, good Shabbos to you, and second, they pinch your face because they love that children like you are here. They lost so much during the War. You represent the best of their past and hope for their future. You are so important to them, to us, and I love you." But I wondered: by pinching my face?

Sabbath eve services at the Quentin Street *shtiebel* moved briskly, lasting around an hour. They included quick afternoon prayers and a Sabbath-welcoming prelude to the evening prayers. When I was younger, around 40 men attended, but as I now looked around, I counted fifteen—including Grandfather and me. There were no children, and I was the youngest by far.

Back at our house, the smell of freshly baked challahs welcomed us. A scallop-edged, white linen tablecloth covered the rectangular dining room table. Sabbath china and wine glasses adorned the table along with a decanter of sweet wine and two seltzer bottles with siphon valves. In the middle of the table, the two braided challahs lay next to each other under a satin, embroidered covering. At a far end of the table sat two trays, each with two silver-filigree candlesticks holding candles lit about an hour earlier. Aliya and my mother stood by the candles. Both wore white lace head coverings. Aliya had changed out of her shorts and tee shirt into a flowered summer dress.

Grandfather, with his eyes closed, sang the blessing over the wine, followed by Aliya holding aloft the two challahs and pronouncing the short *motzi* blessing. Breaking off a piece of one of the breads, she handed a portion to each of us. Before I married, that honor belonged to me, but for the last year whenever we came for Friday evening dinner, Aliya and I switched off, remembering as best we could who had performed the blessing last.

With the pre-Sabbath meal rituals completed, we started eating. Aliya, who always had felt comfortable during dinner conversation, now spoke little and ate even more slowly. After the main course, as was our practice, I helped my mother clear the table and prepare the tea and dessert in the kitchen.

When we came back to the dining room, I saw that Aliya had moved her chair closer to Grandfather and her eyes were moist.

"What's wrong?" I asked, placing my items on the table.

Grandfather gently motioned my mother and me to sit. "Yoeli, there is nothing, as you state, 'wrong,' but your wonderful *kallah* is naturally upset about the Flaum case."

Grandfather's use of *kallah*, the Yiddish term for bride, eased some of the tension. We were married over a year, but Grandfather still used the word. Aliya and I made a bet for how long he would continue. Aliya predicted forever.

Aliya dabbed her eyes and moved her chair back. "I'm upset, I'm frightened, I'm sad, I'm angry, and I've held it together for most of the day since leaving Zaida's office. But if I could talk about it with the people I love for a few minutes tonight, I think I'll be able to handle what will be very difficult days starting tomorrow and Sunday."

And then looking at my mother, Aliya asked. "Would that be okay with you, Mother?"

I knew why Aliya had directed that question to my mother. Since she worried about my grandfather's being a private detective, my mother would find excuses not to listen to Grandfather's "work" conversations. How would my mother answer?

With no hesitation, my mother said gently, yet firmly: "Yes Aliya, I am fine with your request. Please, let's have a family conversation, and I will participate where appropriate."

"But are you okay, Zaida, to discuss a case on the Sabbath?" I asked.

Grandfather preempted any further debate. "My children, I believe we may accomplish both objectives. Let us venture to mitigate Aliya's upset not by an attempt to solve the case of Mrs. Flaum's murder for which we are not nearly prepared, but rather by simply viewing a portrait of the main character in the news of today, Rabbi David Flaum, and the reputation he maintains as a leading Jewish figure in New York. We often discuss news events during the Sabbath, do we not? And in this manner, Aliya may feel unburdened by not carrying her weight in isolation."

My mother, Aliya, and I looked to each other and nodded. Aliya spoke first: "I just want to say that while the Rabbi cheated on Mrs. Flaum, no way did he have anything to do with her murder. I know it's premature to say this because we haven't even started to investigate. But that is how I feel."

Aliya then looked from me to my grandfather. "It wouldn't be fair to our team if I didn't share my convictions up front and promise that I will do my best to keep an open mind as we work together."

Grandfather reached toward Aliya, and she took his hand. "I am sure you will do well," Grandfather said, "and we will do our best to recognize your feelings and perhaps even make use of them in comprehending all emotions surrounding the crime. But for now, Aliya, might you begin telling us about Rabbi Flaum, since you have known him for years? And we will take turns joining in with our own perceptions. Consider that we do not wish for analyses but rather factual information and impressions."

Aliya did not hesitate. "I've known him since I was five. He always seemed a great dad, loves his children, sometimes a bit pedantic to Shoshi and Jonathan but always caring and interested in their thoughts. When I was around, he seemed to be a loving husband, constantly calling Mrs. Flaum an *aishes chayel,* a woman of valor."

Grandfather looked away from Aliya. My mother, to my surprise, responded. "I'll share one impression. Do you remember, Fotter, that I went with Joel and Aliya for a Shiva visit at CPH after the burial, since the Flaum home was still a crime scene and throngs of people were expected? I knew Mrs. Flaum casually, both as one of my customers at the jewelry store and at various women's club functions. After all, she was a leader in Hadassah, ORT, Federation, and several more organizations. I wished to honor her memory by making the Shiva visit. I didn't know many people that evening, so I spent my time observing, especially the Flaum family.

"In the shul's social hall, chairs were set up for the mourners and their visitors. Shoshi looked devastated, her eyes filled with tears. Jonathan looked very uncomfortable, as if he wished to flee. And Rabbi Flaum, though he sat low to the ground on the required mourning bench and was unshaven with a mourner's tear in his shirt, he was composed and holding court, receiving the condolences of a stream of people, bantering, and even smiling at times. I don't mean to be judgmental, but I was struck by his behavior."

My mother looked toward Aliya and blushed as if she had said something wrong.

"I hope, Aliya, I haven't upset you even more," my mother said.

"No, Mother," Aliya answered. "Not at all."

"Do not be uneasy, Malkeh," my grandfather said. "We do not take your words as an indictment or reproach but simply as a reflection to take into account once the work begins on this case."

Aliya looked at Grandfather. "I do know from Shoshi that Rabbi Flaum very much supported his wife starting up her Judaica gift shop. And okay, I did hear the two of them argue at times, and Rabbi Flaum would say, 'Batya, when it comes to matters of the synagogue, I appreciate your point of view, but I will make my decision.' But that happened only occasionally over the course of my being around their house over 20 years."

Glancing at me, Aliya added. "And which couple doesn't have these sorts of fights from time to time?"

I smiled slightly and said: "Rabbi Flaum is a really important figure in the New York Jewish community, especially in Brooklyn. I recall seeing pictures of him in *The Times* with city and state leaders, with Robert Moses at the World's Fair in 1964, and with Shirley Chisholm, the congresswoman from Bed-Stuy, the night she won her first election, I think back in 1968. I also remember the front-page picture of Chisholm coming to services at CPH on a Saturday, and Rabbi Flaum at a community center in Bed-Stuy on a Sunday.

"And, oh yes, he's quite a speaker. He's the only rabbi I know for whom teenagers and college students come into the synagogue's sanctuary to hear him speak instead of heading out to the foyer or street to mingle and flirt when the sermon is about to begin."

No one spoke for several seconds. Grandfather broke the silence.

"Very good, very good, my children. I would like to add that I have for many years followed the career of Rabbi Flaum with great interest. I consider him one of the great Jewish thinkers of our time. His books of commentaries on the Torah and Talmud, along with his critiques of contemporary Jewish life, are marvels in creative thinking. So I tremble to think he was involved in this heinous crime. Are you aware that he also holds a doctoral degree in English literature from the Columbia University, having written his dissertation on *Daniel Deronda*, the magnificent novel by George Eliot? His dissertation was later published with the title, 'Daniel Deronda, George Eliot's Prototype Zionist.'"

"I remember when you brought it home," my mother interjected. "Over 20 years ago when Joel was a toddler, but I never did read it. I'm sure it's in your bookcase for me to pick up."

Grandfather nodded and went on. "It is not only that Rabbi Flaum is a scholarly man, but of greater importance is what he is doing to promote what can be beautiful about Orthodox Jewry."

My grandfather then took me by surprise. "Joel, do you recall when we were working the Yosele Rosenstock case, and you were better acquainting yourself with the tenets and strictures of the Hasidic groups in Williamsburg? You sensed their nature to be closed off, not wanting their children exposed to what some might term the liberal behavior of others. And do you recall what you then asked?"

"I asked, I guess snappishly, if they then reject all the advances that modern life brings us. And I remember, probably verbatim, your comeback of, 'What advances, they would counter, pointing to the slaughter of millions just 30 years before in the Holocaust!'"

Grandfather smiled broadly. "Yes, yes, Yoeli, precisely what we said. But I brought up our past discussion to place in contrast how Rabbi Flaum views Orthodox Judaism. He does not fear the outside world whatsoever. For Rabbi Flaum, Judaism, with its core values and beliefs, can coexist with science, psychology, art, music, literature, with some theological limitations but no basic conflicts. He is quite comfortable blending secular knowledge with sacred wisdom. In this manner, we may make our religion stronger and the world around us better. And really, this recognition has been part of us for millennia."

Grandfather looked down and placed a forefinger to his temple, which I had learned from childhood meant he was trying to pinpoint a certain event in time.

"Please help me, Malkeh," he said, turning to my mother. "When was it that Yoeli had his chicken pox?"

My mother did not hesitate. "March 13, 1954, a day before his fifth birthday."

"Yes, good," Grandfather said excitedly. "Over 21 years ago."

Grandfather lifted his head and swept his hand toward Aliya and me. "The children certainly won't remember, but, Malkeh, do you remember what Congregation P'nai Hesed was called at that time?"

My mother thought for a moment. "Yes, I believe it was called Congregation B'nai Hesed, was it not?"

"Yes, yes!" And surveying the table, Grandfather asked: "What then is the translation of B'nai Hesed?"

Aliya responded quickly: "Children of compassion."

"Yes, yes," again Grandfather responded gleefully, looking from my mother to Aliya as if his daughters had won the class spelling bee.

And referring to his favorite Yiddish language newspaper, he added: "On that day when Yoeli became afflicted with the chicken pox, I read an article in *Der Tog-Morgen Zhurnal* that reported on a new, young rabbi, who had come to Congregation B'nai Hesed and had changed, with the board's approval, the synagogue's name to Congregation P'nai Hesed, meaning…?" Grandfather looked at me.

"The face of compassion," I answered.

Grandfather passed on to me the same proud look he had given my mother and Aliya.

"Yes, the face of compassion," Grandfather reiterated, "compassion within the congregation itself and to the outside world. I was very taken by the newspaper's interview with the rabbi. And going forward from the time of his arrival, he and his congregation have become the face of what we are calling modern Orthodox Jewry.

I imagined that Aliya probably felt the same way as I, and probably my mother, about my grandfather. How in the world did he remember so well an article that he had read 21 years ago? And on the same day I came down with chicken pox?

When Grandfather followed up with, "It is possible that we have participated in a good conversation about Rabbi Flaum," I knew he intended, with his attempt at delicacy, to end the exchange. My mother had pointed out years ago that when he opened a sentence with "Is it possible?" he wished to drive further discussion. But when he opened a sentence with "It is possible," he wished to end the conversation.

So I understood the returned look of concern on my mother's face and why she said: "We all must be very tired, and tomorrow looks to be a very interesting day. So *Fotter*, would you like to retire and prepare for bed while we clear the table?"

"Merely one more question," Grandfather replied. "We have not heard that Rabbi Flaum will not be at his synagogue tomorrow morning for services, yes?"

Aliya answered. "I spoke to Shoshi right before the Sabbath began. She says her father is determined to be at services tomorrow morning. That he wants to address the congregation. And Shoshi will be there but without the kids and Ben."

"Good, let us conclude with grace after our wonderful meal, and then, as my daughter suggests, I will retire."

* * * *

I knew I wouldn't get much sleep that night. The slightly larger than twin size bed of my youth didn't impair our sleep. Aliya and I were young and adaptable. For me, involvement in a murder investigation per se did not contribute to sleeplessness. No, having worked with Grandfather, I had a couple of murders under my belt. Yet just one shot had killed Joe Stein. Just one blow to the head had ended Ori Gold's young life. But the haunting pictures in the police file showed that Batya Flaum's face had been viciously beaten in.

In addition, Aliya and Shoshi were best friends. Aliya knew the Flaum family. We were close to Shoshi and Ben. And on top of everything lay the complication and implication of Rabbi Flaum's affair and possible complicity in the murder. How would we keep our professional distance? And I worried deeply about our investigation finding moral or legal culpability with one of the revered leaders of the Jewish community and the resultant impact.

But my angst was manageable compared with Aliya's. In general, I was less intense and able after a while to compartmentalize and grab a few hours of sleep. Most of the time, Aliya would log-like fall asleep and remain so until morning. But when she had something on her mind, sleep would be unattainable. She would move from side to side, her legs pulsing out a beat that expressed the tension in her body.

After what seemed hours of Aliya's agitation, I interrupted her movements and gently pulled her toward me. Not knowing exactly what to say, I offered: "Is there anything you want to talk about that might help you get some sleep?"

"No… Yes!" Aliya answered, turning her head within the curve of my arm. "Joel, I can't get the picture of Mrs. Flaum's battered face out of my head. I just can't. Am I right that someone hit her over and over, even though the first blow to the head alone might have killed her? Why hit her more?"

I had not fully absorbed the medical examiner's conclusions in the police report, so I said: "I've learned from my grandfather that stuff happens in a moment that begs rational understanding. I know it's awful."

"It is awful." Aliya sat up. "I am also so angry. Her murder cannot become a cold case, and I don't think Rabbi Flaum is involved. I want to contribute to finding the killer."

I coaxed her back to my shoulder. "I'm sure you'll be a big help, and we'll find out who killed Mrs. Flaum. But right now, we should relax the best we can. Tomorrow will be another tough day when we go to CPH."

Aliya made a sound of agreement, but a minute later she left my shoulder, and the night toss and beat continued.

I dozed the best I could.

SATURDAY, JULY 5, 1975

At 7:30, Aliya and I came out of the bedroom and saw Grandfather and my mother at the kitchen table. Grandfather, fully dressed, had his fedora already planted on his head, a sure sign he wanted us to leave on time.

"Good Shabbos," he welcomed us with a smile. He drank his heavily milked coffee accompanied by a cheese Danish, his usual Saturday morning fare when we ate a light breakfast before departing for the synagogue.

My mother, in a black, round-neck midi dress with elbow length sleeves and moderate-heeled gold-buckled shoes, hugged us and said: "Good Shabbos, please have a little to eat."

"You look beautiful, Mother, "Aliya responded before taking a seat.

My mother reddened. "Thank you, Aliya."

We ate quickly and returned to our room to finish dressing. Aliya put on a floral, sleeveless knee-length dress with a white linen jacket. I donned a white shirt, paisley tie, and a two-button, navy double-knit polyester suit with five-inch lapels and large pocket flaps that we called "Mr. Weekend." A year earlier, before I started at PWR, Aliya and I went to the garment district in Manhattan and purchased six suits, naming five for each work day of the week, and one "Mr. Weekend." On my Robert Redford cut hair, I bobby-pinned a black leather kippah.

"And here I thought I wasn't going to see any of our 'Mr.' suits for two weeks." Then I added quickly, "But it's okay, really."

Aliya changed the subject. "Your mom really does look nice today. Did you notice her new make-up?"

"New make-up?" I fumbled. "Uh, maybe."

Aliya laughed and shook her head. I didn't know if her reaction contained amusement or pity. But she said, "I know she's your Mom, and we tend to see our moms as figures who don't appear to change from day to day or even year to year, but others notice her appearance, her personality, her sense of humor, and her generosity."

When Aliya first met my mother, she mentioned to me how much my mother looks like my grandfather. "She has the same thin build as your grandfather, the same roundish face, cheekbones, and skin tone, the sparkly eyes, and the restrained smile. She's short, but maybe had she not been malnourished during those six years in hiding, she would have been taller."

My mother's appearance? I had not thought about it before. But now I expressed interest. "Others? What do you mean by others?"

"Not important right now," Aliya replied. "Let's go, they're probably waiting for us."

Out the door by 8:10. If Aliya and I were walking, it would have taken us around 25 minutes. But given Grandfather's pace, we projected around 45 minutes would get us to the synagogue on East 10th and Avenue I right before services began at 9:00. If anything made my grandfather testy, arriving late did.

We headed north on East 7th toward Avenue I. For early July, it was a beautiful morning, 60 degrees, partly cloudy, and with low humidity. We passed two-story duplexes and single-family homes of dark brick and white siding, a driveway on one side, a narrow alleyway on the other, and aluminum fencing to separate properties.

The fronts presented fenced-in shrubbery and flowers on a lawn no larger than the home's living room. Humming air conditioning units stuck out from windows on the second floors. The owners cared for their homes, the bricks finely pointed, the aluminum siding clean and bright. Many had a five-step stoop leading to the front door.

On Saturday mornings in the spring and summer, men or teenage boys, most of them non-Jewish, whose families went to church on Sundays, mowed grass using reel lawn mowers. I loved the smell of cut grass in the early morning.

Young kids had already taken over the elm- and Norway-maple-lined streets with games of stoop ball, double-Dutch, freeze tag, and on-the-street punch ball. Cars crawled, brakes screeching. Part of me wanted to stop and join the kids, especially when right before Avenue O, Richie Colavito, my stoop ball partner when I was a kid, stopped his lawn mowing and clasped his brick-laying hands around me. Richie married at eighteen, and he, his wife, and three children took over one of the duplex units in which he grew up.

Other Jewish families made their ways to various synagogues in Flatbush. Grandfather and I walked together and set a slower pace. My mother and Aliya, with arms linked, followed behind. I had not accompanied my grandfather to Saturday morning services for a while, but our walk reminded me of when I had. Now, instead of asking me about my studies, Grandfather wanted to know about the types of my accounts at PWR. Even though I worked in the firm's securities division, Grandfather seemed to understand, even my jargon. We talked about our beloved Mets. Buoyed by World Series appearances in 1969 and 1973, we rued how mediocre they were this year under Yogi Berra. And as before, Grandfather offered some thoughts on the Sabbath's Torah portion.

When we turned on Avenue I toward 10th street, I saw on our right the elementary school Aliya and I had attended.

"Joel," I heard her call, stopping us until she and my mother caught up. "Seeing our old school made me think how simple and carefree we were back then, and now I think about…"

Aliya did not complete her sentence, and none of us rushed to fill in the words. I took her hand, and we continued in silence.

Congregation P'nai Hesed was a three-story brick building with Moorish styled, multi-colored bricks. One large and three smaller horseshoed arches defined windows. Two minaret-like structures rose from its roof. At 8:50, as we neared its entrance, I thought it odd seeing streams of people entering the building but not stopping to talk as they usually did. On other Saturday mornings, only a handful of dedicated worshippers such as my grandfather would go in even a few minutes before nine. Many would come later or stay outside to socialize even into the service time.

We were about to follow Grandfather's cue to head inside when I heard, in a slight accent similar to my mother's, "Molly, good Shabbos." We turned and saw a bald, middle-aged, bespectacled man, around 5' 8", his head covered by a large knit kippah. He smiled at my mother.

"Good Shabbos, Martin," my mother responded. "We are about to go in." Did I spot a blush in her cheeks?

"Yes." Martin nodded, taking in each of us. "Then I hope to see you soon, Molly."

Grandfather nodded his head toward the entrance, and we headed through the door. Out of the bespectacled man's earshot, I whispered to Aliya: "Who is this Martin guy?"

Aliya shrugged and nudged me toward the men's doorway to the sanctuary. "Just another congregant," she whispered back as she took my mother's arm and strode toward the Women's section.

As soon as Grandfather and I entered the sanctuary, we worried that all of the seats in the Men's section were occupied. Grandfather gave me a look which said, "See what happens when we don't give ourselves enough time to get to our destination." We turned to head down the main aisle in hopes of spotting some empty seats when two college-aged boys in the last row jumped up and motioned for us to take theirs.

"Please," one said, "we'll just stand in the back."

Grandfather bowed. "Thank you, we appreciate your graciousness."

We sat, and I spotted Aliya and my mother nearing the front of the elevated Women's section. Shoshi stood and had apparently saved seats.

I had been to CPH several times before, but I once again absorbed the beauty and grandeur of the interior. The Men's section, stretching from the back entrance to the front, took up the central area of the sanctuary. Shiny maple pews, with hinged folding desks to hold prayer books, created rows to the right and left of a center aisle.

We faced east toward the sanctuary's front where on a raised flooring platform stood a handcrafted, gold lacquered wooden ark with black doors that contained the Torah scrolls. Words etched in Hebrew atop the ark's center proclaimed *KNOW BEFORE WHOM YOU STAND*.

Three steps both on the left and right aisles led up to the platform. A wooden lectern, also gold-lacquered, with a seven-bulb candelabra in front of it, took up the platform's center.

Two black-padded, ornate, high-backed wooden chairs flanked each side of the ark. Rabbi Flaum sat to our right in a chair closest to the ark, a younger man in a beard whom I didn't know at his left, and a white-haired man sat on the seat near the ark to the left. President of the synagogue? No one sat in the fourth chair to his right, sometimes occupied by a visiting dignitary or a guest cantor.

At the middle of the sanctuary, a rectangular podium with an elevated reading table called the *bimah,* where readings from the Torah and prophets took place, dominated the center aisle. Four shiny brass poles with wreath-like floral patterns and topped by lightbulbs rose high at each corner of the *bimah*. I remembered from my religious school education the practical reason for the *bimah's* placement: from the center of the sanctuary, everyone can hear the reading clearly.

To our right, a five-foot maple wall with carved floral expressions, separated the Women's section with similar pews. I stood for a moment and saw that my mother and Aliya had taken seats on either side of Shoshi.

"I take it your mother and Aliya are well seated with Shoshannah? Yes, I am correct?" Grandfather asked.

I nodded and sat down. With a minute until the start of services, a buzz of whispers ran through the sanctuary along with the mass turning of heads. In particular, heads looked toward Rabbi Flaum and Shoshi.

Grandfather leaned over and whispered: "Might there be someone else present who appeared in the newspaper article?"

I quickly swiveled my head, and my gaze landed on a man sitting on the aisle two pews down on the right. I thought back to the Brennan piece. The man had to be Burton Horowitz, the ex-husband of the *femme fatale,* Barbara Burns. He had a frozen expression as he gazed toward the ark. I whispered his location to Grandfather and then, after a few more swivels, "No one else that I see."

Precisely at 9:00, the prayer leader at the front of the synagogue began his chant of the morning blessings. When he intoned, "Blessed are you, Lord, who straightens the bent," I knew from my religious school lessons, it literally referred to helping us to stand up straight after being in a compacted position as we slept. But I couldn't help thinking that I wouldn't mind help unraveling Mrs. Flaum's murder. And when he chanted "Blessed are you, Lord, who gives the weary strength," I thought of my elderly grandfather facing a daunting case.

Following morning prayers, the parade of the Torah commenced, carried by an individual from the ark to the central podium *bimah*. Along the way, congregants leaned out from the pews to touch it. At the *bimah*, readers chanted the week's Torah portion followed by an extract from the Prophets. At their conclusion, a reverse processional returned the Torah to the ark.

Rabbi Flaum had no role in these rituals.

Then, as hundreds of voices sang the closing verses of the Torah service proclaiming that the *Tree of Life and its ways are pleasant and peaceful*, the doors to the ark closed, and congregants sat down. Rabbi Flaum headed to the lectern in front of the ark. With well-practiced tidying pulls to the broad, woolen prayer shawl draped evenly around his shoulders and back, he stood unbent, presenting a look of confidence. The congregants were pin-drop quiet. His eyes scanned each area of the sanctuary, and I thought his gaze lingered a second longer in the direction of his daughter. He put his hand to his mouth, coughed, and began. He spoke without notes.

"Good Shabbos."

He waited a moment for the usually raised voices reply of "Good Shabbos." But only a few of the congregants in the packed sanctuary murmured responses. He must have noticed.

"A few minutes ago," he began, "we read the combined Torah portions of *Matos/Masei Tribes/Journeys*, which conclude *Bamidbar*, the *Book of Numbers*. In the *Matos* portion, Moses conveys to the twelve tribes of Israel the laws governing vows, their commitments, and annulments. In *Masei*, the Israelites' journeys, from the Egyptian exodus to their location just outside of the Promised Land, are listed.

"Here, at Congregation P'nai Hesed for the past 21 years, I have had the honor of being on a communal journey with you. Our goal has been to make ourselves, our congregation, our community worthy of a promised land. We have journeyed together, dealing with the bumps on our road and valuing the shared effort.

"Throughout our journey, we have made commitments to the probity, sanctity and trustworthiness of our intentions and exertions. And each Yom Kippur eve, at the Kol Nidre service, as we ushered in our day of atonement, we reviewed our vows, asked for release of those impulsively given, and forgiveness for where we have failed. Today, this Sabbath, I stand before you and admit that I have let at least one Yom Kippur go by when I was aware of having broken an essential, most personal vow, and did not change my behavior.

"I am sure you are aware that I am alluding to breaking my marriage vows not only to myself but, of course, to my wife, Batya Flaum, may she rest in peace. I rationalized, I found excuses, I blamed outside forces, and I blamed my dear wife, Batya herself. I am grievously sorry, and I am so ashamed.

"Following her horrible death, I was deeply moved by the outpouring of support for me and my two wonderful children. I will never forget and never adequately be able to express my gratitude."

Rabbi Flaum stopped for a moment and his eyes swept over every area of the sanctuary, once again lingering momentarily on Shoshi.

"But when it comes to my sinfulness, to my shameful behavior, I certainly cannot at this time forgive myself nor ask for your forgiveness. Personal sorrow and shame are not sufficient reasons for begging forgiveness, as I have also brought sorrow and shame to those who expected and deserved better."

Rabbi Flaum paused and looked down before lifting his head: "Thus, I will be taking leave from my beloved congregation to allow time for reflection for myself and for you, for me to heal with my family whom I have grievously wounded, and to provide distance for CPH congregants to mull, to discuss, to debate if there is a desire for me to continue as your spiritual leader should I wish to do so. The correct action may be for me to resign, and I promise I will come to that decision in the shortest period of time after severe contemplation.

"In addition, regardless of the insinuations spun by the recent newspaper article, I swear to you that I had nothing to do with my wife's death. Given my previous dissimulation, I can understand that many of you may not accept my word. Thus, my stepping away also allows time for my innocence to become fully resolved.

"Toward that end," Rabbi Flaum raised his gaze toward the back of the sanctuary where Grandfather and I were sitting, "I am hiring our community's well-known private investigator, Frank Wolf, both to clear my name and hopefully find the real killer."

Hundreds of eyes danced in our direction, and I shrank into myself. Grandfather put his hand on my knee and squeezed gently.

Rabbi Flaum turned and looked at the man who had been sitting near him during the service. "We will now complete our prayers. Know while I am away, you are in good hands with our associate rabbi, Gabriel Abramson."

Again sweeping his gaze over every area of the sanctuary, he ended with. "A good Shabbos to all." Once more hitching up his prayer shawl around his shoulders, Rabbi Flaum returned slowly to his seat.

The crack of a loud, angry voice overtook the buzz that had just started in the sanctuary. I knew to whom the voice belonged before turning to look.

"What an incredible phony you are!" Burton Horowitz screamed. The congregants around him shrank back in confusion and, perhaps, fear.

"Taking leave! Really! Resign now! You are the rabbi of death, one way or another. You may or may not have had your wife killed, but you certainly killed decency! Resign! Get out! I can't stand the sight of you."

Horowitz stormed past us to the back of the sanctuary and the exit. A woman tried to stop his departure. He flew by her, and she quickly ran after him. I recognized her—Martha Brennan.

Following Horowitz's explosion, some congregants headed toward the exits, not so much, I guessed, out of sympathy with Horowitz, but rather for having already witnessed the drama for which they came. Grandfather and I remained with most of the other worshippers for the service's concluding prayers, led by Rabbi Abramson in record time. Grandfather and I had exchanged glances but said nothing. With the final Sabbath morning melody sung, we rose, and Grandfather hugged me tightly. We then exchanged Sabbath greetings with those around us and left. Others who were hurrying out as Grandfather trudged slowly with me at his side jostled us.

We left the building at noon. The July heat had expelled the morning's coolness. Several hundred congregants had now taken over the corners along Avenue I and East 10th Street spilling out of the sidewalks and onto the streets. Traffic backed up, and angry honks reverberated loudly in contrast to the whispered talk of those clumped in small groups, looking around constantly to determine who or what else they could spot.

Grandfather and I didn't see Aliya or my mother, so we waited on the sidewalk near the synagogue entrance. I took the opportunity to survey the crowd for Burton Horowitz or Martha Brennan. I didn't locate either. I looked at Grandfather, who shook his head sadly.

"A terrible morning, yes, Yoeli? But might we not discuss the events we just observed, as it is the Sabbath? Let us use the restfulness that the Sabbath offers to separate from the ugly and rejuvenate our spirits for the work we have promised. Tonight, after darkness descends, we will spend a few minutes reviewing our thoughts, yes?"

"Okay," I replied, even though I would have loved to get into the case right then and there. "But I must tell you I spotted Martha Brennan at the back of the sanctuary as Horowitz stormed out." I once again surveyed the crowd. "Right now, I don't see them anywhere."

I had expected anger to flash across my grandfather's face for the offense, I believed, the woman gave to the Sabbath service. Instead he said calmly: "I did not see her, so I thank you for your keen powers of observation. Might you remember what she was wearing?"

Why did he need to know that? I closed my eyes and pictured those chaotic seconds. "A white, long sleeve blouse over a black, knee-length skirt. More, I cannot be sure."

"Did she carry some sort of purse, pocketbook, or notebook?"

Still confused, I replied: "No, not that I remember."

"Good. Let us please return to my request that we delay any further discussion of the case until after the Sabbath."

Within a few minutes, Aliya came out and hugged us. "Shoshi rushed off to be with her father, but she sends her Sabbath greetings."

"My grandfather has once again asked that we don't discuss the case until after dark tonight," I offered in exchange. "But where's my mother?"

"Oh, she just stopped to say hello to a friend."

"To a friend?" I persisted, but before I could go any further, I saw my mother come out with the bespectacled man, Martin. I didn't hear what they were saying to each other, but the man looked toward us and nodded in greeting before turning back and giving my mother a smiling goodbye.

* * * *

On the way home, my mother and grandfather walked ahead. We couldn't hear their conversation, but they appeared relaxed and unhurried, as they usually did on a Sabbath afternoon returning from services. Aliya and I hung back, partly to give them space to be together, but, if truth be told, mostly to hide our agitation and desire to discuss the morning's events. Did Grandfather's not hearing somehow rationalize violating his trust?

"Martha Brennan was at CPH," Aliya gasped. "Wow! That takes some chutzpah."

"And Grandfather doesn't seem to be bothered," I added. "He asked about what she was wearing and if she had a pocketbook or a notebook. Strange, but I know better than to relegate a Grandfather question I don't understand to irrelevancy or weirdness. We'll ask him tonight. What did you think of Rabbi Flaum's talk? Shocked that he's taking leave?"

"Not really," Aliya answered, her voice rising. "I think he was pompous when he elevated himself while in self-censure mode. He made his decision to take leave with the possibility of resigning a virtue instead of explaining he really didn't have any other option."

Aliya's response surprised me, but before I could say anything, she went on. "It's as if one moment I was prepared to listen to and accept the words of a man I utterly respected for most of my life, but suddenly I heard the voice of a betrayer and manipulator. I'm not saying that now I believe he had something to do with the murder, but I am very troubled that I harbor some suspicion. And it makes me feel terrible. I love Shoshi. She's my best friend, and it's her father. I don't know what to think."

"And Shoshi, how did she take it all, including the Horowitz outburst?"

"It was awful, Joel. At first she was relieved that your mother and I had joined her. 'Aliya, I feel the whole congregation is looking at me,' she said. When services began, her hands lay knotted in her lap, and she prayed fervently with her lips moving and eyes closed.

"When her father approached the lectern, Shoshi grabbed my hand. She kept looking at her father and then away, as if she thought it her duty to be respectful but in conflict doing so. At one point, she whispered, trembling, 'I think my father just looked right at me. Aliya, I don't know what to do.'"

"And when Horowitz exploded?"

"Shoshi recoiled as if a bullet had struck her. Your mother put her arms around her. As soon as Horowitz finished, I don't know if you saw, Shoshi left through the sanctuary exit to Rabbi Flaum's office."

I shook my head, and Aliya went on. "'I need to be with my father when services are over,' Shoshi told me as she left. 'I think he's going to head straight to his office.' Also, I'm sure Shoshi didn't want to push through the crowd with us to the main exit."

* * * *

Back at the house, we ate lunch with halting, polite conversation as if each one of us may have been afraid that a certain word or a certain memory of the morning might lead to the case being brought up.

Around 2:00, Grandfather announced wanting to take his usual *Shabbos* nap. My mother enthusiastically encouraged his pronouncement.

"I think everyone can use some rest," she said, glancing at each of us. "But first I will take a leisurely walk in the shaded area of the park and return to join you for a nap. I sit so much at the store during the work week."

A sudden drowsiness urged sleep. A year of short nights and long days had accumulated. Aliya's sleeplessness the night before and the events of the last two days had piled on to my exhaustion.

I welcomed Aliya's words: "Joel, your mother's right, we can all use some rest." She took my hand and headed us to the bedroom.

We didn't even try to talk about the case. Our eyes closed quickly, and we slept until 5:00 when the sound of the front door opening and closing woke us. We came out of the bedroom and saw my mother taking off her summer hat before joining my grandfather in the living room. He sat in his worn, vinyl-clad easy chair with his feet on a matching footstool. He was reading a Talmudic tract.

A bit cobwebby from the long nap, I blurted: "Mom, you're just getting back?" along with, "Zaida, what are you reading?"

My mother and grandfather gave each other a "that's our Yoeli" look. Aliya laughed.

"Well, since you started with me," my mother responded, "I went over to a friend's house after we met in the park. I'll be okay without a nap today."

Before I could ask anything further, Grandfather said: "I am reading from the Talmudic tractate of *Sanhedrin* that deals with criminal law and definitions of homicide."

Grandfather placed a bookmark in the volume before closing it. "Although the subject does touch on our investigatory work that will continue in a few hours, it is permitted on the Sabbath to study the writings and wisdom of the Torah and commentaries such as the Talmud, even if the subject ties to one's work. After all, is there anything worthwhile that one can read from our teachings that does not have a connection with everyday challenges and questions? I believe, my children, that we can rest and grow at the same time."

After a light, dairy-based dinner, I accompanied Grandfather to his *shtiebel* for Sabbath ending prayers. I'm glad I went because without me, there would not have been a *minyan*, a quorum of 10, for the service to proceed.

Back home after darkness descended, we performed the *Havdalah* ceremony of holding a large lit candle aloft, drawing in pleasant smells from a spice box, and sipping wine as we declared the Sabbath to be over and wished each other a coming good week. My mother said she was going out again to visit a friend. Aliya and I gathered around Grandfather in his easy chair. Just as my mother closed the door behind her, the phone rang.

When I answered, I heard the fright in Shoshi's voice: "Joel!" I quickly motioned for Aliya to come to the phone. "Is everything okay, Shoshi? Do you want to speak to Aliya?"

I was about to hand the phone to Aliya, but Shoshi replied: "I can talk to you. I won't be long. I need to get back to my father because things are not okay."

"What's happened?" I held the phone away from my ear so that both Aliya and I could hear.

"A terrible thing. I walked with my father from morning services back to our house. In front of the house, Burton Horowitz, came out of nowhere and confronted my father. He started yelling the same things he yelled at services, so loud that neighbors could hear and started to come over. My father tried to calm Horowitz down, but he became even more enraged. He stepped close to my father and grabbed his suit lapel. When my father tried to defend himself, Horowitz pushed him. My father fell. He scraped both hands badly and the back of his head a bit.

"Horowitz continued snarling at my father and then stomped off. A neighbor helped my father up and wanted to call the police. But my father said he wasn't hurt badly and that it wasn't a police matter. I took my father into the house and cleaned him up. He says it's just a matter of time for his scrapes to heal. I am so upset about my father—and with myself."

Aliya took the phone. "Why Shoshi, why are you upset with yourself?" Aliya moved the phone away from her ear.

"Because," and we could hear Shoshi weeping, "I didn't do anything. I just stood there, petrified, like one of Lot's daughters, unable to move or cry out until Horowitz left. That's why."

"Shoshi," Aliya answered in an almost whisper, "you experienced a terrible shock back in February, and shocks again in the last two days, culminating with this attack on your father. I'm not sure if I—" Aliya looked at me. "—or even Joel would have acted any differently."

I blinked and almost showed disagreement. Had Aliya included me to make Shoshi feel better? Of course, I assured myself, I would have taken action.

"Do you need us to come over tonight? Is your father still meeting with us tomorrow afternoon?" Aliya asked.

Shoshi's voice crackled, but I could make out: "No need to come tonight. I'm staying with my father. Hopefully Jonathan can be with him when I go back to Ben and the kids in the morning. And yes, my father insists that he must see Mr. Wolf tomorrow. I'm hoping that Jonathan will drive him, but if not, my father will take a car service."

Grandfather listened intently as we relayed our conversation with Shoshi. Arthritic pain had intermittently beset his body, revealed in grimaces, quickly suppressed. While he hadn't seemed afflicted in the last few days, as soon as we began speaking, that look appeared. When we recounted Horowitz's attack, the constrictions spread more deeply, with Grandfather narrowing his eyes in what I took as painful empathy.

When we finished, he said: "Genius is to be found in various places, including in the Shakespeare's *Macbeth* when the witches chant the seemingly childish rhymed verse of 'double, double, toil and trouble.' There is much wisdom in the five words. Various factors, which we must determine, led to Mrs. Flaum's slaying. A crime, a murder left unresolved, begets multiple furies, distress, and further wrong-doing, including violence."

"So, you don't think Mrs. Flaum was murdered as part of a robbery?"

Grandfather gave me a glance as if to say, "Not so quick, Joel." Then he continued.

"First, allow me to respond by saying even if the slaying was part of a robbery, is not the slayer still at-large and possibly committing additional crimes? Joel, we are at the beginning of the investigation, and as you had learned previously, all possibilities must be laid before us so that our critical analyses may be employed."

Aliya leaned toward my grandfather. "And I want to say that after this morning, I am sadly open to the possibility that Rabbi Flaum was complicit in his wife's death." Aliya then shared what she had confided to me on our walk home.

Grandfather extended a wan smile toward Aliya. "I am glad, my child, that you are open to all considerations, but are you doing so for the wrong reason? Is it possible that in your distress and in your solicitude for your friend, what you interpreted as the rabbi's pomposity has pushed you to wanting to punish him for your disappointment? If so, you would be entering the case with a bias, yes?"

I thought I knew exactly how Aliya felt at that moment, having gone through that sort of introspection before with Grandfather. On the one hand, I would feel defensive, reflexively wanting to deny the imputation, and on the other hand, I would allow an emerging admittance to suggest he might be right.

"Thank you, Zaida," Aliya responded quickly. "I fully understand and will work to keep my emotions in check."

Grandfather swept his arms open to include both of us. "And a further word on emotions as they lead us to bias. We are taught that for justice to prevail, we must remove bias for and bias against both the rich or poor, the famous or the uncelebrated, and, as it may apply in our case, the arrogant or the meek. Each is capable of being misunderstood, each is capable of being victimized, and each is capable of criminality.

"As it applies to our detective work, it is not an individual's position, or reputation, or display of persona that drives our analyses, but rather how these surface factors contribute among many other considerations to comprehending the facts, environments, and emotions within which the crime was committed."

Aliya put up her hand to stop Grandfather for a moment. "I'm trying to follow you, I'm trying very hard, but my head is swimming. Forgive me if I'm not totally with you."

Grandfather smiled. "I do not understand this modern term of 'being with you.' Even if you do not comprehend everything I have said, I am sure you are with me as you didn't allow me to continue further without sharing your confusion or pretending you understand. I am proud of you for 'being with me,' and it is altogether possible that it is my own failure to explain well that causes the lack of understanding. Therefore, I shall try again by assessing our thoughts about Rabbi Flaum as we now begin our case. Aliya, how did you find his words?"

"I thought they were self-serving and only alluded superficially to Mrs. Flaum. I thought she deserved more from him in expressions of affection and loss. I'm sure he said *Kaddish* during his requisite 30-day mourning period, but there's something wrong, at least in my expectations of him.

I think I understand what Mother observed about Rabbi Flaum when she went to the *Shiva* visit. I spent almost all of my time that week with Shoshi and didn't pay much attention to her father."

Grandfather pivoted toward me. "And you, Joel, you experienced the same while you were at services?"

Should I support Aliya as much as possible? I wrestled with how to couch my answer. Truth would surely serve us all for the best. "I didn't feel that way until Aliya brought it up on the way home, so I understand what she's saying. To a degree, especially about his spoken treatment of Mrs. Flaum. But Rabbi Flaum is a very confident man who has worked tirelessly for his community and for the city of New York, and he's been phenomenally successful. Maybe as Zaida just cautioned us, I am caught up with the rabbi's reputation and contributions. But I wonder, Aliya, had you listened to another rabbi whom you did not know talking about his murdered wife, would you have left with the same impression?"

Aliya thought for a long moment. "Maybe not, but for me it was a disappointing sermon. It still bothers me."

Grandfather sat up straight and leaned toward us. "Your thoughts are helpful as we look toward our interview tomorrow with Rabbi Flaum. Might I request a favor? If you will allow me to assume the lead tomorrow, I would be pleased."

Aliya and I let out a duet chorus: "Of course."

After a moment, I asked: "Zaida, why did you ask what Martha Brennan was wearing at CPH this morning?"

Grandfather stroked his chin. "I wished to understand something of her character before we met her. She dressed tastefully for our service and did not violate sensibilities by carrying a purse or pocketbook. It is a small indication that we might trust her to help us."

"Help us, how?"

"With interviewing Barbara Horowitz, which I will explain in a few moments. But first, please, Joel, call *The Daily News* night desk and ask to speak to Martha Brennan. Please advise them that it is about the Flaum case."

"She'll be there? At this hour on a Saturday night?"

"A high possibility. You must understand that her business, and I'll say unfortunately, is a 24-hour operation. If she is not there, they will know how to contact her, and she will call you back quickly. And when you speak to her, please ask her to come to my office tomorrow at 3:30, after our interview with the rabbi."

"You think she'll come?" Incredulous, I looked at Aliya. She smiled and shrugged.

* * * *

I called Information and got *The Daily News* night number. A man's voice snapped, "Brennan's not here. What's it about?" I followed Grandfather's instructions and relayed the message. When I hung up, I thought, *if she calls in the morning, I'll be surprised.*

But I had barely seated myself when the phone rang. Aliya jumped up and answered. After a short conversation, Aliya hung up and smiled at me.

"That was Martha Brennan. She will be at Zaida's office tomorrow at 3:30."

Nearly 11:00. My mother hadn't yet returned, and I decided to assume her family role. "Zaida, it's late, and we're all tired. I think we should call it a night and see what we learn tomorrow before we proceed further. Make sense? Also, Aliya and I will stay over another night. We can take a cab to the precinct and then to your office since the trains are on a Sunday schedule."

Good thing Aliya and I had thought ahead to bring another change of clothes.

Grandfather did not hesitate. "Yes, your plan is sensible. But we will not add our travel fares to the expenses we will charge to the rabbi. Until we establish terms with him tomorrow, he is not yet our client."

Grandfather rose slowly and extended his arms to us. "Good night, my children."

SUNDAY, JULY 6, 1975

The next morning, Aliya and I were up at 8:30. Grandfather was at the kitchen table slowly eating wheat toast and a soft-boiled egg along with his morning coffee. He wore his usual brown suit, white shirt, and tie, but I noted no vest. He obviously anticipated the July heat.

"Good morning," he said. "Our meeting with Detective Carlucci is at 10:00. With my slow walking pace, is it possible to be on the Kings Highway by 9:30 to obtain a taxi for our trip to the precinct?"

We assured him that we could leave in a few minutes, even though my mother was peppering us with suggestions for breakfast. We both opted for scrambled eggs, toast, and coffee.

"What time did you get in, Mom?" I called.

"Around 12:30," my mother responded from the kitchen. "Have a good day. I'm heading out to open the store." My mother worked a six-day week running the jewelry shop with Sunday, open just from 10:00 to 3:00, the busiest day of all.

"Joel." Aliya put her hand on my shoulder. I took the hint and sat beside her at the table. "Let's concentrate on eating so that your grandfather doesn't worry that we'll be late."

After a quick breakfast, we returned to our room. Aliya pinned her hair back in a ponytail and threw on a light, knee-length dress with a rose petal pattern and short sleeves. She had packed tan summer sandals to make walking easier.

I wore khaki pants with flared bottoms, a striped short-sleeve shirt, white socks, and Converse sneakers. When I came out of the bedroom, I looked toward Grandfather for any reproof, but he had his suit jacket on and just seemed glad to get going. I also had tucked a kippah into one of my pockets. Would I wear it when we met with Rabbi Flaum? I wasn't sure.

* * * *

With Kings Highway bustling even on the Sunday morning of a holiday weekend, it took just a few minutes to find a cab. We arrived at the precinct at 9:45, and the cab pulled up at the front entrance. As I helped Grandfather out of the back seat, we both looked up at the imposing three-story building. With its plain limestone walls, it could have passed for a turn-of-the-twentieth century public school or perhaps an orphanage. The first and third floors showed rows of rectangular windows bordered by plain masonry, while the second had smaller windows edged by artistic stonework with a triangular hood above each. Filigreed masonry bordered the roofline.

As we approached the entrance, I counted seven steps up to the red, wood double doors with a stained glass above indicating **61st PRECINCT**. Two Doric columns bordered the doors. Above them a pinwheel design frieze fronted a stone balcony. There wasn't much activity going in and out. Had crime taken a summer holiday? That, or the 61st did a pretty good job.

I opened the door for Aliya and Grandfather. Inside, fluorescent ceiling lighting shone down from a Lady Justice frescoed plastered ceiling. Half-empty metallic furniture occupied the far end of the room where officers talked with individuals who were agitated, disconsolate, or bewildered. We heard muffled sounds of clanking and a series of epithets. I knew from my experience in other precincts that they were coming from the basement.

Aliya walked haltingly next to Grandfather as we made our way toward an enclosure with a name plate that indicated *Desk Sergeant*. I caught up and linked arms with her. Just three days ago, I thought, she never would have imagined being in a police station investigating a murder.

The desk sergeant, with a buzz haircut and jowly face, told us to wait as he pressed a phone button to call Detective Carlucci. "He'll see you now, Room 305," and nodding to Grandfather, "Are you okay, sir, to go up there? We don't have an elevator."

"Yes, I will be fine," Grandfather said. "I thank you for your concern."

Through an open door, Detective Carlucci spotted us. He sprang up from behind his desk and met us at the door.

He was a little over five feet tall. His black hair was graying at the temples. I pegged him to be around 50. Though he moved well, he showed a paunch covered by a yellow dress shirt with gold cufflinks. Black and gold suspenders that latched onto baggy gray pants pressed down the shirt. Suspenders! I stared for a moment—I hadn't seen suspenders for quite a while.

"You're the incredible Mr. Wolf," he said, pumping Grandfather's hand. "I know Fink in the 90th and Rooney in the 34th. They both go on and on about you and how you solved those cases."

"It is good to meet you," Grandfather responded, extricating his hand from Carlucci's. Grandfather was turning to introduce Aliya and me, but Carlucci beat him to it.

"You're the grandson who helps out, right?" He tightly shook my hand. "Forgot your name. Sorry."

"Joel, Joel Gordon," I had barely answered before Carlucci dropped my hand and moved in front of Aliya, eyeing her out of curiosity and the way some men eye attractive women.

Carlucci did not extend his hand. "And you are?"

Aliya moved slightly forward, looked Carlucci squarely in the eye, and extended an open right hand. "I am Aliya Blum, Joel's wife, and will be assisting in the investigation." After shaking hands, Aliya moved past Carlucci and stood between Grandfather and me.

Grandfather put a hand on Aliya's shoulder. "She will be of immense assistance, with her excellent knowledge of the Flaum household and the community served by Rabbi Flaum."

"Well, well, well, a real family affair." Carlucci laughed, returning to the swivel chair behind his desk. "Okay, Frank Wolf and family, how can I help?" Carlucci pointed to three chairs in front of the desk. "Make yourselves comfortable."

We sat down as Aliya plucked from her large handbag copies of the police report, a notebook, and a Bic pen. She handed reports to Grandfather and me, kept one for herself, uncapped the pen, and opened the notebook to a blank page.

Grandfather began. "It is greatly appreciated, Detective Carlucci, your meeting with us to review the Batya Flaum murder case, particularly as it is a Sunday of a holiday weekend."

Carlucci waved his hand. "Sunday, Monday, makes no difference to me. Work gotta get done. As long as I took in an early Mass this morning, the wife's fine with my schedule. What do you want to know?"

Grandfather opened his copy. "We have carefully reviewed the police report, but to begin, please allow us to go over some facts and hypotheses. Mrs. Flaum died between 9:00 and 10:00, when her body was found by her business partner, a Marcia Gelb, if I remember correctly, yes?"

"Yep, the Gelb lady said the door of the house was open when she arrived around 10:00, so when there was no answer to her knock, she walked in and saw Mrs. Flaum lying in the entry foyer. Coroner thought closer to 9:15 from the warmth of the body when he got to her."

"How was the 9:00 earliest time established?" I asked.

Carlucci looked at me as if to gauge how much gravitas I carried. "The Flaum son, Jonathan, lived in the house at that time. He told us that he had gotten a call the previous night for a job interview in the City at 9:00 the next morning. With rush hour and all, he didn't want to be late and left at 7:30. His mother was alive at that time."

"Did he arrive on time for his appointment?" Grandfather asked casually.

Carlucci gave Grandfather a look that said to me, *so you think you're smart.* "Turns out that he became nervous about not getting there on time taking the train, so he took a cab at the Avenue H Station to Manhattan. We did our leg-work and found the cabbie. Yep, he dropped the kid off at 63rd and Madison at 8:50. Tough traffic slog, the cabbie told us. Also said the kid was nervous he would be late."

Looking pleased, Carlucci was about to continue when Grandfather asked: "And did the Flaum son have his job interview?"

Carlucci gave out an exasperated sigh: "Hell if I know! What's the difference? He was in Manhattan at 8:55, and the partner lady found the body at a little after 10:00. Do you think he put on wings and flew back?"

I disliked Carlucci's sarcasm and wanted to snap back. But I held it in.

"Detective," Grandfather said. "Please forgive my having elicited your irritation in response to what may be nothing more than idle curiosity."

Carlucci stared at Grandfather, and his expression softened. "It's okay, it's okay, tell you the truth, I'm frustrated not solving the case. Don't get me wrong, I'm glad you're going to be looking into it. You're probably better making your way with your people than I am."

"Your frustration is very understandable," Aliya said.

Carlucci nodded his head, returned his gaze to Grandfather, and continued.

"The rabbi himself left the house at 7:50 for a synagogue monthly seniors 'bra cha and breakfast' discussion group at Kornblatt's Kosher Deli on Coney Island Avenue and Avenue J that started at 8:00."

"Bracha," I corrected Carlucci, emphasizing the Hebrew/Yiddish guttural pronunciation. "It means blessing." He had pronounced it with an ending similar to the dance step. Out of the corner of my eye, I could see that Grandfather frowned.

"Okay," Carlucci responded, sounding more bored than angry. "Bracha." He still mispronounced the word. "We confirmed with the folks there that the rabbi stayed at Kornblatt's until 8:50, when he headed to the synagogue. His secretary, a Mrs. Hirsch, said he was behind closed doors with a family planning a bar mitzvah till 10:00. Then at 10:00, he met with another family planning a wedding. Mrs. Hirsch was there when the 10:00 family arrived."

"And she was there when the nine o'clockers arrived?" I asked.

"No, she got there around 9:10, but she says she could hear talking in the rabbi's office. I know what you're thinking. There was a 20-minute window between 8:50, when Rabbi Flaum left the deli, and 9:10, when Mrs. Hirsch arrived. And the Flaum house is very close to the synagogue. Thing is, he couldn't have killed his wife during that time. The plumbing folks, the Chanskys, father and son, arrived at 8:00 to work on a bathroom leak. Mrs. Flaum was still alive when they left just after 9:00."

"And you've cleared the plumbers?" I inquired.

Carlucci did a quick eye roll but answered neutrally: "Yep, they're part of the rabbi's flock, been members of the congregation a long time. Been servicing the Flaum house and synagogue for years. Mrs. Flaum had set up an appointment two days before. But we still looked at them carefully. Had Jacob, the father, and Asher, the son, in several times, together and alone. Said they always record the time they come and leave on a log. Showed it to us. Showed us the pipe and bolt they replaced under the sink to fix a leak. The replacements fit what they carry in their truck. They were at their next call in Sheepshead Bay before 10:00. Homeowner corroborated. Also, since the murder weapon wasn't found at the crime scene, we went over their truck, their shop, their home, their clothes with a fine-tooth comb. No blood residue on anything."

Grandfather asked: "The police report indicates that Mrs. Flaum was struck on the front of her left temple with a heavy instrument. A weapon such as a wrench or a hammer, would that be correct, Detective?"

Carlucci nodded.

"And you say, Detective, that the murder weapon was not discovered at the Flaum home. Might you assess if that is common in cases of robbery?"

Carlucci thought for a moment. "Usually not. A burglar won't carry something heavy, and an armed robber will use a gun to threaten the victim and shoot if there's resistance. Especially in this kind of robbery, where we're not looking at a huge haul. To kill for the week's receipts, $715, from that little store, well that's not your John Derringer at work. Probably some guy or kids on drugs."

Grandfather continued as if he and Carlucci were having a casual chat. "But yet, no murder object was left behind, and I am sure you went over the house from top to bottom and found no object with blood residue that could have killed the poor woman. I am therefore thinking that the murderer escaped with the lethal object, and therefore we are not dealing with a typical behavior, yes?"

"You got me there," Carlucci answered, shrugging. "Something doesn't add up. But that's why we examined everything the Chansky plumbers owned, and again zilch, plus they got a pretty good alibi."

No one spoke for a few seconds until Aliya asked, her voice quavering slightly: "And Marcia Gelb, did you have any reason to suspect her?"

"Young lady," Carlucci snapped his head toward Aliya and then away toward Grandfather, "when we start an investigation, we have every reason to suspect everyone. But there wasn't anything on her, near her, or hidden anywhere that would suggest anything other than she was the one to come across the body. We examined her hands, fingernails, hair, and clothes. No blood anywhere."

"Okay, then," I asked. "Does *The Daily News* piece mean you're going to look at the case from a different angle?" I glanced at Aliya. "With Barbara Burns coming forward about the affair—and Rabbi Flaum not denying it—does that establish motive for looking more carefully at the two of them?"

"Thought about it," Carlucci answered quickly, "but there's not much point with the rabbi. He's got an ironclad alibi for where he was at the time of the murder. And the Burns lady, I guess I hadn't mentioned it, but I had her in again for an interview last Friday after the story appeared. Asked her to come to the station, and she had no problem with it. First question we asked her: Where was she on the morning of the murder? She looked at me from across the interview table with her eyes flashing and said, 'Doing the weather live on the WPIX morning show.' We checked. She was. And do you think either needed to steal the money when they killed her?"

"But—" Aliya burst out. "Never mind," she said quickly. "Please go on."

Carlucci continued. "So I'll sit tight and let the, uh, the three of you see what you can find out. Of course," and Carlucci opened a palm toward us, "I am at your disposal. Just let me know what you need."

"Again, Detective Carlucci," Grandfather said, rising, "it is most gracious of you to share your time and information with us."

We made our goodbyes and started toward the door when Grandfather turned back: "It is not precisely in the police report, but did we hear you correctly that the son, Jonathan, was called for his appointment the evening before? And there is also no mention as to what establishment wished to interview him."

Carlucci scratched his head. "Not in the report? Huh! Well, I don't think we ever asked the kid who wanted to interview him, but I remember for sure he said he got the call in the evening."

Grandfather doffed his hat toward Carlucci. "In that case, Detective, might we take you up on your offer? Is it possible to examine the phone records of the Thursday evening before the murder to determine what calls came into the Flaum house?"

Carlucci stood. "Easy enough. Should have it to you sometime Tuesday."

* * * *

We walked slowly out of the precinct and down its steps following my grandfather's careful lead. I wanted to hold on to him, but, I thought, he goes up and down the three flights to his office without incident when I'm not around. I harnessed my worry.

From the past I knew that Grandfather did not want to discuss the meeting we'd had with Detective Carlucci until we were in his office. Aliya did not press as we walked in silence toward the Avenue U station where we found a Yellow Cab. It was 11:10, and Rabbi Flaum was expected at 1:00.

The cabbie, Konstantin, whose name I could read on his badge taped to the right side of the dashboard, spoke in a heavily Slavic accent to ask where we were going and then said nothing more during the 35-minute trip. The air conditioning was not working. Konstantin kept the front windows open through which he discarded chain-smoked cigarette ash on the driver's side. The three of us packed into the bench-like back seat. None of the seatbelts worked, and Aliya, who insisted because she was the smallest, sat in the middle. The day's summer heat had intensified. We sweltered as Konstantin pulled out.

I was probably bothered less than Grandfather and Aliya as a drive along Ocean Parkway, even to this day, brings back memories of Sunday excursions with my father and mother before my father passed away. From the moment my father steered our Buick Electra onto the Parkway at Avenue P, I half sat and, to my mother's chagrin, half stood in the back seat and imagined the Parkway to be America's grand highway traversing the country from ocean to ocean. I was half right as it did start around Brighton Beach off the Atlantic, but later I would learn that the Parkway was only five miles long going south to north toward Queens. I'd crane my neck in all directions to take in the three-lane road we were traveling with a turn lane to our left that separated us from another three lanes of traffic headed in the other direction.

Each side had grassy medians with a bike lane, along with pedestrian paths. Triple rows of trees—elms, maples, sycamores, oaks, and even ginkgoes from saplings to well-mature—offered shade to benches and game tables and created a sense of being outside of a city. I ignored the high rise apartments dominating the two service roads and sidewalks. Instead I kept my eyes out for engraved mile markers, stubbornly insisting that the numbers going up to five had nothing to do with the length of the Parkway but only to help young children learn how to count.

Konstantin took us onto the Brooklyn-Queens Expressway, jolting me out of my reverie as we hit the first of several potholes. I sensed Grandfather's wince with each bump. I looked over and saw him sweating profusely. Aliya held his hand, and Grandfather nodded slightly at her as if to say that he was well enough.

I had expected Konstantin to get off at Atlantic Avenue and head straight to Joralemon, but for some reason he took the Brooklyn-Queens Expressway farther north and came back down what is Brooklyn Bridge Boulevard to Cadman Plaza and Boro Hall. Along that stretch of the BQE, we passed the Watchtower sign atop of what we called when I was young the old J Witnesses headquarters building. Its red letters indicated it was already 90 degrees at 11:45.

After being dropped off, we walked slowly up the three flights to my grandfather's office. Immediately feeling the inside heat, I rushed to the window air conditioner and turned it on. I was glad we had purchased a top-of-the-line model. My stomach growled. Was I the only one hungry? When could we eat given that Rabbi Flaum was coming at 1:00, and then Martha Brennan at 3:30? About to ask, I turned around. Grandfather pointed to three paper bags as he scanned a note.

"Is your mother not a wonderful person? She has left a lunch for each of us. She writes, 'I was worried you would not have much time to eat something with your busy schedule, so on the way to the store, I thought I would drop off some sandwiches.' We must remember to thank her, yes?"

Some sandwiches! Labels on each bag with our names. Each tuna sandwich had the type of bread we favored along with the individualized accompaniments. My mother did not forget a thermos with tea for Grandfather and water bottles for Aliya and me. And for dessert, she included left-over mandel bread from Friday night's dinner.

Grandfather took off his suit jacket and fedora and hung them on a wooden coat rack near the door. He took his seat behind his desk. Aliya motioned me to sit in the guest chair. "Fair is fair, I got to sit last time."

I was about to argue when Grandfather opened his desk drawer, took out a key, and motioned me to take it.

"Joel, you will please go next door to the Acme Loans office and bring us two chairs. I have made such an arrangement with Mr. Khan, to borrow them on Sundays or evenings when his office is closed. You will please arrange the chairs at 45 degree angles to the right and left of where you are now sitting, yes?"

I quickly brought in two folding chairs, placing them as directed. Aliya sat on the folding chair on the left facing Grandfather, and I switched to the chair on the right.

The unoccupied guest chair dominated my mind. In just a matter of minutes, Rabbi Flaum, an iconic leader in the New York Jewish community, would fill the chair. How would he respond to being interrogated? He intended to hire Grandfather to clear his name. But he would be questioned as a potential suspect.

And how would I react? Part of me wanted to establish his role in Mrs. Flaum's killing based on his affair with Barbara Burns. But another wanted him cleared so that he could continue his leadership role. Might I cause further damage to my religious community? And Aliya? I could see the strain on her face, probably taking into account the same emotions and more as his daughter's best friend.

I kept listening for the sounds of someone in the hallway. I was glad that Grandfather would take the lead. I didn't trust myself.

Grandfather leaned back in his chair and opened his hands to Aliya and me. "Before Rabbi Flaum arrives, what are your thoughts about our meeting with the detective?"

"May I just get out of my system that I didn't like the man and am dubious about his crime-solving skills," Aliya quickly volunteered, throwing me a look that I took as, *Yes I'm emotional but trust me*.

She continued, turning toward Grandfather. "And you're going to ask me why, so let me just say it. How in the world does the Brennan article not demand that both the rabbi and Barbara Burns be further investigated, whether together or individually! Sure they may not have wielded the weapon, but they may have hired a hitman to do it, right?"

We waited for Grandfather to reply, but instead he sat for a minute with his hands cupping his face and eyes lifted in thought. Finally, he said:

"Aliya, it is not that I am dismissing your observation, but please allow me also to consider any other reactions from our meeting. Joel, may we hear your thoughts?"

"Okay," I spit out, "here goes. I also didn't like the man. I hate when someone uses the phrase, 'your people' as if we're a different breed of humans. But that aside, I thought he was indifferent to finding out who murdered Mrs. Flaum. As Aliya said, it's obvious that it needn't have been the rabbi or the Burns lady directly, but they could have hired someone to do it."

"You say 'they,'" Grandfather questioned. "You are at least assuming that it was a conspiracy, that together they had Mrs. Flaum murdered?"

"Well," I retorted, "or even individually without the other knowing. Doesn't make much difference does it?"

Grandfather's eyes narrowed. "Joel, I believe your anger is undermining your reasoning. For the pursuit of justice, it certainly would make a difference, no?"

I felt the sting of his comment. I knew he was right. I said nothing, and Grandfather continued, his voice calmer.

"Let us put this question aside for a moment as we quickly examine some other emotions that we harbor as they may touch on the critical analyses skills we require to work on this case? Joel, you seem to be imputing anti-Semitic tendencies to Detective Carlucci which may affect his resolve to find the killer, might I be correct?"

"Yes, perhaps."

"But," Grandfather continued, "is it possible that the detective, living in our New York City of today, is, like so many people, ethnically insensitive and not necessarily anti-Semitic? Is it possible if the murder had occurred in the Greek, or Irish, or Puerto Rican community, would he not use the same words of 'your people?' Might we be more careful in ascribing hateful motives to someone when it is a human tendency to identify certain, non-malevolent distinctions in others and, in the case of Detective

Carlucci, that he is not sensitive enough to comprehend that his frankness may be hurtful? In the end, should we not judge the detective by the work he produces and not his surface tendencies?"

Grandfather stopped and picked up the police report. "You both read the contents of this report? There are weaknesses, such as not indicating more definitive information on Jonathan Flaum's interview in Manhattan, but otherwise does it not appear to be well constituted and thorough up to the point of *The Daily News* article? Detective Carlucci stated that he is open to our helping in the investigation. Let us proceed."

Aliya looked at her watch: "We've only got a few minutes left. Might we examine Detective Carlucci's point about both suspects not needing the money that was taken? I was going to challenge him, but I thought I'd wait until we discussed it. We've all watched enough detective shows to know that stealing money can be a ruse to distract attention from the real motive, which in this case may have been the hiring of a hitman to get Mrs. Flaum out of the way of their affair. Right?"

I interjected: "What company calls the night before to set up an interview? Someone wanted him out of the house in the morning. The murder was planned, and taking the money was probably a ruse to plant robbery in the police minds as the motive. Indeed, Rabbi Flaum or Barbara Burns could care less about the money."

Grandfather smiled while giving me an admonishing wave of his hand. "But in addition, Yoeli, why dwell only on the rabbi and Barbara Burns? Is it not possible that whoever called may have wanted Jonathan out of the house, perhaps to effect Mrs. Flaum's murder or perhaps to plan for the robbery during which she was killed. Is it not possible that $715 is a significant amount of money to some person?"

Flummoxed at not arriving at certainty, I just nodded.

It was 12:55 when Aliya said: "This isn't to question our role in trying to solve Mrs. Flaum's murder, but Zaida, you say that Carlucci is a good detective. Then it should have struck him that someone wanted Jonathan out of the house at the time of the murder. Shouldn't he have some idea how to follow up on the new information about the affair and how it may have played in the murder? What makes us better positioned to work the case than the NYPD?"

Grandfather looked at the door. "I will give you short answers to your very important questions. We must consider how overwhelming it must be the work Detective Carlucci has before him. It is entirely possible he and his officers overlooked some aspect of the investigation before the article appeared. But more to the point, when it comes to this particular case, as was true in the previous cases your husband and I worked, we possess certain skills and inclinations that a detective such as Carlucci may be lacking such as an understanding of the Jewish community and its culture in which Mrs. Flaum's murder took place. If we were to try to solve a crime in, let us say, an Amish community, would we not encounter the same difficulty? As we proceed with the case, I think you will comprehend better what I am imparting, yes?"

Aliya nodded, and I looked at my watch. Right at 1:00, we heard a knock on the door. I quickly pulled out my kippah and bobby-pinned it to my head. Rabbi David Flaum may have been a suspect in this case, but there was nothing yet definitive. Affair or not, I felt he still deserved the respect he had otherwise earned.

* * * *

Rabbi Flaum entered. Grandfather stood, and we followed his lead.

"*Sholom aleichem*," the rabbi uttered using the millennial-old Jewish greeting.

"*Aleichem sholom*," we responded according to the welcoming formula, with Aliya's response constrained.

Rabbi Flaum moved with confidence into the office and extended his right hand to Grandfather and then to me. The hand showed some scrapes at the knuckles. His left hand was lightly bandaged with gauze and adhesive tape.

Though he walked ramrod straight, a belly bulge through the vest of his well-tailored blue pinstripe suit compromised his bearing. A gold and blue silk paisley tie perfectly matched the suit. A large, crocheted blue and white kippah covered most of the slicked strands of his light brown hair and hid any sign of a contusion from the incident with Burton Horowitz. Clear aviator glasses allowed his hazel eyes to pierce through. I recognized the Faberge Brut cologne that he wore. My father had also used that scent. It's Sunday and a holiday weekend, and he's dressed to the hilt.

"Mr. Wolf," Rabbi Flaum said slightly bowing, and to me, "Joel, how are you?" He did not shake hands with Aliya but smiled at her and said, "Aliya, thank you very much for the support you are extending to Shoshannah during these difficult times. My appreciation is boundless." Aliya did not reply.

Grandfather indicated the open seat between Aliya and me, and Rabbi Flaum moved toward it. A big man, around six feet two inches, he sank awkwardly into the small guest chair. The chair's burgundy fabric back pushed out, and the metal frame creaked.

The rabbi cleared his throat, preparing to speak. To control the room, I guessed, but Grandfather grasped the initiative. "How may we be of assistance, Rabbi Flaum?"

The rabbi crossed and uncrossed his legs. "First, allow me to congratulate you, Mr. Wolf, and also Joel, on solving a few months ago the Ori Gold killing. The bravery you showed in bringing the Charnick boy down from the roof was extraordinary. I am well acquainted with Sam Gold and his family, and I am also a member of the Manhattan Jewish Academy High School board. I'm not sure if the school has sent you word of its appreciation for your work, but I would like to thank you personally."

"We haven't heard a word from the school," I said. Grandfather pinched his lips.

Rabbi Flaum turned toward me. "Yes, the wheels of bureaucracies grind slowly, do they not? I am sure you will receive a note from the board. I know we are all grateful."

"Thank you for your kind words, Rabbi Flaum" Grandfather said evenly, "but again, how may we be of assistance?"

The rabbi thought for a moment. He looked at Grandfather. "I can see, Mr. Wolf, that you very much like to get to the heart of the matter quickly. I imagine that is why you have been able to solve your cases in little time and thus have gained a well-deserved reputation. I also wish to find resolution speedily, so I will be direct. I am here to request your assistance in clearing me of the murder of my wife. I understand that following the publication of *The Daily News* story a few days ago, there may be some reason to suspect my involvement. But I am fully innocent. I wish to hire you to establish my innocence."

Grandfather picked up a paper and a pen. "Rabbi Flaum, as it is usual when I entertain a request, I draw up a contract that establishes the nature of my services and the rate which is eighteen dollars per hour, plus judiciously charged incidentals such as transportation. But before I offer this contract for your review, please know that not anywhere in this contract does it commit me, as you put it, 'to clear' you as a suspect. I will, if it is your desire, work to determine all of the facts in the murder of Mrs. Flaum, may she rest in peace. If the facts demonstrate that you were not involved in any way, then certainly your innocence will be established. But I will not begin with the objective of establishing your innocence. To establish your or anyone else's innocence, then one must find the guilty party, whoever it may be. Does such a distinction make sense to you, and do you then wish to sign the contract based on such a stipulation?"

Rabbi Flaum rose and took the paper and pen from Grandfather, perused it for under a minute, and placing the paper on the desk, signed and handed it back to Grandfather who added his own signature.

"Tomorrow," Grandfather said, "when the library is open, I will create a duplicate copy and mail it to you, if that is acceptable? I am sorry that we must attend to such business at the outset, but it is the way of my profession."

Grandfather opened his hand first toward me and then Aliya. "Also, my grandson, Joel, will assist me, but there will not be a charge for his work, nor for that of Aliya, who will serve as a consultant to the case."

Rabbi Flaum nodded and returned to his seat. He did not give me or Aliya a glance. "Very good, Mr. Wolf, please let me know what else you need from me to proceed. And is it proper to call you 'Mr. Wolf?' I am on good terms with Rabbi Koenig in Williamsburg, the leader of the Hasidic community in which you solved the kidnapping of the little boy over a year ago. Rabbi Koenig mentioned to me that you also were ordained a rabbi in the old country before the War. Would it be proper to call you 'Rabbi?'"

Grandfather shook his head. "It is not proper. I did not use my *smichah* to practice when I was ordained in Europe and, as you also surely know, I took a university teaching position instead. And now as a private detective, it is simply appropriate to refer to me as 'Mr. Wolf.'"

Was Rabbi Flaum being coy and flattering? I wondered how much he knew about my grandfather's history. If he had spoken to Rabbi Koenig, he was aware that raised an Orthodox Jew in Vienna, my grandfather was born Velvel Franck, but in a transposition of his first and last name and play on the translation of the Yiddish "velvel," translated as "wolf," he used Frank Wolf as his professional name in America. Yes, as my grandfather told Rabbi Flaum, although he had completed rabbinical training, he did not employ his ordination but instead accepted a professorship at the Vienna university where he had completed his doctorate. But Rabbi Flaum probably did not know that at 23, my grandfather was the university's youngest professor at that time.

Rabbi Flaum and my grandfather were engaged in a chess game of probes and counter moves. Trying to appraise the situation as Grandfather might, I pushed myself to see the well-respected, well-dressed, and seemingly well-composed Rabbi Flaum as frightened. Grandfather would want me to set aside a gut response to the rabbi's behavior and wait for the facts to arise. As Grandfather had enjoined us, the haughty and frightened also deserved justice.

"Rabbi Flaum," my grandfather said, his voice strong, "we will need your assistance tomorrow in allowing us access to your house to gain a picture of the murder scene. I know it may be painful for you. If you do not wish to be present, we will understand. Might we visit in the morning?"

"Mr. Wolf, I can make my house available at any time. Would 8:45 be convenient? I will need to leave at that time to go into the City for a Federation meeting."

The rabbi followed with a forced chuckle. "That's if they'll still have me. The phone has not rung yet to request I do not attend. I will depart as soon as you arrive, and I would ask you to please lock the door from the

"Indiscretion!" Aliya burst out. "Is that what you call it? How many times had I sat at CPH and heard you label what you did an *averah*, a sin? If I remember correctly, it's a violation of the seventh commandment, and you call it an 'indiscretion!' Oh, and it's really not your fault, is it? What male could resist Barbara Burns? What middle-aged male doesn't suffer the irritation of a tiresome wife? Just one of those 'indiscretions!' Really!"

I listened amazed. Aliya had just echoed what my grandfather had repeatedly said to me when I, as a child, exhibited impulsive, inconsiderate, or hurtful behavior.

"Yoeli," he would begin, and after a while I knew the next words would be, "what separates us from the animals and their natural-given drives to hunt, protect territory, or find a mate? Is it not our brains and the ability to exert control of our impulses, to inhibit harming others, to negotiate our differences without killing others, to find a mate through love and not brute strength? And when we fail, whether in the small violation which you just exhibited or as on the mass scale which we saw just a few years before in the Holocaust, do we not forsake that trust which has been granted to us?"

Rabbi Flaum said nothing for several seconds. Finally, he looked down and uttered softly: "Aliya, I understand why you are angry with me."

I got it. Grandfather wanted Aliya to question Rabbi Flaum for a couple of reasons: to throw the rabbi off balance so as to both expose his emotional side and to observe what he lets others see when he is not displaying his strong, physical presence and intellectual forcefulness. He had also, in his own words, given us reasons to think why he might have been involved in his wife's death. With a neutral tone, I probed:

"Rabbi, are you able to accept why, given what you said, we must consider you a suspect in Mrs. Flaum's killing?"

Without looking at me, he pursed his lips and nodded slowly. I had the momentum and continued by asking if the timeframes in the police report for his movements on the morning of the murder were accurate. He looked at me and confirmed the information.

"And you arrived at what time at CPH?"

"A minute or so before 9:00."

"And Mrs. Hirsch was already there?" I asked, thinking of what inconsistency traps I could lay.

"No, although her day should start at 9:00, she often arrives somewhat ʳ after taking care of family matters. Her lateness is acceptable to me as ʳwise she is a wonderful secretary."

ʼAnd you had a meeting scheduled for 9:00?"

ʼYes," the rabbi answered, his voice stronger. "It was with the Mosʳ family to discuss their son Ari's upcoming bar mitzvah."

bbi Flaum took a folded paper from his jacket pocket and placed it on Grandfather's desk. "I assume everything I am saying is in the police report, but I thought you might want to check my memory by contacting David and Bella Moskowitz. Their phone number is on the paper along with that of Mark and Mira Jacobs with whom I met at 10:00 to begin planning their daughter Becky's wedding."

I paused. The rabbi did not cede control easily. Grandfather filled the breach. "I believe it will not be necessary for us to contact those families, but please tell us about your son Jonathan, I believe, is his name."

Rabbi Flaum's eyes flared. "Jonathan had nothing to do with his mother's death. Look in your police report. Clearly, he was in the City when Batya was killed."

"It is surely due to a fault in how I expressed the question," Grandfather replied, his voice slow and steady. "I did not mean to inquire as to your thoughts about his guilt or innocence. We very much would like to learn about your son from his father's perspective."

I rushed to add: "And let's be clear. One didn't have to be at the scene of the murder when it occurred to be involved. For instance, Rabbi, you remain a suspect even though we may be certain you were at CPH when it happened." I glanced quickly at Grandfather. He nodded once.

Rabbi Flaum looked straight ahead. "Yes, I acknowledge that reality. And about my son, he is a good boy, sometimes troubled by not having a rudder in life. I love him dearly. He was very close to his mother, closer than he was to me with our common father/son struggles. I did want more from him, and I believe I could have been more forgiving. I am determined to make every effort."

"More forgiving? Of what, Rabbi?" Grandfather asked.

Rabbi Flaum thought for a moment. "A good question, one much deeper than the facile answer I was about to give, which is he did not rise to meet my expectations in scholarship, in fortitude, in religious practice, and I can simply summarize by saying in my thinking, my one son was a failure. If I bare my soul, I find that I hold a grudge against him for not speaking to me directly about his feelings, for not confronting my rigidity, for not striking out more manfully against me. Instead he belabored his thoughts and feelings to his mother who tried to convey them to me. I would not have it that way. As a result, he would at times express his anger against his mother for her failing him through not intervening effectively. But be assured, he was not involved in any way in her death. He loved her too much to have gone that far with any anger against her."

Aliya asked. "And did you speak to him directly with any compassion? Did you confront your own rigidity? Or did you yourself strike out manfully to belittle him?"

Grandfather grimaced and started to speak when Rabbi Flaum turned to Aliya and said: "I have made mistakes, Aliya. Again, I can understand your disappointment."

Grandfather brought the rabbi's attention back to him.

"Rabbi, on the morning of your wife's murder, your son left for a job interview in Manhattan. Do you know if he indeed had the interview?"

Rabbi Flaum looked glum and narrowed his eyes. "No, I don't know if he had the interview. I never asked. Jonathan moved out shortly after Batya's death. He said he could not sleep in the same house where his mother's murder occurred."

"Thank you, Rabbi, and you must have given this question thought. If I were to tell you that robbery was not a motive in your wife's killing, who might you suspect committed the murder?"

"Robbery, not a motive?" Rabbi Flaum stammered. "Then I don't know who might have wanted my wife dead. She was beloved by everyone in the family, at the *shul*, and in the community."

I couldn't tell if Aliya had noted Grandfather's displeasure with her last utterance, but if she did, she wasn't backing down. "Rabbi, you say she was beloved by everyone? By you? By Barbara Burns? Is there anyone else who loved her that way?"

Grandfather's expression was blank. Keeping his gaze down, the rabbi responded, "No, I cannot say."

He then looked at his watch and said: "It is now a few minutes before 2:00. I took a car service here and asked that they pick me up at 2:00. If there are no further questions, I must leave. If you will have any questions or need my assistance in any fashion, I am at your disposal."

Aliya and I looked at each other and then to Grandfather and shook our heads. Grandfather once again stood and, as when the rabbi entered, Aliya and I followed. "We thank you for your visit, Rabbi Flaum," Grandfather said, "and we will see you tomorrow morning at your residence."

Rabbi Flaum heaved himself up slowly, nodded to each of us, and walked wearily to the door as if he were carrying more than his own body's weight.

* * * *

As soon as Rabbi Flaum had closed the door, Grandfather took out his frayed address book from his desk, thumbed to the end, picked up the phone, and began dialing. "I am calling Detective Carlucci to ask him to obtain the bank records for Rabbi Flaum and Barbara Burns for the two weeks prior and two weeks after the murder. As the detective is dealing with a murder investigation, I am confident he will be able to find a judge tomorrow morning to obtain the subpoena and perhaps have the information to us along with the phone records on Tuesday."

Carlucci answered right away, and the two talked as if they were old friends. He told Grandfather that he would do his best to obtain a subpoena tomorrow along with a trip to the banks to obtain the records. After hanging up, Grandfather looked pleased.

"My children, it appears that as part of the earlier investigation, the good detective identified the banks with which the rabbi and Mrs. Flaum did business. As for Ms. Burns, he is hopeful that her records will not be difficult to obtain."

I admired the flexibility my grandfather showed, at his age, in adapting the newly introduced designation of *Ms.* for women.

Aliya brought me back to the discussion at hand. "Are you angry with me, Zaida?"

"Might you explain, my child, why you think I might be angry with you?"

Was Grandfather being coy? Aside from interrogations of witnesses or suspects, he was never coy or disingenuous. Was he not sure to what she was referring? Was it Aliya's eruption in response to the rabbi's use of the term "indiscretion" or her sarcasm when the rabbi described his relationship with his son?

Aliya responded. "I lost my temper, Zaida. I thought Rabbi Flaum was self-righteous by devaluing Jonathan and not being aware of the role he himself played in the bad relationship."

Grandfather put his left hand to his chin. "I would not term my reaction 'angry' but rather concerned. Your expressed anger at that moment he was informing us about his son was counter-productive. It was quite different from when you challenged him about his describing his affair as an 'indiscretion.' In that instance, I found your question, though fraught with emotion, most appropriate as it went to the heart of the matter—that is, what role did the affair play in the murder of Mrs. Flaum? But your denunciation of his disappointment in his son? Does it not close down conversation, driving him deeper into himself and fearful of sharing information, those emotions that we need to understand along with the facts of the case?"

In the few years we'd known each other I had seen Aliya, as any person might be, defensive when shown to be guilty of one's own "indiscretion." But she did not flinch from Grandfather's reprimand. "You're right, Zaida, I should have known better, even from my own training in clinical psychology. Maybe I'm too close to the case, maybe I shouldn't be on it with you and Joel. Do you forgive me?"

"Sha, sha, sha, Aliya, we also do not need over-dramatization. Forgiveness is required for much larger transgressions than an error in detective methodology. There are violations much greater in our personal lives and societal interactions. As to your remaining on the case, I hope you will not let one misstep deter you from providing the very assistance we need in terms of your intelligence, emotions, and knowledge of the Flaum family and community. Yes, you will stay?"

A tear rolled down Aliya's cheek. "Yes, I very much want to stay."

Grandfather opened his arms toward both of us. "What have we learned from our interview with Rabbi Flaum that we did not know prior?"

I answered first. "For me, I learned that when it comes to his being a suspect in the crime, Rabbi Flaum is no longer an iconic figure whose reputation I need to protect or that I am afraid of offending."

"And I'm learning," Aliya added, "that because I'm emotionally angry with or disappointed in a person, in this case Rabbi Flaum and his affair, I shouldn't automatically associate his adultery with involvement in the murder."

Grandfather thought for a moment. "Certainly such an assessment of the suspect along with oneself is critical to the evolving analyses of the case, but in addition to learning about our own selves, is there anything factual we learned that we did not know from the police report?"

Aliya and I looked at each other and waited for the other to reply. I finally said: "Nothing really factual, right Zaida?"

Grandfather replied, "Nuh, you will please go on, Joel?"

"Well, I think we can go over the route he took that morning and time-frames he gave for going to the synagogue and his meetings, but we will find nothing to contradict what he told us. I agree there isn't any point in calling those two families to corroborate their meetings with him. But we did learn a lot about the psychological make-up of the man, didn't we Aliya?"

Aliya did not hesitate. "We did, but as we were saying a moment ago, as much as we think we learned about the rabbi's psychological make-up, we also dealt with our own emotional propensities in how we listened to and assessed the man. There is a difference, and we've got to get it right to solve the case. For instance, I don't think at the time of her murder he loved Mrs. Flaum. But does that make him more of a suspect than if I felt he loved her deeply? I just don't know."

"Yes, yes," Grandfather exclaimed excitedly. "I very much am impressed how both of you are peeling away your own layers of emotions to allow critical analyses of the crime to take place. And I also am not sure discerning whether he loved his wife or not is productive. I believe he did, Aliya, but there is no such thing as uncompromised love. Are there not multiple examples of what we call a 'lover' killing the object of that love for various reasons? Let us point to jealousy as one. Is it possible that Rabbi Flaum entered his affair while still strongly loving his wife? Perhaps we overstate the role of love when it comes to murder. I may be wrong, my children, but at this moment, I posit that Rabbi Flaum does not believe he had any involvement in his wife's murder, whether he loved her or not."

Why didn't Grandfather believe that Rabbi Flaum had anything to do with the murder? I also didn't know how Aliya was reacting overall. I'd ask her later. She was a much more complex thinker than I, especially when it comes to factoring in emotions. I looked at my watch. 2:15. With Martha Brenan arriving at 3:30, I thought it helpful if Grandfather rested, closed his eyes even for a few minutes, to keep up his strength. I didn't think we should address my confusion. I looked from Grandfather to Aliya and said:

"I guess we move on with our interviews and examinations of locales tomorrow. And Zaida, I think Aliya and I need to stretch our legs by taking a few minutes walk until Martha Brennan arrives. Is that okay?"

Grandfather did not object. "Yes Joel, please take a walk while I review some thoughts. Such a hiatus will benefit all of us."

* * * *

Aliya was quiet as we left Grandfather's office and headed toward Montague Street. I had suggested a 10-minute walk to the Brooklyn Promenade. Thirty minutes on the promenade along with the time to and from would get us back around 3:15, enough time for pre-interview planning with Grandfather. Aliya had not objected to the destination. While on Court Street, right before we turned west on Montague, Aliya stopped me and said:

"I think I understand what your grandfather was telling us about not letting superficial notions guide us while investigating. We're brought up to believe that love drives everything in how we behave, so we may overlook any destructive forces that operate within the complexity of that emotion."

"I'll have to think about it," I replied. It wasn't just that I was being kind to Grandfather. I needed separation from the case at that moment as much as he did.

Clouds hid the sun and made the walk bearable. During law school, I had done a summer clerkship at the Brooklyn DA's office on nearby Jay Street and was familiar with the Monday through Friday bustle of activity around the imposing Boro Hall and the Kings County Supreme Court buildings. So the quietness and emptiness of our surroundings on the Fourth of July Sunday seemed eerie, the occasional flying of wrappers carried by a slight breeze momentarily startling.

Montague Street was a mishmash of mom-and-pop haberdashery, lingerie, drug, hardware, dress, thrift shops, and walkup apartment buildings, along with franchise stores such as a Key Foods, Nathan's Hot Dogs, and a Nedick's restaurant featuring its signature orange drink that exclaimed **Always a Pleasure.** Most were closed except for Key Foods and the Nedick's, its orange-faced man encased in a flashing circle.

Between Clinton and Henry Streets, the old St. Ann's Episcopal Church with its Gothic Revival spires, situated on the highest point in Brooklyn Heights, loomed over us, dark and mostly abandoned. I wanted to grab a drink at the King George Coffee House on Montague and Henry, but it was closed. Continuing down Montague toward the promenade, we walked by three- and four-story immaculately maintained brownstones shaded by vibrant pear trees. At Pierrepont Place, we turned north and onto the promenade.

The desolate promenade reminded me of the Coney Island Boardwalk on a cold winter's day. A few couples strolled slowly, but otherwise it was abandoned except for several homeless men who occupied the wooden benches that lined the promenade on its east and west sides. Flower beds on the east side sprawled with milkweed, asters, and goldenrods, many withered from the summer sun. In some places they spread onto the promenade. Wrappers, flyers, cartons, bottles, and cans littered the beds. Dirt grimed over the hardwood planks, and bird droppings and dog excrement created an eyes down obstacle course.

I linked arms with Aliya as we headed toward the Brooklyn Bridge. Every few minutes, I checked my watch to make sure we would not be late returning to Grandfather's office. Had I locked his door from the inside upon leaving? I was pretty sure I had done so.

Despite the rumble of the Brooklyn/Queens Expressway below, we took in spectacular views of the Statue of Liberty, New Jersey, and Governor's Island behind us, Manhattan to our left, and the Brooklyn and Manhattan Bridges straight ahead. At our left on Furman Street, the bleak sign identifying the sprawling limestone and granite building as the **National Cold Storage Co**. marred the view. As a child, I would take autumnal walks with my parents and, sometimes, with Grandfather on the Promenade, and when I would see the sign, I would grab an elder's hand. What if I was trapped in the frozen interior of the building with no way out.

Aliya and I made small talk, mostly about how nice it would be that evening to return to our apartment later and what we would have for dinner. We planned to take a cab back to Flatbush with Grandfather and then take the train home. We had decided on pizza.

A man who had been sitting on a bench with an overstuffed backpack filling a Bohack shopping cart approached us. In a soft voice, he asked if we had "some spare change?" Aliya tightened her hold around my arm.

Back then these men were called "winos" as we were sure that whatever money we gave them would go toward their alcohol dependency. Most were in what I thought to myself a "wino uniform," olive army fatigues and, regardless of the weather, a dark, wool cap and military boots. Perhaps many were Vietnam War veterans who had returned to a frosty reception from the American public, seared by their experiences, and lacking skills, resources, and treatments to reestablish their lives. Most did not shower for days, and the distinct smell emanating from this man made it difficult for us not to recoil, even as we felt sorry for him.

I took out my wallet and, silently, gave the man a dollar. He said "thank you" brightly and returned to his possessions. I invariably acquiesced to these requests. I still remember vividly the evening of December 1, 1969 during my junior year in college. With my mother and grandfather, I watched the Selective Service Lottery for men born between 1944 and 1950. Tension had pervaded our house for at least a month leading up to that evening. My mother's composure had worsened each day as December 1 loomed. When the broadcast began, my mother removed herself to her bedroom and asked that we tell her after the lottery number for my birthday, March 14, was called.

"Mom," I shouted, "it's okay, I got number 354." Those with numbers over 195 were not to be drafted. She burst out of the room, tears streaming from her eyes, and crushed me in a hug. Grandfather stood for a moment saying nothing until he gently tapped my mother's shoulder and coaxed, "Malkeh, maybe now you will want something to eat, yes?" He never said a word to me, one way or the other, about my escaping the draft.

But was it really "okay," as I had exclaimed to my mother's relief? I have always carried some guilt. Did I hand out a dollar bill to the man out of generosity? Or was there more to it?

I looked at my watch again. At Columbia Heights, we turned back and retraced our steps to Grandfather's office.

* * * *

We arrived back at 3:15. The sight of the door slightly ajar momentarily made my insides jump, but I heard voices inside that didn't sound threatening. Aliya and I went in. A woman with long, wavy red hair sat in the guest chair leaning toward Grandfather, who in turn sat behind his desk and leaned toward her. They seemed to be chatting amiably.

The woman rose quickly and walked toward us. She was about 40, tall with an angular freckled face. She wore light makeup, but her pinkish-red lipstick focused the eye on her lips. She was dressed in a khaki safari suit with a wide belt and tapered pants. Her open-toed sandals matched perfectly the color of her lipstick.

Holding a spiral notebook and pen in her left hand, she extended her right and shook first Aliya's hand and then mine. "Hi, I'm Martha Brennan of *The Daily News*. Aliya. Mr. Wolf was just saying some nice things about you. And you must be Joel."

"Ms. Brennan," Grandfather announced, "arrived within the previous few minutes, and I told her my grandson and his wife would soon return. We have been exchanging pleasantries and have not delved into the heart of her gracious visit. It seems that Ms. Brennan comes from a large family, seven brothers and sisters if I remember correctly and is fortunate that all live in the New York area."

Brennan laughed. "For the most part, 'fortunate.' Once a month we come together for a potluck lunch in Queens at my parents' house after mass at St. Mel's. No excuses permitted. Well not so much 'luck,' as it's carefully coordinated by my sister Maureen. With grandchildren, there are now 29 of us."

Brennan caught my eyes first and then Aliya's. "I think I could spend hours in relaxed conversation with Mr. Wolf, but we do need to get to, as you put it, the heart of my visit. Another story needs me to be back in Manhattan as soon as possible. Please tell me why you asked me to come?"

Grandfather leaned back and looked toward Aliya and me. "I have not yet possessed the opportunity to discuss with my colleagues, but, Ms. Brennan, I would like you to arrange, please, a meeting for Joel and Aliya with Ms. Burns as soon as it is possible. I am sure she trusts you and will be more accommodating if the request comes from you."

Before Brennan could reply, Grandfather added: "In addition, I would like you to publicize my involvement in this case. And in exchange, you will have exclusive rights to report on the meeting with Ms. Burns and subsequent developments. But I must hasten to add you will not be with them for the meeting. My colleagues will not convey to you what information they obtain from Ms. Burns until after the case is solved, if, and only if, that information will be appropriate to share."

As Aliya confirmed later, we had comprehended Grandfather's trying to take advantage of Burns' trust in Brennan. But to ask for publicity? Grandfather had studiously refused interviews and media appearances after the Ori Gold case. Why now?

Brennan also seemed taken aback. "Okay, I think I could do that. In exchange, you'll let me use personal background on your life, a picture of you if not your whole team, at least one quote for my first mention of your involvement, and updates on the case as they occur? Also, I can't be prevented from reporting information I find on my own."

Grandfather laughed. "It appears we are in a negotiations phase. Please hear my revised terms which will not be renegotiable. Yes, a picture of me behind this desk is acceptable, but not of Joel and Aliya. Their private lives should not be infringed upon. You may write about my personal life that I lived in Vienna before the Holocaust, the loss of my wife to that genocide, how long I have been a private detective, and even my office address. More information, especially about what I and my daughter endured during the Holocaust would not be appropriate. Of course, any information you obtain through your own investigation you are free to publish."

Grandfather paused for a moment. "And please use a version of the following quote: 'I would like to share a thought with the person or persons involved in Mrs. Flaum's murder. Our Jewish tradition teaches us to pray with humility but to do so, we also must possess a clear conscience.' Are those terms acceptable?"

Before answering, Brennan retrieved a Ricoh 35 camera with built-in flash from a large, red handbag. Aliya and I had recently purchased a similar model. "Okay," Brennan bowed to Grandfather, "you're a tough negotiator, but you have a deal. Let's start by taking some pictures."

Grandfather patiently followed Brennan's direction on various poses behind his desk. After a half dozen shots, she placed the camera back in her bag.

"When do you want to meet with Barbara Burns?" Brennan asked, turning toward Aliya and me.

We looked at Grandfather. "Joel, Aliya, if it is convenient for you and possible for Ms. Burns, could you engage her tomorrow evening?"

"Yes, sure," Aliya responded for both of us.

Brennan once again reached into her bag and took out a large, cloth covered address book with the initials **MB**. Opening it, she rose and made her way to Grandfather's desk. "May I?" she asked, pointing to the phone. "I have Barbara's personal number."

Grandfather still used a rotary dial phone. He turned it toward her. Brennan spun the finger wheel seven times, and upon the first ring, we heard a voice say, "hello."

"Barbara, it's me, Martha Brennan. I'm at the office of Frank Wolf, the private detective who has been brought in by Rabbi Flaum. Mr. Wolf's two associates, a Joel Gordon and Aliya...", and here Brennan looked at Aliya, who responded. "...Blum, would like to interview you tomorrow night. Would that be possible?"

I'm not sure what Burns said for the next 30 seconds. Brennan intermittently said "yes" or "no." But at the end, Brennan gave a slight smile and asked us: "Tomorrow night at 7:00, at Barbara's home in the Jamaica Estates?"

I quickly nodded. Brennan concluded the conversation: "No, Barbara, I won't be with them. I have another commitment. Thanks and talk to you soon."

Brennan tore a serrated piece of paper from the book and wrote down Barbara Burns' address. She handed the paper to Aliya, slung her handbag over her shoulder, and started toward the door. Aliya stopped her.

"One more thing, Martha," Aliya hastened to ask. "How should we dress when we visit Ms. Burns?"

"I would dress up, especially you, Aliya," Brennan responded.

Aliya nodded, and Brennan moved to the door and left the office. She was very attractive, and perhaps my gaze followed her too intently.

* * * *

I came back to myself and said with a bit of an edge:

"Aliya, do we need Brennan to tell us how to dress?"

"Yes, because in some ways, Joel, Martha Brennan knows people better than we do at our age." And then looking at Grandfather, "Perhaps better even than Zaida with some people."

Grandfather was beaming. "Joel, does not your *kallah* have good instincts?"

I quickly agreed, but my racing mind had fixated on the "deal" Grandfather made with Brennan. "Zaida," I asked, "I don't get your wanting Brennan to publish personal information about you including a picture. What was that about?"

"Good, Yoeli, your question is of course expected, and had Ms. Brennan not arrived early, I would have prepared you for my tactic. It has been a long day. I will give you a brief, but I hope, satisfactory explanation. It involves what my fictional predecessors Sherlock Holmes to Sam Spade and Lew Archer might term "flushing out the suspect." I believe a planned murder took place. Whether one person or more committed the heinous act, the responsibility lies hidden within the Jewish community. Just as with our previous cases, the otherwise excellent New York Police Department does not possess the history, the language for communication, or the knowledge of the culture to extract the requisite information for analyses. I am, whether famously or infamously, known to Mrs. Flaum's community. I want to arouse nervousness that someone who has achieved success in those other cases where secrets were cloaked within Jewish life is now involved. My hope is that such a threat causes impulsive behavior, compromising testimony, or other errors in judgment as we proceed with our investigation. Joel, this explanation is satisfactory, yes?"

I wanted to ask much more, but I could tell that my grandfather considered his words sufficient. I turned to Aliya who seemed lost in thought. "Aliya, should we accompany Zaida home, get our stuff, and head back to the City? We're all tired, and we start again tomorrow morning with our visit to the Flaum house at 8:45."

Aliya stood. "Yes, I think we should, Joel. I have no questions for Zaida at this time. We should go."

Grandfather also stood, gathered up the police report and other documents on his desk, and headed to the coat rack for his fedora and suit jacket. "Before we leave, my children, might you return the two chairs to Mr. Khan's office? As you indicated, Aliya, we will be elsewhere in the morning when Mr. Khan's office opens at 9:00."

Grandfather waited in the hall as we returned the chairs. He then locked his office and, carrying the Flaum police report, headed to the stairs with Aliya and I a step behind. He held on to the railing and descended slowly. We stepped out onto the pavement and headed toward Boro Hall to find a cab. Aliya took Grandfather's arm. He did not resist. Within a block, I hailed a cab. We were silent the whole way back to East 7th Street. Grandfather never discussed a case when he thought a stranger might overhear the conversation. I tried some small talk with Felix, the cabby, but he just puffed on a fat cigar.

Aliya rarely admitted to being weary during the day, but on the train heading to our apartment, she put her head on my shoulder: "Quite another day, three in a row."

"Yes, that's the way it is working cases with Zaida."

"I'll get used to it. Joel, Martha Brennan is very attractive, isn't she?"

I don't know if Aliya felt my flinch. "Martha Brennan? I'm not sure if I noticed."

Aliya lifted her face and looked squarely at me. "Joel!"

My face warmed. "Okay, yes, she's very attractive."

MONDAY, JULY 7, 1975

The previous evening, after our pizza and salad dinner, Aliya had called Shoshi as promised to check in on her. She let Shoshi know that her father had retained Grandfather's services, but, explicitly, without the assumed objective of "clearing" him. She also forewarned Shoshi of the article that would appear the next day in *The Daily News*.

Before the call, we had discussed the limitations on what Aliya could share with her best friend. "After all," I had said with some unease, "we hate that Shoshi is a potential suspect, but as a Flaum family member, she is closely involved with other suspects."

Aliya did not protest. "I'm learning a lot quickly from your grandfather and," after a momentary pause, "from you. I think I can separate my emotions from what I need to do."

An hour later, after I had showered and looked over the mail, Aliya was ending her conversation. I heard her say, "I love you too, Shosh, and say hello to Ben and the boys for me."

She cradled the phone and immediately told me about a conflict between Mrs. Flaum and her partner that Shoshi had just shared. Mrs. Flaum had caught Marcia Gelb embezzling at their store.

"What? Why did Shosh tell you now? Odd that she didn't mention it before."

Aliya stiffened. "Not odd at all. Shoshi said with everything else going on, it slipped her mind until I asked about her mother's relationship with Marcia Gelb."

"You asked?"

"Yes, I did. We don't know much about Marcia Gelb. So I asked Shoshi about her, and she told me about the stealing and how disappointed and upset her mother had been. And now we may even have motive."

It was after 9:00, and I was sure my grandfather had gone to bed. "You've got to tell Zaida, but tomorrow, right? Let's call him in the morning before he heads out for the Flaum house."

At 7:00, Aliya called Grandfather. "That's correct," Aliya said emphatically, "just a week before the murder, Mrs. Flaum informed Marcia Gelb that she was going to end their partnership. It seems she had caught Marcia stealing from the till. Mrs. Flaum told her she wouldn't report her to the police and that she had seen a lawyer to start drawing up a business severance document. Mrs. Flaum was to buy out Mrs. Gelb according to what the store was worth."

Aliya listened intently for a minute and said: "Okay, Zaida, we will discuss what Shoshi told me about Mrs. Gelb after we visit the Flaum residence."

Aliya hung up. "Joel, does Zaida not think much of what I told him, or does he always take new information in a perfectly neutral stride?"

I laughed. "Always the latter, but what he thinks of what your sleuthing brought up, well, I have no idea."

* * * *

On the way to the subway, I placed a quarter on a stack of *Daily News* papers at a kiosk and took the top copy. We easily found seats on the Q Train leaving the City toward Brooklyn. We looked at the paper. Martha Brennan's story wasn't page one. A murder in the Bronx held that prominence. We found it on page three. Taking up the whole sheet, the piece showed a picture of Grandfather at his desk, along with regurgitated photos of the murder scene, Rabbi Flaum, and Barbara Burns under a heading of **SUPER SLEUTH HAS ADVICE FOR RABBI'S WIFE KILLER**.

Brennan repeated a summary of the material from Thursday's story and added information on Grandfather, including his Holocaust background and previous successes. She ended with: "This cagey, white-haired super sleuth wants the killer to know that in the Jewish tradition, 'We are instructed to pray with humility but to do so, we also must possess a clear conscience.' If you are involved in the murder, Frank Wolf is talking to you!"

Aliya and I got off at the Avenue J Station and walked toward the Flaum home. On the way, I kidded with Aliya that even though we had given ourselves plenty of time and would be fifteen minutes early, my grandfather would already be there.

I was right. As we turned from Avenue J onto East 10th, we saw Grandfather pacing on the west side of the street across from the Flaum house. He stopped in front of three homes, looked at each, and then shifted his gaze back and forth from each home to the Flaum residence.

Grandfather stopped when he saw us approaching and waved. "Good morning, my children, you are right on time."

"What are you doing, Zaida?" I asked. Aliya gave him a hug.

"Your mother kindly transported me here on her way to the store in Manhattan. As you may have noticed, I am perambulating the street where the crime occurred and making observations."

Grandfather took out a small notebook from inside his suit pocket. "Once we complete our examination of the crime scene, let us remember to call Detective Carlucci to burden him more for the names and ages of the homeowners of these three homes I have written in my notebook. They have the best view of the Flaum residence, particularly this one."

He pointed to the home furthest south on East 10th with a prominent bay window toward the street and at a diagonal to the Flaum residence. The other two homes had their view at least partially blocked by the cedar tree in the middle of the small Flaum front lawn that would have kept its needle leaves in February at the time of the murder.

Grandfather motioned us to cross the street to the Flaum home. We approached a two-story brick structure painted white with a wooden bay window to the right of the entry doors. The top floor featured a brick and wood dormer that projected vertically beyond the plane of a pitched gray roof with a loft window and two rectangular windows below each side of the dormer. To the right of the house, a new model Dodge Monaco sat on a grayish-white crushed limestone driveway.

We walked up three steps to a paved walkway with a black metal bench to the left. Two urn-shaped hedges fronted five stoop steps up to a black metal grilled outer door that opened to a white, solid wood inner door.

As we stood on the landing, the door opened and Rabbi Flaum, dressed in another well-fitting three-piece pinstripe suit, brown rather than yesterday's blue, motioned us to come in. He again wore a large, crocheted kippah, this one gold and white.

"Sholom and good morning," he said brightly.

We returned his greeting, and he ushered us into an entry foyer. "I am glad you are a bit early. The Federation has not rescinded the invitation for me to attend the meeting in the City."

Holding car keys, Rabbi Flaum moved past us. "I am feeling well enough to drive today, and so as not to be late and perhaps acerbate some unwelcome feelings, I will depart now. Stay as long as you wish and, again, please lock the front door from the inside when you leave."

Grandfather and I moved slowly forward, but Aliya remained in place. I looked back at her pale face and understood her reluctance. The previous evening, we had again reviewed the police report, including the photos of Mrs. Flaum with her shattered face lying dead in the foyer. Aliya had not been to the house since the murder, and now, although no signs of the brutal event remained, I knew that in Aliya's mind, Mrs. Flaum lay with blood oozing from her head. The thought also stopped me in my tracks, and I tapped Grandfather's shoulder. He also looked behind him and immediately understood. I turned back to Aliya.

"Would you like to take a minute? We think we know what you're feeling. Zaida and I are not in a hurry."

Face ashen, Aliya's eyes locked into mine, and fear gave way to steely determination. "No," she answered, taking a small step forward, "I wanted to be a member of this team, and that's who I'll be. I know this house well. Let me tell you about the layout."

Aliya pointed to a wooden staircase to the right. "These stairs go to the upper level with two bedrooms, two bathrooms, and a loft that served as Jonathan's bedroom when he lived at home. Should we take a look at the upstairs?"

"There is no need at this point," Grandfather answered softly, "to violate a family's privacy. If the necessity arises driven by a future finding, then we shall do so."

"Okay, good," Aliya said, inching forward. She hugged the area closest to the left wall and halted at an opening to a living room on the right. Aliya pointed down a long hallway that ran from the entry foyer to a self-enclosed kitchen on the left, a small television room with a couch across from the kitchen, and a bathroom and guest bedroom at the end.

Aliya led us into the living room with its gold and cream colored décor including a sofa and two armchairs, a mantle, a walnut coffee table with picture books of Israel and New York City, built-in shelves with Hebraic and secular books, and a glass stand of four levels displaying a black and white wedding picture. Rabbi and Mrs. Flaum, I guessed. The woman's youthful face and smile echoed back and forth in my mind with the police report photos.

A hinged, large painting in an ornate gilded frame on the center wall over the sofa caught my eye. The hinged painting swung partly open revealing an open, small black wall safe. The safe was empty, except for a few coins. Perhaps Rabbi Flaum had left it in that position for our viewing benefit.

The painting portrayed a wedding scene that to me seemed from the 18th or 19th century. A bride and groom stood with their heads covered by a prayer shawl under a marriage canopy. The bride, eyes downcast, extends her right index finger to receive the wedding ring. The bride and groom do not look at each other.

"It is a 19th century Moritz Oppenheim painting titled, 'The Wedding,'" Grandfather offered. "Oppenheim, born in Germany, though currently little recognized, is our first great Jewish painter. He did not, as did many of his contemporaries, take the easy path toward recognition by rejecting Judaism, but instead employed his historical and religious roots to influence his works. The scene takes place in the courtyard of the "Old Synagogue" in the 18th century Jewish Frankfurt ghetto, with the community gathered around the wedding couple. It is not the original, which is held by a private collector in New York. But it is quite a good copy, yes?"

Aliya and I nodded. Later I would tell her, only half jokingly, that when you're on a case with my grandfather, you learn about lots of things that seemingly have nothing to do with the investigation.

To the left of the living room, curtained glass French doors opened to the dining area. The room contained a walnut table, eight upholstered chairs, and glass china closets showing dishes and Judaica items such as *Kiddush* cups, menorahs, Sabbath candlesticks, and *Havdalah* pieces.

Grandfather sat on an armchair to the right of the couch and opened his police file. He retrieved various documents, mostly the photos, and several times lifted his gaze from the documents to the painting and safe before him, and to the hallway. Twice he walked to the hallway and back to the armchair.

Finally he said: "I believe we have a good indication that the savage murder of Mrs. Flaum did not occur solely as the result of a robbery."

I jumped in. "Because Mrs. Flaum was attacked in the foyer and not near the safe. Is that what you're thinking, Zaida? If the primary intent was robbery, then the murderer would have needed to determine what valuables were available and where to find them. If Mrs. Flaum, frightened, told the perpetrator about the money in the safe, then she would have been led into the living room, forced to open the safe, and then assaulted. One way or another, the attacker had to have been familiar with the Flaum home, known about the safe, and that there was money in it. As such, I would guess that robbery was not the primary objective."

Grandfather beamed. "Ah, Yoeli, that is exactly what I am thinking. But still, we will ascertain if Mrs. Flaum kept the safe open awaiting the arrival of Mrs. Gelb."

I glanced at Aliya who gave me a proud look. Grandfather continued: "To cement our hypothesis, please take out from your police file the tragic photos of Mrs. Flaum lying on the foyer floor. From what position was she attacked? How did she fall?"

Aliya quickly removed the file from her bag, and we huddled over the pictures.

"Zaida," Aliya began, "I'm not an expert on these things, but the police report says she was hit on the left side of her forehead along with smashes to her face, mostly on the right side. She seemed to have been facing her assailant and fell back to the right wall of the foyer after the first blow to the forehead."

Aliya halted, shuddered, and continued. "Then the assailant struck her repeatedly on the right side of her face."

Grandfather looked grim. "And I would surmise from immersing myself in that moment of the attack that Mrs. Flaum was hit moments after she allowed in the murderer, whom she probably knew."

"How will we find out if the safe was already open when Mrs. Flaum was murdered?" I asked. "The police report indicates that only Mrs. Flaum's fingerprints were lifted from the lock's turning face and, for that matter, from the painting's frame. But of course, whoever killed Mrs. Flaum may have worn gloves."

Grandfather nodded. "We will pay an unannounced visit to Mrs. Gelb's store after we depart from here in a few minutes. There are times when an unannounced visit serves the investigative process well. And for corroboration, we will ask Jonathan Flaum when we speak to him. Aliya, might you be in possession of a phone number to reach him or might Shoshannah provide it to you?"

"I don't have it, but I'll call Shoshi and ask her. Do you think we could call Detective Carlucci for the information you requested earlier and Shoshi from the phone in the kitchen?"

Grandfather shook his head. "While convenient, that would not be appropriate. There are message unit charges for each call. We had not asked Rabbi Flaum for permission to do so, and he is not here for us to ask. I am sure there will be a phone booth on Avenue J on the way to Mrs. Gelb's store."

Grandfather jingled a trouser pocket. "And I have much change for these situations."

Grandfather turned toward the foyer. "Good! My children, our mission is done at the Flaum residence, yes?"

We left the house, each of us walking on the far side of the foyer wall from where Batya Flaum's head lay after being struck. We locked the inner door from the inside and closed both doors behind us. Aliya and I started to walk down the stoop. We glanced back at Grandfather standing on the landing and staring, one after another, at the houses across the street in which he had shown interest previously. In particular, he appeared to measure the view between the Flaum house and the house diagonally across to Grandfather's left.

He pointed again to the house. "I am particularly curious to know who lives in that dwelling and if anyone was inside on the morning of the murder."

* * * *

We walked slowly toward Avenue J with Grandfather's silence setting the limitation on discussion. As usual after an interview or visit to a crime scene, Grandfather retreated into himself, taking with him what he had learned about the setting of the crime including its geometry, its characteristics, and its contradictions to place himself at the exact moment the act occurred.

As we neared Avenue J, Grandfather broke the silence. He stopped and turned toward Aliya. "On the phone this morning, I had stated that we would discuss the information that you had received from Shoshannah about her mother's broken relationship with Mrs. Gelb, yes? I have just one question. How would you describe the tone of your very good friend's voice as she related the information to you?"

Aliya did not hesitate. "Calm, neutral I'd say."

"So without rancor, anger, or suspicion, yes?"

"Yes," Aliya responded.

"Good, then we at least know that Batya Flaum's loving daughter seems not to harbor thoughts of Mrs. Gelb's involvement. It is far from sufficient for our drawing a final determination, but we shall consider its influence as we proceed with our visit to Mrs. Gelb."

At East 10th and Avenue J, we came across a phone booth. Grandfather delivered a handful of change to Aliya. She called Detective Carlucci first who told her he could have the information on who owns the three homes within a few hours and to call him in the afternoon. "He's certainly cooperative," Aliya said, poking her head out of the booth before dialing Shoshi. "But I wish he wouldn't call me 'honey.'"

After reaching Shoshi, Aliya immediately began writing. Again, she poked her head out of the booth while holding on to the receiver. "Shoshi wants to know if she should call Jonathan or if we want to call him to set up a meeting. He's now living in an apartment off Prospect Park. She gave me his number."

Grandfather answered. "Please let her know that we will call him to make arrangements to come to my office. Also, please let Shoshannah know that we would like to have her come in for an interview tomorrow."

Aliya clamped her hand over the phone's speaker. "Zaida, you want Shoshi to come in for an interview? But she told me all she knows. Why?"

Grandfather did not immediately reply. I, of course, knew the answer and hoped Aliya would come to it on her own. She didn't disappoint as she disconsolately looked to me and then to Grandfather: "I guess I know why. Shoshi can't be ruled out as having involvement in the case. I took in what she told me as a friend. Her emotions became my emotions."

Aliya smiled wanly. "I didn't use critical analyses. I will ask her to come in."

Grandfather laughed and turned to me. "Did I not say, Yoeli, from the first moment I met your *kallah* that you have come across excellence?"

Aliya blushed, and while she had not closed the door to the phone booth previously, she now did so. After dropping in several additional coins and after a few minutes of conversation, Aliya hung up and came out of the booth. We had also heard her dialing anew. I wondered to whom?

"Okay, I took the liberty to ask Shoshi to come in at 10:00. That'll give her time to take the kids to her in-laws. Will that work?"

Grandfather was enthusiastic. "Yes, of course, well arranged."

I could tell that Aliya had more to say, and it would be in her proud tone. "I also reached Jonathan. He has no problem coming to your office tomorrow, Zaida, but it has to be no later than 11:00. He is still working on getting a job and hopes for an interview in the afternoon."

"It is close upon the heels of our questioning of Shoshannah," Zaida said beckoning to restart our walk toward Marcia Gelb's store. "But we will do as we must. Again, splendid initiative, Aliya."

We crossed Avenue J to its north side and turned right. The storefront, *Bezalel Judaica,* located between East 12th and East 13th Streets, stood between a *Key Food* market and a kosher butcher shop. It was a few minutes after 10:00, and the store had just opened according to a cardboard sign of hours in the front window. Before entering, I looked down Avenue J just past East 13th to the protruding black marquee of the *Midwood Theater.* In 1975, the *Midwood* showed second run movies. The marquee featured the previous year's hit, *Blazing Saddles.*

A clinking at the top of the door announced our entry. We brushed against a revolving rack of Jewish-themed greeting cards and looked down the aisle of the small, rectangular store stocked to overflowing with merchandise on counters, shelves, and glass cases. *Kippot* of all sizes and shapes took up a prominent position on the right wall next to folded prayer shawls and rows of phylacteries bags. Framed pictures of rabbis, prayer scenes at the Western Wall, and women blessing Sabbath candles hung for sale where space allowed. Counters held a wide variety of Sabbath candlesticks and Chanukah menorahs. A table held an assortment of children's games.

The glass case to our left displayed gold and silver necklaces along with *mezuzot* and Stars of David pendants for attaching. The case also contained brooches, rings, watches and, in the custom of those times, *Cross* pen and pencil sets for bar or bat mitzvah gifts. Thirteen years later, I still had two unused sets.

Between the glass case and the left wall, a heavy-set teenage girl in a white blouse and navy blue skirt affixed price tags to merchandise. She did not look up as we entered, but a middle-aged woman sitting next to her, who had been pecking at an adding machine, greeted us: "Can I help you?"

But before we could respond, she glanced at the morning's *Daily News* lying open to the Martha Brennan story. She looked back at us: "Oh yes, I imagine you do want me to help you. I've been wondering when you would come or call."

She directed her gaze to Grandfather and then to Aliya. "Mr. Wolf, I believe, and aren't you Aliya, a friend of Shoshannah? What is your connection to Mr. Wolf?"

"And you are Mrs. Gelb, yes?" Grandfather replied, bowing toward the woman. "It is quite reasonable for you to wonder why Aliya is here with me."

Grandfather gestured toward me. "Aliya is married to my grandson, Joel. Both he and Aliya are assisting me in the investigation of Mrs. Flaum's death."

"This is my daughter, Raisel," Gelb said, pointing to the girl next to her. When the girl said hello, heavy upper and lower teeth metallic braces glinted under the fluorescent lights.

"Raisel," the woman ordered gently, "you will mind the store for a few minutes? I will meet with our guests in the office?"

Her daughter nodded, and Mrs. Gelb came out from behind the counter. "Please come this way," she indicated toward the back of the store. We followed. Short and corpulent, she waddled as she walked, as if her legs had trouble bearing the weight they transported.

A narrow hall separated what she called an office from a door marked "toilet." The room we entered did double-duty as a storage area for the various types of merchandise featured out front. A large card table served as a desk with a metal folding chair between the table and the back wall. Gelb pointed to a folded chair near the door and asked me to place it for Grandfather. I did so, and Grandfather sat. Aliya and I wedged behind Grandfather and between boxes with "Chanukah Games" scrawled in magic marker.

Mrs. Gelb opened the top drawer of a ragged cardboard filing cabinet to her left and took out three folders. She carefully opened each and turned them toward Grandfather. "Mr. Wolf, I am sure you are as busy as I am. So let me say you need not start by asking me about my relationship with Batya Flaum. You are aware that Batya and I were at the end of our business partnership when she was killed. Batya was working with an attorney to draw up a business termination agreement in which I was to be bought out of my share minus," and here the woman stammered and blushed, "what I had embezzled over the previous three months. I presented no protest. Batya was not going to the police or in any way publicizing my crime. I saw it as a supreme kindness. I will never live down my shame."

Grandfather spoke with no rancor in his voice. "Why, Mrs. Gelb, may I ask, did you steal? If my phone book research is correct, you live in a fine apartment on Ocean Parkway, and your husband is a successful dentist. Please, why embezzle?"

I anticipated agitation and even tears, but Gelb responded steadily and firmly. "My husband," she began, "is a gambling addict. He loves the horses, he loves the dogs that race in Florida, he loves the Mets. I should just say he loves to gamble on everything. Through the years, his gambling got worse and worse."

Mrs. Gelb shook her head. "His rationalizations for not stopping were extraordinary. I remember the first day the New York State Lottery began maybe eight years ago. He came home with $100 in tickets and said cheerfully, 'See Marcia, gambling is not all bad. It says right here on the tickets, **YOUR CHANCE OF A LIFETIME TO HELP EDUCATION**. You see it is my way of providing charity to the needy and enjoying doing so.'"

I snickered, and Aliya nudged my arm. The woman continued: "It would have been acceptable if Arnold restrained himself with just lottery tickets, but he kept up his illegal sports and numbers betting. Our savings were being drained to the point where rent payments were a few months behind, and I feared that we would not be able to feed the children. Last Yom Kippur, while others were asking for repentance and forgiveness, I, on the other hand, made three vows: I vowed to give Arnold an ultimatum to stop gambling or I and the children would leave him; I shamelessly vowed to keep a roof over our heads and food on the table by embezzling from the business for a short period of time; and I vowed to repay every penny I stole.

"And so, beginning in mid-October, when I was alone in the shop, I would skim each week about a hundred dollars from the register. Since we are still mostly a cash business, it wasn't hard, and I would carefully alter receipts to match what I pilfered."

Gelb pointed to one of the open folders. "Here are records of all of my thefts that show the original receipt and its alteration. A total of $1,350 over a thirteen week period."

"And your husband, I take it, wouldn't stop gambling?" I asked.

Mr. Gelb turned to me with a flash of happiness in her eyes. "Quite the opposite. When I gave Arnold the ultimatum, he broke down in tears and promised he would quit. I told him his empty promises weren't good enough, that if he agreed, I had arranged for him through the Rav, Rabbi Flaum that is, in total confidence, to be admitted to the **Your Worth Rehabilitation Center** in the Catskills for a month. The Rav graciously worked it out for CPH to cover the admission from the Rabbi's Fund until we got back on our feet to pay the money back. Arnold left the next day, and he hasn't gambled since.

"In mid-January, I was ready to stop embezzling and even start paying the money back by altering receipts in the reverse fashion. Arnold had been back to work for several weeks, and our finances were returning to normal. But for that three-month period when I was stealing, Batya was confused and worried.

"'How is it that we've had a drop in revenue all of a sudden?' she would wonder aloud.

"I tried to present an equally bewildered face and disingenuously would respond, 'I guess sales are down after the New Year holidays.' And Batya would look slightly annoyed and counter, 'but they're down week after week from last year. I just don't understand.'

"But of course the snake from the Garden of Eden that still infests our lives to this day and leads us into sin gets the last satisfaction. The question kept nagging at Batya, and one evening a few weeks before her death, she went back over all of the receipts since October. I had been sloppy just once, but that was enough. I had left an original receipt along with its altered version. The next morning, Batya confronted me, and I confessed immediately. I explained why I stole, but I did not use my explanation as an excuse. I had committed a grave *averah*, a sin, which, to make matters worse, I had planned on Yom Kippur."

Silence greeted her confession. What happened next made me recall a few months earlier when I gathered with PWR colleagues by the large glass windows facing Lexington Avenue to watch the planned implosion of a smaller building on 56th to make way for a high-rise apartment. As we watched the detonation, we, along with the erupting building, seemed to suck into ourselves and then, with a loud sigh or a large breath, felt our own deflation as the building disintegrated. One minute, Marcia Gelb sat confidently and steely, and then, suddenly, sank back and erupted into uncontrollable tears.

Grandfather leaned toward her and placed his hands on the desk. She was not a relative, and he wasn't going to touch her, even as a gesture of comfort. To have done so would have been inappropriate. Instead, he said:

"My dear Mrs. Gelb, I sense from what you have communicated to us that you are a righteous woman who in desperation allowed yourself to be driven into a wrongful act. That the thought occurred to you on Yom Kippur makes it no worse than had it been a day later. Despite all of the tutelage we receive to stop those impulses that steer us in the wrong direction, we are often weak, especially when the well-being of our families influences our decision making. I also sense that you are grievously sorry, and as you started to say a moment ago, you had plans to repay what you have stolen and live with your guilt, yes?"

The woman began to control her sobbing. "Yes, thank you, you are correct. I couldn't forgive myself, but I hoped desperately that Batya might find it in her heart to do so. But she said back then, herself crying along with me, 'I can easily forgive you, but I can't live in distrust of you. God in heaven knows, I will not report you to the police, but we cannot remain partners in the business.'

"The next day Batya told me that she was going to draw up a business severance agreement, and she would buy me out for a fair price. She said she trusted me to let her know how much I had stolen, and that amount would be subtracted from my buyout share. She also said that we would continue to operate the store for a month as if nothing had changed until the agreement was formalized. Whether 20 years of friendship would now be buried, Batya said she wasn't sure. And so it was until that morning when I found the body."

Grandfather leaned back. "And now you will assume full ownership of the store?"

Gelb pointed to the other two open folders. "I will, and if you are suggesting I had a motive for killing Batya, I understand it is your job to suspect me. But put that awful thought out of your mind. I did not kill her."

"Nor arrange for her to be killed or know who did it?" Aliya asked.

Gelb's cheeks flushed. "No, I did not arrange her killing, and I don't know who killed her." Gritting her teeth, she continued. "In this folder is a record of the monies I have returned to the business for my embezzlement. And in this folder is a record of weekly transactions along with canceled checks made out to Rabbi Flaum for half the store's revenues and expenses since the partnership still exists. Rabbi Flaum knew about my thefts. I imagine Batya told him. But after the murder, he said he was not ready to discuss partnership severance as long as I was comfortable running the shop on my own. I agreed. But sometime soon, I hope, we can conclude a formal arrangement to either sell or close down the store or for me to purchase it outright."

I had a few questions, and I remembered Grandfather's coaching in previous cases to smooth the way toward the heart of the matter. "Mrs. Gelb, might you tell us when and how you formed your friendship with Mrs. Flaum?"

Her shoulders relaxed. "It was a little over 20 years ago that Rabbi Flaum, Batya, and their young family arrived at CPH. Batya got involved immediately with sisterhood, Hadassah, charitable giving, food for synagogue events, and book club. I remember well getting to know her and, in particular, our first book club discussion of Herman Wouk's novel, *Marjorie Morningstar*. We hit it right off, constantly visiting and exchanging views about our families, Judaism, politics, and the arts. I was honored but not really surprised that she thought of me first when she insisted this area of Flatbush very much needed a Judaica store. I jumped at the partnership offer."

I waded in further. "Even with the discovery of your embezzlement, Mrs. Flaum still wished you to accompany her to make the weekly deposit?"

"Yes," Gelb answered quickly. "Batya said that we would continue business as usual which meant I came on Friday mornings with my car to pick her up around 10:00 to drive to the Chemical Bank branch on Kings

Highway. We made our weekly deposits in the morning so as not to bump up against the beginning of the Sabbath after the store closed on Fridays. And Batya never wanted us to take the deposits alone fearing a holdup. From there we were to go to the store for short Friday hours until 2:30."

Grandfather spoke. "And may I ask you how much was to be the deposit?"

Gelb dug deep into the third folder and extracted a deposit slip. "Seven hundred and fifteen dollars."

Grandfather thought for a moment. "And 38 cents?"

She looked down in amazement: "Yes, that's right, and 38 cents."

A picture of the open safe at the Flaum residence flashed before me, empty except for some loose change. Grandfather had peered in, and he must have done a quick count of the coins. I regained my bearings. "On the morning of the murder, what time did you arrive at the Flaum house?"

"At 9:58, I remember distinctly. WINS 1010 had come on with its *You give us 22 minutes, and we'll give you the world* on the car radio. I stopped right in front of the house. Often Batya was already waiting at the door when I'd pull up, but this time she wasn't there. I could see the inner door was ajar. I waited a couple of minutes, and when she didn't appear, I went up to the house and rang the doorbell. After another few minutes, I became worried and went in.

"Oh, God of the Universe, I saw her immediately in the foyer, lying with blood oozing from her head. I wanted to scream, but nothing came out. I stood over her not knowing what to do. She wasn't moving. Should I lift her up? Try to stop the blood coming out? Finally, I tiptoed into the living room and called 9-1-1. I don't know how long before the police arrived, but a few times I walked over to Batya to see if perhaps she was moving or trying to speak. Back and forth I went between her body and the living room. And of course, even at that moment as life was leaving her, I probably thought more about myself than about her. 'Batya,' I said even once aloud, 'now you can never trust me. Despite what you said, I held out hope that over time our friendship could return to the way it was. Now it cannot happen.' The little person that I am, I felt more sorry for myself than for my battered friend."

Tears rolled down Mrs. Gelb's cheeks, but without the racking sobs. Grandfather once again leaned toward her. "We must not keep you from your business, but might you have a memory if the safe in the Flaum living room was open or closed?"

Mrs. Gelb did not hesitate. "It was open, for sure it was open. I remember looking at it, empty except for the few coins on its black felt tray, slightly pulled out. Come to think of it, whenever I came into the house to pick up Batya, the safe was always closed and the painting back in place."

"And would you always deposit the change along with the cash?" Grandfather asked.

"Yes, Batya was very precise, down to the penny."

"And how would you carry the change to the bank?"

"In a small plastic bag, like for sandwiches, rubber banded to a sealed envelope that held the cash, Batya always put it in her handbag."

Grandfather rose and bowed toward Mrs. Gelb. "Ah, thank you for your time and openness. We are sorry for the difficulties you have experienced."

"But I have one question," Aliya spoke up softly as we turned to the door. "Did you ever mention the thefts to Shoshi Flaum?"

Looking confused, Mrs. Gelb responded: "No, I spoke of them only to the Rav."

* * * *

The temperature was already in the low 80s when we left *Bezalel*. I worried about Grandfather's overheating, even though it was just two short blocks down Avenue J to Kornblatt's Deli. I was about to suggest that we combine business with a catch-a-breath break while we were at the deli when Grandfather stated a similar idea.

"My children, we had resolved yesterday to traverse the ground Rabbi Flaum covered on the day of the murder. But obviously we made an additional stop to interview Mrs. Gelb. Might we benefit ourselves with a Danish and a cup of Sanka at the Kornblatt's Delicatessen where we had planned to stop, in any event? As we sit and refresh ourselves, might we also review what we learned from Mrs. Gelb that adds to our analyses?"

While Aliya and I weren't Sanka drinkers, we smiled and enthusiastically endorsed his proposal. Placing himself between us and enfolding our arms, Grandfather led the way with strong steps.

I put on my kippah as we entered Kornblatt's. I immediately became hungry even though I had eaten a large breakfast. The pungent smell of brine and vinegar coming from the pickle barrels to the right and left of us stirred my appetite. I wanted a corned beef sandwich but decided against it.

The deli's breakfast rush was over, and we easily found a booth with a red vinyl upholstered double bench toward the back where we could speak easily and not be overheard. A few customers stood before a counter loudly placing orders, and a deli man and woman repeated and clarified the requests.

The glass and metal counter cases bulged with a variety of salads along with fish choices: lox, whitefish, pickled herring, matjes herring, and kippered salmon. I imagined the members of the *Bracha Breakfast Club* thoroughly enjoying their breakfast, even though *pareve* margarine and a milk substitute such as *Coffee Mate* had to substitute for real dairy products.

A neighboring case held on a top shelf an assortment of cold cuts and accompaniments: salami, bologna, corned beefs, pastrami, tongue, liverwurst, roast beef, and turkey breast. Prepared foods lay below: stuffed cabbage with ground beef, schnitzel, goulash, chicken with mushroom sauce, chicken and vegetable barley soups, noodle and potato kugels, and stuffed derma. The case closest to the doors overflowed with pastries, pies, cakes, and cookies: babka slices, linzer tarts, black and whites, brownies, and rugelach. The wall behind the counter with divided wooden shelves sent out the delicious aromas of freshly baked ryes, pumpernickels, Russian black breads, bagels, and bialys.

Aliya and I sat on one bench across from Grandfather. From the corner of my eye, I could see a man standing at the far counter looking back and forth from us to an open *Daily News*. When he started our way, I guessed what was coming. I guessed right.

The man, our presumptive waiter, was around Grandfather's age. He wore tuxedo pants with a black satin stripe down the left leg, a white shirt, black bow tie, and a cummerbund around a large pot belly. He had a full head of gray hair tufted in the middle over which sat a worn, white velvet kippah with "Mo" stitched on the front.

Mo ignored Aliya and me and, with the expression of someone who hadn't come across an old friend in years, zoomed in on Grandfather while at the same time calling out to someone unseen in the back, "Jack, guess who we got here, a celebrity, that detective, Frank Wolf."

Aliya nudged me in the ribs. Was she as humorously taken by Mo's behavior as I was? Mo went on just addressing Grandfather: "You're Frank Wolf, that famous detective, who's gonna solve the rabbi's wife murder. Well, I'm glad you're on the case because our cops, God bless 'em, haven't come up with anything. Either like *The Daily News* story is sayin', someone close to the family may have done it including, God forbid, the rabbi, or we got a murderer runnin' around, which hasn't been too comfortable for us in this neighborhood, I can tell you."

I couldn't help thinking back just a few years ago when Grandfather would have been a persona non grata at Kornblatt's after solving the Stein murder case. Some members of the Jewish community considered him a betrayer for causing a widow to lose the money from her husband's insurance policy.

Grandfather didn't miss a beat. "It is a pleasure to meet you, sir. Your name, I believe I can see, is Mo?"

"Yes sir, Mo, short for Morris. And I guess you're here to ask me questions about the rabbi with his *Bracha Breakfast Club* bein' here during the morning of the murder. I had gone over it with the police, but I'll be glad to repeat it to you since you might get somethin' they didn't. But first, let me take your orders. You're probably thirsty and maybe hungry."

Mo returned a few minutes later with an almond Danish and Sanka for Grandfather, a glass of Lipton tea and brownie for me, and a regular coffee and a small rugeleh for Aliya.

"So what would ya' like to know?" Mo asked, eagerly standing before Grandfather.

"It is much appreciated," and Grandfather waved toward Aliya and me, "your wishing to help us solve this horrible tragedy. Just a question or two. On the morning of the murder, are you able to recall with confidence the time when Rabbi Flaum left his morning gathering?"

"Sure am," Mo responded proudly. "I'm always on Friday mornings, and I've been takin' care of the *Bracha Breakfast* group since the rabbi started it about fifteen years ago."

"And the police report says the rabbi left Kornblatt's at 9:50. On what basis was that precise time established?"

Again, Mo grinned broadly. "Easy again. The rabbi always signs off on the check just as he's leavin', and we write in the date and time off the wall clock over there at the front."

Mo took out a paper from his shirt pocket. "I thought you were gonna want to see it, so as your order was bein' prepared, I went and got the receipt, the very original that shows what I told you."

Grandfather perused the paper and handed it to Aliya and me. We read quickly and returned it to Mo.

"One last question, please sir," Grandfather said. "Might you recall how Rabbi Flaum seemed on that particular morning?"

Mo answered confidently. "No different than any other Friday morning. The same look like he knows he's an important person. At least until a few days ago, people would call him 'King David' for all the good stuff he would do for CPH, the Jewish community, other communities, and tons of charities. But at the same time he tried to be just one of the guys knowin' everything about your family, talkin' sports, Mets, Yankees, Giants, Knicks, you name it, and lots of kiddin' around. You know what I mean?"

We all nodded. Mo lingered a few moments, probably hoping for additional inquiries. Finally he said: "Well, if there ain't somethin' else, I guess I'll leave you alone for a while. By the way, Mr. Wolf, your Sanka and Danish are on the house. Let me know when you want a refill."

Before Grandfather could object, Mo shuffled away. We smiled at each other. "A helpful gentleman, yes?" Grandfather said. "But as we refresh ourselves, let us take a few moments to reflect on what we learned from Mrs. Gelb. Yoeli, would you like to begin?"

I had finished off the brownie in a few bites. In the midst of taking some final sips of my tea, I responded: "Well, as much as she first tried not to show it, she's really upset about what happened, wouldn't you both say?"

"I grant you," Grandfather came back, "that she is upset, but you stated, 'about what happened.' What exactly happened about which she is upset?"

I was about to say something about Mrs. Flaum's murder, when Aliya broke in: "She's upset about her embezzlement and the whole rationale web she wove: how she had to do it, that she would pay it back, and even after she was discovered, that over time she would regain her friend's trust. But she's much more upset about the unraveling of her web than her good friend's brutal murder. She feels sorry for herself because she'll now have to live with what she's done with the web, never to be rewoven."

Grandfather looked sad, an expression I had come to connect to memories of his European past. "Yes, I think you are correct, Aliya. I believe for many people the pain we feel from our errors in judgment that satisfy our own needs and drives, when brought to naught, trouble us much more than the actual harm we do to others, whether on a personal or mass scale. But does our philosophizing bear on the case in eliminating Mrs. Gelb as a suspect? I think not. While at this point I think she had nothing to do with the crime, I may have overlooked something that would suggest otherwise."

I jumped in. "I tend to believe the factual stuff we learned from her, regardless of whether we can yet strike her as a suspect. She may have had some complicity, but she did not strike the blows. Putting things together with what we concluded from our visit to the house along with what Mrs. Gelb told us, three things emerge: one, the assault had taken place just a few minutes before Mrs. Gelb arrived in her car, and by that time she saw no one leaving the house; two, the safe would not have been open, and the money was still in the safe when Mrs. Flaum was struck. Batya Flaum wasn't waiting for her, money in hand; and three, she was attacked as soon as she opened the door to someone she certainly knew. Or she encountered someone who didn't need her to open the door, and the attacker left without closing the inner door."

"And so," Grandfather added with a satisfied glint in his eyes, "the murderer opened the safe after felling Mrs. Flaum, and that means..."

Aliya shuddered and answered: "What we surmised earlier, that someone didn't force Mrs. Flaum to open a safe that was hidden by a large painting. As we said, the person would have forced her into the living room and probably have killed her there. Also, the person knew about the safe, and" here Aliya's shudders increased, "knew the combination. Someone, oh my God, in the family!"

"Or again," Grandfather said, his expression flattening, "the person was given the combination to make it appear as a murder resulting from a robbery. But yes, on first appearances, it reinforces our consideration of the involvement of a family member. Our conclusion at this point cannot be absolute, but yes, I am led in that direction."

"Why was the change left behind in the safe?" I wondered aloud. "And if the assailant didn't want it, why not just leave it in the plastic bag?"

"I am envisioning," Grandfather answered, his eyes closed, "that whoever killed Mrs. Flaum and for whatever reason made it appear as part of a robbery, was annoyed with the change and did not want to bother with it as part of a hasty escape. We must digest this indication of character as part of our analyses. I am picturing the person ripping the rubber band and plastic bag away from the envelope, and the change falling into the tray with the plastic bag and rubber band discarded on the living room carpet."

"That's quite a hypothesis," I retorted. "How do you guess, Zaida, that the rubber band and plastic bag were on the carpet?"

Grandfather rose and waived to Mo for the check. "It is not a guess, Yoeli. How carefully did you examine the police photos? Did you by any chance examine the photos with a magnifying glass? If so, you certainly captured the presence of a plastic bag and rubber band on the carpet near each other in the vicinity of the safe."

I blushed and grabbed the check from Mo, left two dollars as a tip, and headed toward the cash register by the deli entrance. As Grandfather and Aliya moved by to leave, I saw Grandfather looking back at the Kornblatt's clerk returning change to me and writing in the date and time on the paper check.

* * * *

As we started heading toward Congregation P'nai Hesed on Avenue I, Grandfather stopped and looked at his watch. "It is now 20 minutes after eleven. I know you are prone to walk more slowly when I am with you, but if you will indulge me, please let us establish a brisker pace as we make our way to the synagogue. In this way, we may judge how long it took Rabbi Flaum to arrive from the delicatessen that terrible morning. Yes, you will do so?"

Though we were a bit worried because of the growing heat, we agreed. Both Aliya and I realized that there was no point in objecting.

"Good," Grandfather said, "then Joel, you will please set the pace as if you were Rabbi Flaum."

I did my best to gauge how quickly Rabbi Flaum had walked that morning up Coney Island Avenue to Avenue I. I looked back occasionally to my grandfather and Aliya who were just a few steps behind. CPH appeared just ahead to the west as we turned left on Avenue I. Walking toward the building, I marveled how comfortable the builders of this synagogue had felt incorporating architectural influences from the Jewish past such as this

Moorish look with minarets, along with classical, Byzantine, Romanesque, and even church Gothic design.

We stopped at the awning-covered entrance that we used the previous Saturday. It had taken us ten minutes at our moderate pace. Grandfather was perspiring, but he appeared pleased and indicated that we should enter. We did so, but instead of heading straight toward the sanctuary doors, we walked a few feet toward the east side of the building and turned into a long hallway that paralleled the sanctuary and beyond. We looked for Rabbi Flaum's office where we were to meet his secretary, Mrs. Hirsch, who would orient us along with the custodian, Eli Schorr.

We found the office at the far end of the building. Along the way, we passed other synagogue offices, a gift shop, rows of Judaica encased in locked glass cases, walls showing dedication and donor plaques, and brass boards filled with electric memorial bulbs located above the name and life span of the deceased, both in English and Hebrew. A few lit bulbs marked this day, the 28th of the month of Tammuz in the Jewish calendar.

The eastern sun filtered into Rabbi Flaum's spacious and bright office. Two window air conditioners hummed in the background. A thin woman with silver flecks through short, brown hair sat at a large desk facing the entrance doorway. A framed poster depicting the Lower East Side at the turn of the 20th Century decorated one of the golden papered walls, a black and white photo labeled the 'Original Congregation B'nai Hesed. 1929' on another wall, and a framed poster of the Jerusalem hills featuring the Western Wall on a third.

An assortment of silver picture frames containing what I took to be photos of family members at various ages neatly picketed the woman's desk. The closed door behind her read **RABBI'S STUDY**. She tapped with two fingers on a manual Remington typewriter, but as soon as she saw us, she jumped up and, with a smile, said. "Hello, sholom, I am Mattie Hirsch, Rabbi Flaum's secretary."

Looking first at Grandfather, then at me, and at Aliya, she added: "You are Mr. Wolf, and you are his grandson, and you, young lady, I do remember you well, you are Aliya, Shoshannah's friend. When you were children, you would come and run around this office. I would pretend to be stern and shush you. The rabbi said to expect you all and to have Eli show you around the *shul*. I'll just page Eli to come by to escort you and answer any questions along the way."

"Thank you, Mrs. Hirsch," Grandfather replied, "but before you call Mr. Schorr and we commence our tour, might we sit for a few minutes so that we may ask you a few questions?"

Mrs. Hirsch pointed to a nearby couch that had room for the three of us. She walked over to the outer door and closed it. Returning, she said, "Certainly, please sit. I will bring my chair over. What is it you wish to ask me?"

Grandfather looked at me, and I knew how to start. "Mrs. Hirsch, how long have you been Rabbi Flaum's secretary?"

She again smiled. "Oh, for about nineteen years now, a little while after he came to us at CPH, well, then CBH."

"You were a member when he arrived?" I followed up.

Her smile flattened. "Yes, my first husband and I were congregants, and I was coming out of a divorce with two young children and no skills, not even typing, beyond a philosophy major's proficiency in ontology and metaphysics."

She blushed, looking at each of us as if, she hoped, we wouldn't take what she said as bragging about her intellectual credentials.

Grandfather, always ready to respond to another's discomfort, said gently, "Ah, Mrs. Hirsch, I would very much enjoy a discussion with you at a later date on those subjects to which I had some exposure when I too was younger."

"Exposure!" I contained myself. Before the Holocaust, Grandfather had taught those subjects on a graduate level as a professor of philosophy at his Vienna university.

"I'd like that," Mrs. Hirsch said, brightening. "Feeling down and a bit desperate, I came to the rabbi for pastoral counseling, and right then and there he offered me this position, first on a trial basis. With its salary, free daycare at the synagogue's pre-school, along with the alimony, allowed me to get by. But even a few years later when I married Max, a loving older man with no children of his own and more than willing to share his life and ample earnings, I still stayed in the job. I was born Jewish, but when I had joined the congregation with Henry, my first husband, I knew very little about Judaism. But as Rabbi Flaum has observed to me many times over the years, there are those like me born as assimilated Jews or converts who just take to the religion."

She was beaming. "Now I read Hebrew fluently and lead a monthly ladies Torah discussion group. Somewhere along the line, my trial basis must have ended because here I am, and I have loved every minute of my job."

Mrs. Hirsch looked away. "At least until recently, I'm afraid to say."

"We may guess," Grandfather said, "as to your meaning of 'at least until recently.' But perhaps in your own words explaining when loving your position became circumvented and why it occurred would be helpful to us."

"When?" Mrs. Hirsch became flustered. "Well, of course last February when Batya was murdered." Pausing for a moment, a flush coming to her cheeks, she went on. "Well, actually some time before that day. You're trying to solve a horrible crime, and the rabbi would want me to be totally honest with you. I know him so well. Things were concerning me for several months before the murder."

"Could you please tell us more?" I requested.

"Yes, well, I sensed that Rabbi Flaum was bothered by something, or perhaps many things. He did not smile as much. He didn't crack his great jokes as much. He stayed much later at work and took on many speaking engagements and out-of-town committee meetings, which I thought must have been wearying him.

"Rabbi Flaum is an extraordinary man in what he accomplishes for CPH, for the New York Jewish community, and for the well-being of all citizens. When someone is in trouble, he will fight tooth and nail to help. I guess I'm an example, and of course Eli, our custodian, who was an addict and petty criminal when he came to Rabbi Flaum for help. The rabbi saved him. And for years, Eli has been on the straight and narrow, our invaluable custodian who meets the everyday maintenance needs of CPH. I'm not giving away any personal secrets; you can ask Eli, himself. He loves telling his story and how wonderful the rabbi has been to him. But we are a 1500-member congregation, and you can imagine how many people wish to see their rabbi on any given day for marital counseling, advice on child rearing, depression and anxiety, and so many other matters."

Mrs. Hirsch laughed. "And even to receive a blessing that they are choosing the right stocks and bonds for their portfolio or, and you'll be amazed, how many congregants just like to hang out with the rabbi in his study talking sports or politics. Which, by the way, he always refuses to do, talk politics, that is, on or off the pulpit. When we hired Rabbi Abramson as the Associate Rabbi a year ago, it helped a little, but still Rabbi Flaum hadn't come back to himself for some other reason."

Aliya chimed in. "Did you consider what another reason might be, Mrs. Hirsch?"

Her face became redder, and she looked down. "There was certainly the disappointment that he was experiencing with his son Jonathan who had difficulty completing college and then holding a job."

"And there still may have been other reasons?" Aliya prodded.

Mrs. Hirsch lifted her head and directed her response toward Aliya. "Well, yes, and it's hard for me to say, Aliya, since you are such good friends with Shoshannah, but I think the rabbi and Batya were having problems in their marriage. I think it started a few years before her death and just got silently worse."

Grandfather's eyes narrowed. "An interesting phrase you created, Mrs. Hirsch, 'silently worse.' Might you explain?"

"I guess, Mr. Wolf, I mean, between them as a couple, I never saw or heard them screaming at each other, but after years a secretary knows when something important has changed with her boss. When he spoke to Batya on the phone, there was an edge to his voice. When Batya called to speak to him, she was always gracious and asked after me and my family, but there was a tension when she asked to talk to the rabbi. For years, I would hear his cheery voice while saying goodbye on the phone or in person when she visited, but then, starting a few years back, he would say things such as, 'Ah my wife is a smart woman, but there is much about what I do and the decisions I make that she does not understand fully.' Or 'You probably know, Mattie, from your first marriage or even now with Max that after many years, two people can get on each other's nerves. My Batya, at times, can be troublesome.'"

"And how did you feel after Rabbi Flaum shared his thoughts with you?" Grandfather asked.

Mrs. Hirsch raised her hands to either side of her face and spoke as if between two hands folded in prayer. "I must be honest and say I took the rabbi's side. I am his secretary, charged during working hours to look after his welfare, sort of a wife away from home, and so I saw things only from his perspective. Even though Batya had been wonderful to me through the years, I started to resent her. For all I know, at least some of the tension I felt when she called was induced by my attitude. After her murder, I felt shame in how I had reacted to her."

She lowered her hands and looked at us. "Are there any other questions?"

Aliya asked: "And that is the extent of why you think Rabbi Flaum seemed different and you experienced tension?"

Her face became full crimson. "I think so, yes I think so."

"Mrs. Hirsch," Aliya countered, "is there really nothing else? Certainly you saw the newspaper article that exposed Rabbi Flaum's extra-marital affair with Barbara Burns. You knew nothing of it? You did not suspect?"

The flaming brightness did not recede from Mrs. Hirsch's face. "Looking back, I suspected, but I ran from the knowledge. I remember making that first appointment for Barbara Burns to see the rabbi. I have the calendar entry where I wrote 'wishes to discuss a personal matter.' She came back regularly, and the rabbi kept seeing her. She is a very attractive woman, a television personality, always dressed to the hilt and wearing gorgeous clothes and expensive perfumes.

"It may have been a few months later when I meekly questioned the rabbi about all of the time she was taking up. He said that she was greatly in need of his help. When she left his office, for quite a while she seemed happy, and the rabbi's mood was somewhat relaxed. And so, to get to the point, I did suspect an evolving emotional entanglement. To my sorrow today, I blamed Batya and her failure to make the rabbi happy and not Barbara Burns. I feel very ashamed."

"'For quite a while,'" Grandfather said, "suggests to me that different behavior eventually set in, yes Mrs. Hirsch?"

"Yes, about a month before Batya's death, they began arguing with raised voices, especially Barbara. When she was in his study, I kept the outer door shut so no one could come in here. I thought I heard sobs a few times, and I was right because when she came out, her makeup would be smeared. I never could make out exactly what was being said, but her voice often sounded threatening, and the rabbi's voice under control. And when she left, she no longer looked pleased and even rushed out once without any sort of goodbye."

Mrs. Hirsch looked around the room, stopping her gaze at the door to the Rabbi's Study. "I'm sorry I tried to hold back telling you everything. That Rabbi Flaum had an affair has been hard for me to accept. Please forgive me."

"There is no need to ask for forgiveness, Mrs. Hirsch," Grandfather replied. "As you stated, a secretary's duty is to protect her employer, and you have ably done so for nearly two decades. And in the end, you told us what you thought important for us to know, for which we are grateful. But please, one more moment. Were you here when Mr. Schorr began his duties?"

Mrs. Hirsch relaxed. "Oh yes, of course, how could I possibly forget. It was about seven years ago, late one afternoon on a hot, sunny day. I saw this man standing in the doorway with wild curly, greasy black hair, a dirty beard, glasses flecked with grime, and rumpled and torn clothes. I don't mind saying that he frightened me.

"He said that he had come to see 'the Rav.' Those were his words, and I was about to tell him that Rabbi Flaum was busy when the rabbi came out of his study. The rabbi listened for a minute to the man and invited him into his study. I am not ashamed to say that I stood close to the door in anticipation of trouble. But after 30 minutes, they came out, and the rabbi said: 'Mattie, this is Eli Schorr. Since our custodian just left us, Eli will be assuming the position and residing in the custodian's basement apartment beginning tonight. Could you please place Eli on our payroll and advance him $100 against his first paycheck so that he can go shopping tonight for clothes? I will let the Board know.'

"After I showed Eli to his new quarters, I returned to my office. Rabbi Flaum told me that Eli grew up in Boro Park in a religious family, had fallen prey to addiction, served six months in Riker's for possession, and was just released from a city-run rehabilitation program and had been drug-free for over a month. While he was a high school dropout, he did well in his vocational training classes and had held down various maintenance jobs in between drug rehabilitation. 'We will take a chance on him,' the rabbi said. 'As you know, one of my favorite Talmud dictums is, *whoever saves a single life is considered to have saved the entire world.*'

"And that was that. Eli's been with us ever since, no troubles, keeps himself clean in all senses of the term, maintains the building beautifully, and except for long conversations with the rabbi, doesn't have a great deal to do with anyone else including, from what I can observe, his own family members. Eli can be quite intense, at times, but we have gotten used to him."

Grandfather thought for a while and then stood up. "Good, very good, Mrs. Hirsch. And now, would you please call Mr. Schorr, and we will take up only a few minutes of his time for us to tour the synagogue. And while we wait for him, is the Rabbi's Study unlocked? If not, would you have the key to it, or must we wait for Eli? We would just like to take a quick look inside."

Mrs. Hirsch sprang up. "Oh, you don't need Eli for that. I have keys to the outer office and to the Rabbi's Study. But Eli will have the keys to everything else."

Mrs. Hirsch moved to her desk drawer, took out a set of keys, and walked over to open the door to the Rabbi's Study. Grandfather motioned for all of us to enter. The brown lacquer on the mahogany desk and bookcases gleamed. Books, folders, and notepads lay on the desk in square or rectangular arrangements, with distances between each remarkably the same. A finely buffed, dark brown phone with extension buttons sat to the right within easy reach of whoever sat in the matching leather swivel chair. A Tiffany lamp of multicolored glass on a brass base suggesting a tree trunk and spread roots sat precisely at the back center of the desk. I looked at the silver framed photos at the desk's left and recognized the cheerful faces of Rabbi Flaum's two grandsons, Shoshi's children, the only family photos in the room.

The bookcases filled with Jewish writings in Hebrew and English took up most of the gold papered walls. But one smaller bookcase in particular caught my attention. Classical British and American novels in chronological order from 18th century Henry Fielding and Laurence Sterne to more recent writers such as William Styron and Saul Bellow filled this bookcase. Intermittently and thoughtfully placed along the walls hung various diplomas, Rabbi Flaum's bachelor's degree, doctorate from Columbia, and a beautifully embellished declaration of rabbinical ordination from Yeshiva University. Spaces in bookcases were also reserved for photos of the rabbi at synagogue milestone events, interactions with celebrity figures, and moments captured with well-known clergy from all branches of world Jewry.

"If you will indulge me for a few minutes, Joel," Grandfather asked, "would you please join Mrs. Hirsch in the outer office and close the door behind you? Then please take a position near Mrs. Hirsch's desk. And Aliya, you will please stay with me?"

I didn't question his request and followed Grandfather's instructions. Mrs. Hirsch sat back at her desk. "They'll be out in a moment," I said with no further elaboration since I had none.

After a few minutes, we could hear voices coming from the study. At first, a steady murmur of conversation, and while I could make out Aliya's voice as distinct from Grandfather's, I couldn't comprehend what either was saying. Then the voices, especially Aliya's, became louder and strident, but still I couldn't make out what was being said besides a word or two. When I distinctly heard Aliya sobbing, I wanted to rush in, but, bewildered, I held my place. Mrs. Hirsch said nothing, and I thought her self-restraint and trust in us remarkable.

Finally, the door to the study opened and Grandfather, with Aliya clasping his elbow, came out. I was really confused. Although her cheeks were wet, she smiled as she walked over and whispered, "later."

* * * *

"Later" would have to wait as Eli Schorr came bounding through the door. Short, around 5'3", and V shaped from the small head down to a rotund stomach and stubby legs, he appeared like a cartoonish gnome come to life. His jet black, long curly hair had a clean sheen, and the locks partially hid a bobby-pinned black satin kippah. His long, but groomed black beard with gray speckled wisps, along with his thick Coke bottle glasses, made me think of a mad scientist. He wore a gray, one-piece jumpsuit with CPH in large letters on the back. The left front lapel read, *Eli Schorr, Maintenance Director*.

I couldn't help but stare at the opening at the jumpsuit's waist that Eli must have cut and tailored to allow the four-corner fringes of the rectangular vestment worn underneath to be visible in the manner of many Orthodox Jewish males.

When Eli spoke, his high-pitched voice had a slight lisp, often accompanied by a chuckle. *"Sholom aleichem, sholom aleichem,"* he addressed the three of us and ran over to shake Grandfather's hand and then mine. He bowed slightly toward Aliya. "Mattie, I'm here because you're ready for me to show our guests around as the Rav requested?"

"Yes," Mrs. Hirsch replied, "this is…."

Eli interrupted. "Mr. Frank Wolf, his grandson Joel, and his wife, I forget her name, and they're going to try to find out who killed Mrs. Flaum so the Rav is no longer a suspect. I also saw the story in this morning's *Daily News*."

Aliya took a step forward. "My name is Aliya Blum, and we are here as part of our investigation into who murdered Mrs. Flaum. Thank you for your assistance in showing us around the *shul*."

"Nothing to it, nothing to it," Eli chuckled, turning his attention back to Grandfather and me. "Anything I can do to clear the Rav's name."

"Then we will follow you according to your pace to see all of the floors," Grandfather said. "There is no need to take us into the sanctuary with which we are familiar." Grandfather motioned toward the door. "Please, Mr. Schorr." And turning back to Mrs. Hirsch, "Thank you for your immense help. We are grateful."

The tour took an hour. Eli at first spoke non-stop. On the main level, which we had already traversed, he told us about synagogue politics, who was vying for the presidency, what prominent figures belonged to CPH, who of importance recently passed away, and the very strong state of the synagogue's finances.

"And Mrs. Flaum, was she much involved in synagogue matters?" Grandfather asked.

Eli did not hesitate as we kept walking. "Mrs. Flaum, Mrs. Flaum, I guess, especially when I first started at CPH, and not so much since she started her store. Volunteered at the gift shop, sisterhood events, other clubs, didn't play mah jong, but was on some of the more important committees such as Education and Religious Activities. And I'll tell you, she didn't always make life easy for the Rav on those committees. Didn't make life easy, sometimes openly disagreeing with what he was proposing. Can you imagine?"

Grandfather did not follow up. We made our way to the second floor. Eli kept up his chatter as he identified the grade levels for the classrooms, each with walls featuring a chalkboard, the flags of the United States and Israel crossing each other, along with children's artwork and short essays that appeared more sophisticated and elaborate as the grades rose. Melamine-topped student desks with black, sliding book and accessories boxes, along with matching chairs filled the classroom. The meetings rooms all had similar metal rectangular tables, folding chairs and a rolling chalkboard.

"Do you want to see the basement?" Eli asked hesitantly after completing his narration of the last room on the second level.

"If you would be so kind, yes," Grandfather replied. "But while we are standing here a moment, could you please tell us how well you knew Mrs. Flaum?"

"How well did I know her, how well did I know her?" Eli tittered. "Pretty well, pretty well, I guess. When I first came to CPH, the Rav would invite me over often for a Sabbath eve meal, and I'd see her at CPH a lot, but in the last few years, not so much, not so much as she didn't come as often, and I didn't go over to their house much. She was a nice lady, I guess, but nothing special if you ask me, nothing special. There are a lot of nice ladies at the shul."

"Such as Barbara Burns?" I asked. I gave a quick glance toward Grandfather who didn't look displeased.

Eli's eager response surprised me. "Yeah, yeah, like her. What a great lady! Beautiful, isn't she? Beautiful! And elegant the way she dresses. I'm not one to judge fashion, but she was unlike Mrs. Flaum who always looked frumpy to me. Mrs. Burns, I guess that's the right way to call her, always smiling with those beautiful eyes of hers, not afraid to come near me, like some people around here, and often bringing me treats such as cakes and candies, always considerate, with a *hechsher*, with a *hechsher*, you know a certification of their being kosher on the packages."

Aliya asked. "And was Mrs. Flaum one of those people who was afraid to come near you?"

"Nah, she didn't have that attitude. But she couldn't make me feel special the way Mrs. Burns did."

With no one asking any further questions, Eli headed us down two flights of stairs to the basement level. We followed with Grandfather holding the railing in the darkened stairwell. Eli descended quickly as Aliya and I kept the slower pace with Grandfather.

He held the door open as we passed through. "Basement's got three things. Three things: storage rooms for all sorts of stuff like prayer books, school supplies, and outdated junk. The Rav doesn't like anything thrown away but insists we try to find folks who could use what we no longer need. Second, what I call the guts of the *shul*, the guts of the *shul*, what makes it keep functioning: the boiler room with its plumbing, heating, cooling, and water supply."

We kept moving down the hall until Eli abruptly stopped. "And here," he pointed proudly to a door, "is the third, what I call 'my pad,' my own apartment, 'my pad.'"

We gazed at the door which displayed Eli's first and last name above a hand-written admonition not to enter without knocking. Eli started moving on when Grandfather stopped him: "Mr. Schorr, it would be possible for us to look into your apartment, perhaps just to stick our heads in? We like to obtain a complete sense of an environment, and the home of the synagogue's Maintenance Director certainly has prominence in our overview."

Eli turned back. "Well, okay, it's a bit messy in there, but take a peek."

He opened the door, and we each looked in, one at a time, not crossing the threshold. A quick observation showed a room that served as a studio apartment with a sink, two kitchen cupboards without doors, a small refrigerator, gas stove with an oven below, sofa bed, television, small bookcases, and a curtained area with a shower head peeking out from the top that must have been his bathroom. On the wall above the sofa bed hung a large framed picture that announced at the top, **REFUAH ADDICTION CENTER,** and its address. Below was a drawing of an Orthodox young man in a large kippah, white shirt, dark trousers, and fringes at his side sitting before syringes, white powder, and marijuana cigarettes, eyes wide in fear, his face ringed in sweat droplets. Beneath were written the words, I recognized, of a Hasidic sage: **G-D is wherever you let Him in**.

On a coat rack close to the door hung three Yankees baseball caps of different styles, a tan wool newsboy hat, black fedora, white panama with a purple band, two tightly rolled black umbrellas, and a tool belt with hammers, wrenches, and screw drivers wrapped evenly around the lowest branch.

"A bit messy," Schorr had advised us.

Not in the least. The kitchen sink shone brilliantly, the dishes in the cupboards arranged meticulously, no dust and no clutter anywhere.

"That's it, that's it." Eli muttered with less enthusiasm than when he began on the main level. "I'll walk you upstairs."

"Yes, thank you, it is proper that we now depart," said Grandfather. "But just two more questions, please. Would you have an opinion as to who murdered Mrs. Flaum?"

Mirthless, Eli responded. "I have an opinion, but it's not about who killed her but who didn't do it. And that's the Rav. I get it, I get it, Mrs. Burns may be angry that she made the Rav fall for her and he didn't want to divorce Mrs. Flaum and marry her, but the Rav would never have murdered his wife, never! He would have gone to the end of his days in an unhappy marriage, but he would never kill her. Never! Must have been a robbery gone bad just as the cops first thought!"

"Ah, your perspective is most helpful, Mr. Schorr," Grandfather replied. "And the very last question as we trust your memory and sensitivities. How was Rabbi Flaum's mood around the time of the murder?"

"His mood, his mood! It wasn't that great. Things were troubling him, and it's not that I just could tell, which I could, but you know he would confide in me. Sometimes when we were alone late at night in his office at the *shul* and we would have a glass of schnapps together, he would say, he would say, 'You know Eli, life sometimes is *shver*.' That means if you don't know Yiddish, 'difficult.'"

"We know, yes, please go on," I snapped.

Eli ignored me and quickly continued. "He sometimes carried the whole Jewish world on his shoulders and on top of that New York City itself with its race relations issues, and the jockeying for leadership at the *shul*, and the politics at the Rabbinical Council, and add to that not having comfort in his own home. In his own home! Once, just once, the Rav had more than one glass of schnapps and said, 'where there is no *sholem bayis*, peace in the home, there is no peace elsewhere.'"

Grandfather asked, "And you believe he was referring to his relationship with Mrs. Flaum, and not, possibly the absence of peace at the synagogue or the Rabbinical Council?"

Eli responded with a chuckle that also contained a sneer. "Of course it was Mrs. Flaum. She was the cause of his sadness, she was."

Eli lifted his head. "And I'll even tell you, I knew for a while about what was going on with Mrs. Burns. And I didn't care. Didn't care! Who could blame an important man with a wife who causes him trouble for falling for such a beautiful woman!"

* * * *

We walked out into a steaming, hot day. Grandfather halted immediately.

"There is much for us to digest utilizing our critical analyses skills, yes? I would like to return home and proceed to unravel my thoughts. It is quite a hot day, no? Might we obtain the services of a taxi to convey us? If we walk one block back to the Coney Island Avenue, taxis can be found, yes?"

Aliya and I agreed. He was right about easily finding a cab on Coney Island Avenue. We dropped Grandfather off at East 7th and Avenue P and, feeling too lazy to drag ourselves to the subway and probably into an unventilated hot train, we told the cabbie to take us home to Manhattan.

Although Grandfather had trained me not to discuss a case in anyone else's presence, the music from a Middle Eastern radio station blared loudly, so I whispered to Aliya: "I'm dying to know, what was going on in Rabbi Flaum's study when you were behind closed doors with my grandfather?"

Aliya laughed aloud for the first time in several days and answered, lowering her tone to a whisper. "Your grandfather wanted to test how well voices in the study could be heard from the outer office. He's amazing. First he said we would engage in regular conversation, so he asked me to explain what I had learned about cognitive behavioral therapy. Then after a minute, he asked me to pretend I was Barbara Burns and he Rabbi Flaum. As Rabbi Flaum, he said, 'Barbara, you know I cannot marry you at this time. My wife is in the way.' And he told me to react emotionally and say, 'But we care for each other so much. I can't go on this way.' I take it you couldn't hear exactly what we were saying, am I right?"

"No, not even when you raised your voice, only that something nasty was being exchanged. But I saw tears on your face. You were actually crying when you shouted those words?"

Aliya placed her head on my shoulder and looked up at me. "You've got quite a wife, don't you Mr. Gordon. Remember attending one of my plays in high school? *A Doll's House*? I was Nora. I took acting lessons and learned how to show emotions, including crying on cue. I haven't lost the touch."

I kissed Aliya and relaxed the rest of the way home.

* * * *

As much as one gets absorbed in a case, one still has to attend to everyday demands. Aliya and I had expected to be on vacation, so when we arrived home, the proverbial cupboard, refrigerator, and freezer were bare. After an hour of relaxing in bed, we made a quick shopping list and headed out. We stopped at a nearby Shop Rite that had a kosher meat case and purchased some packaged cold cuts and chicken, along with a few other grocery basics, enough to cover us for a few days since we didn't want to lug too much in the heat.

We returned to our apartment around 4:00 to the phone ringing. I picked up the receiver just in time.

"Joel," my grandfather said after his greeting, "I have just been in receipt of a telephone call from Detective Carlucci. He conveyed to me the name of the occupants of the three homes across from the Flaum residence. Please ask Aliya to record the following in her notebook."

I called over to Aliya who had finished putting away the groceries to come over and bring her case notebook and pen. I held the phone away from my ear so that Aliya could also hear. "We're ready, Zaida, Go ahead."

"Very good. I will speak slowly. The Flaum house is at 1073 East 10th Street. If we are standing in the front of the Flaum house and gazing across the street, the house diagonally right is 1070 East 10th Street occupied by a Michael Harris and his wife Susan, both aged in their 40s with young children. The house directly across is 1074 occupied by Jerry and Ruth Weinberg, in their 50s with college age children. And in the house diagonally left, 1078, dwells a Mrs. Gianna Caviglia, age 78, a widow with no one else living with her."

Grandfather paused. "My children, have you successfully recorded what I have transmitted so far?"

We assured him that we had, and Grandfather went on. "If you remember what is written in the police report by house number identification, the dwellers at 1070 and 1074 reported that no one was home at the time of Mrs. Flaum's murder. But Mrs. Caviglia at 1078 indicated that she had observed the plumbers coming and going and nothing else. I believe it behooves us to re-interview Mrs. Caviglia. Toward that end, I have called the lady and arranged for us to visit her tomorrow at 2:00. Does anything stand in the way of your accompanying me at that time?"

"No, no," both Aliya and I answered.

"We'll finish our interviews with Shoshi and Jonathan in the morning, have some lunch, and go over to this Mrs. Caviglia's home at 2:00," I said, placing the phone to my ear. "Is there anything else to plan for tomorrow?"

Grandfather laughed. "We shall see, Yoeli. At present, it is only today."

There was a good deal left to do this day. "Joel," Aliya pronounced after I hung up. "We're due at Barbara Burns' home in Jamaica Estates at 7:00. We should make sure we're on the train by 6:00. Let's make ourselves a quick bite and discuss the questions we want to ask her and our approach. I think I should take the lead. Are you okay with that?"

I was fine with Aliya's proposal, but I asked anyway: "Just curious, why do you think you should take the lead?"

"Because Burns was responsive to Martha Brennan, Burns thinks another woman would understand her anger and grievance. I can be empathic."

Aliya came over and draped her arms around me. "And as much as there are times when someone like Barbara Burns would like to direct her attention to and flirt with a strong, handsome guy like my husband, I think she's now in a 'I'm sour on men' frame of mind. Trust me. I come out of a girl's locker room."

I was putty in Aliya's draped arms. "Sure, I absolutely trust you and will follow your lead."

Aliya kissed me: "Thank you. I'll also need about an hour to get ready. As for you, Mr. Handsome, no *shlubby* dressing for this visit. Good slacks, shoes, dress shirt, and your one and only navy sport jacket. Okay?"

Although my puttied state hardened somewhat, I answered: "Okay, I wasn't going to go *shlubby*, but probably not that dressed up. An hour? You need an hour to get ready? You never take that long."

"Trust me," Aliya repeated as she went into the kitchen to prepare our food.

When Aliya came out of the bedroom at 5:40, I had already been dressed and waiting for 30 minutes, my clothes just as Aliya instructed. I looked up and looked again. Aliya was wearing a plum-colored chiffon midi-dress, with a small rounded neckline and sleeves half way to the elbows. She had on stockings and heeled open toed shoes. But I stared, actually gawked, at her wearing full makeup, perhaps the most made up I could remember since our wedding. She had abandoned her ponytail for hair elegantly pinned back. Instead of her large handbag, she now carried a small, black, rhinestone-adorned shoulder purse. I sniffed. She was also wearing perfume, Lanvin Arpege I guessed. Aliya had received a bottle as a bridal shower gift, and it had remained sitting unsprayed day after day on our bedroom dresser.

"Wow," I exclaimed, jumping to my feet, "you look…"

"Like Aliya under strategic camouflage?" she laughed. "That's what you were about to say, right, Joel?"

"Well, not exactly, but good to know that you'll always put one on for the team. Do you really want to go on the subway, all dressed up like that? Should we take a cab?"

"Nope, we're train people, right, unless we really have to take a cab such as when your grandfather comes with us or we're totally exhausted."

Aliya had anticipated my worries about a beautiful woman riding the subway. "And if anyone makes an advance toward me, I think my big, brave husband will protect me."

"I sure will," I responded, picking up my keys and offering my arm to Aliya. "I absolutely will."

* * * *

Despite its being rush hour, we rode the F Train to the Jamaica Estates neighborhood of Barbara Burns uneventfully. Although we stood the whole way, we didn't have to endure the press of person-on-person, usual for that time of day. The air conditioning also worked.

We got off at the 179th Street station at the end of the F line and walked up into the lingering heat of bustling Hillside Avenue. The smell of Hebrew National hot dogs from a kosher kiosk tempted our appetite. But with fifteen minutes to go before we were to arrive at Barbara Burns' home, we resisted.

We crossed 179th heading east for a few blocks and joined a multitude of ethnic groups and languages jostling by us. Aliya walked slowly in her heeled shoes. Within our four minutes walk, we passed a Dunkin' Donuts, kosher bakery, McDonalds, laundromat, candy store, check cashing and bail bond shop, large Sloan's supermarket, jewelry and watch repair, storefront law firm specializing in visa cases, and a few entrances to walkup apartments thrown in between the commercial sites.

When we came to Midland Parkway which joined Hillside at a perpendicular, we turned, crossed Hillside, and immediately encountered the Jamaica Estates gatehouse. It stood on four columns of river stone buttressing a clay tiled roof with a cupola and flagpole in the center. Metal railings set off a monument of stucco and stone with a star at the top and plaque in front honoring the memories of the ten men from the Estates who lost their lives in World War II.

We were in a different world. Just yards away from the grime and blaring car horns of Hillside Avenue, we had been transplanted to an English countryside with large, mostly Tudor-style houses, some with circular driveways, and along the parkway, flourishing trees, mostly oaks but some yews and dogwoods. Lush vegetation filled each lawn.

Nor did we hear the hum of hundreds of window air conditioners. Rather, I marveled how all the homes seemed to possess central air conditioning. As we walked and talked, we found ourselves lowering our voices as if we were walled off in this rustic refuge from the previous demand to speak over the din of Hillside Avenue traffic.

We could also hear the conversations of others who passed by. Two men, both with clear Irish brogues, heatedly discussed the Northern Ireland "Troubles." An elderly couple, the white-haired man wearing a richly embroidered satin yarmulke hat, and the woman wearing a summer coat dress well below the knees, the fabric richly colored and embroidered with lace and silk, passed us speaking rapidly. They were Bukharan Jews who had started to move into Jamaica Estates some years before. I recognized the Bukhori language. My high school friend, Abramov, or Abie, as we called him, tried to teach me. I learned enough for my ear to identify it, but besides "hello" and "goodbye" which were the same as the Hebrew "*sholom aleichem,*" I didn't comprehend a word.

Another couple, our age, strolled by discussing, in strong New York City accents, where they would have dinner that night.

Barbara Burns lived on Dalny Road near Avon Street, a perfect name for the neighborhood. When we stopped in front of her home, I looked at my watch. 6:58. We only had a minute to take in the expansive, golf-greens lawn with surrounding azaleas, laurels, liriopes, hollys, nandinas, and other varieties I couldn't identify. The red brick, Tudor-like house also featured a large, white Greek style portico with four Doric columns rising to a triangular shaped entablature, its frieze presenting a non-distinguishable coat of arms. Three steps led up to a rust-colored wooden front door framed by white stucco molding that rose to the center top where an American eagle held arrows in its talons. To the right and left of the door, two oval shaped windows kept the viewing eye balanced.

"Should we wait a few minutes to be fashionably late?" I asked.

"I don't think so," Aliya replied, heading toward the walk. "Let's take after your grandfather and be punctual. I think that will work best with Barbara Burns."

We tapped our fingers to the polished silver mezuzah attached horizontally to the right door frame. Aliya rang a red doorbell. We could clearly hear the chimes inside. After a few seconds, the door opened half way, and a woman peeked out.

"Yes, hello, you must be the two young people working with that detective, Mr. Wolf. Martha Brennan called me about setting up a meeting. I think it's Aliya and Joel, am I right?" The door swung fully open. "Please come in."

We entered and re-introduced ourselves. We stood awkwardly in an expansive foyer. Wide-planked, moderately dark oak flooring and a beautifully ornate Turkish rug centered the eye between an arched entryway to a library on our left and an open white molded portal, the size of a double door, to a living room on our right. She motioned us to enter.

I gaped as we entered. That one room held more furnishings than were in my whole house when I was growing up. I hoped she hadn't noticed my awe-struck response. A classic Tudor rose décor pattern wallpapered the room. The windows facing the front of the house still had ample light pouring through sheer white curtains topped by heavy golden drapes. From the center of a cream-colored ceiling, spaced by oak beams, hung a gleaming glass chandelier with small flame bulbs that mimicked a dozen candle holders.

In the middle of the room sat a richly dark round coffee table on four sculpted legs. An ornate, flowered china tea set with three cups had been placed on lace doilies, along with an assortment of sandwiches cut into quarters on rye and wheat breads. A velvet sofa took up one side of the table, and across from it, stood an oak wood arm chair, with a cushion matching the velvet of the sofa. Love seats in matching upholstery lined the two walls perpendicular to the front windows. An assortment of chairs in various English styles from Tudor through Queen Anne to Victorian, along with a writing table and desk, filled the rest of the room. The far wall contained a tall fireplace, gold enameled over a brown metallic frame that could have passed, at a quick glance, for wood.

"Please have a seat," Burns instructed us, indicating the couch for two. "I thought you might be hungry so I prepared some tea and *pareve* sandwiches, tuna and egg salad. Kosher of course. I didn't know if you have dietary restrictions. Please help yourselves."

I was prepared to see Barbara Burns as I had imagined her from *The Daily* News articles, but the thoughtfulness of her hospitality made me take another look. Thin and lanky, she dressed in a light blue denim jumpsuit with a thin brown belt. Her lush, ash blonde hair, falling to her shoulders, shone. Carefully penciled eyebrows emphasized her gray eyes, and her foundation, rouge, and powder were discretely applied. Each ear had a small, diamond stud, and the pinkie finger of her left hand showed an onyx on a gold base ring. Working part-time at my mother's jewelry store as a kid contributed some knowledge of gemstones.

We sat, and Aliya took a napkin from the table and spread it over her lap. "Thank you Ms. Burns. As it happens, we are hungry. Also, thank you for your consideration. Joel and I can eat tuna and egg salad any time of the day." Aliya poured herself some tea and chose egg salad. I smiled at Burns and followed suit.

"Did you want to ask me anything in particular, or do you just want me to tell you what I've been through and why I went public about Rabbi Flaum?" Burns did not reach for food or drink.

I waited for Aliya to answer. "If you would, Ms. Burns…"

"Barbara, please call me Barbara, and I'll call you Aliya and Joel." She had a wide and engaging smile.

"Yes, that would be great," Aliya continued. "Could you just briefly tell us about your background? You don't sound as if you grew up in the New York area."

"You've got a good ear, Aliya. I didn't. I'm from Kansas City and first came this way to attend Barnard. And yes, my last name really is Burns, changed from Bernofsky almost a 100 years ago when my great-grandfather came as one of the first Jews to Kansas City. And while the family has married Jews down through my generation, particularly from western Missouri, I grew up very assimilated.

"At Barnard in the early 1950s, I was in a way a misfit. I always had loved math and the sciences and wasn't going to major in English or education like almost all of the other girls. Thanks to my parents who encouraged my interests and who bought me a telescope when I was 10, I particularly loved meteorology and astronomy and wanted to do something with my interests. But Barnard offered very few courses, especially on the upper levels, in these disciplines. I wrote letter after letter to incredulous deans at Barnard asking that I be allowed to take courses at Columbia as a geology/earth sciences major."

Burns frowned. "You know what they say—'beware of what you ask.' The harder slog was after they finally agreed."

Burns' voice lifted. "Columbia is all male. I was the only girl in that major attending class after class with guys. I knew I was considered attractive, so I decided to play down my appearance by not putting on makeup, pulling my hair back, and wearing loose-fitting sweaters and pants. Boy did that backfire! The snickers when I came into a class and when I left were never-ending. Loudly whispered jibes branded me a lesbian, while at other times I was cast as being promiscuous."

I thought Barbara had given me a quick glance as if I may have been part of such a revolting group, but it may have just been my discomfort reacting.

She continued. "Professors were condescending and openly questioned my 'intentions' to be in a man's world. My fury kept growing and, one day, before I exploded, I decided on a different tactic. I was taking an upper-level geophysics course that featured a lecture for about 50 students. I dressed to the hilt with full makeup, bouffant hairdo, pendant earrings, tightly fitted dress, hose, and heels. I waited until a minute before class was to start and walked in and made my way up the middle aisle to the top of the lecture hall.

"Immediately, stunned silence! Not one cat call, snide vulgar comment, or derisive laugh. The professor, who was probably in his 50s, stammered through the lecture. I don't think those boys heard a word of what he was saying as they tried as sneakily as possible to transfer their eyes to the back of their heads. It was as if I had turned every male in that room, including the gray-haired professor, into timid adolescents.

"And that's how I got my degree in geology with emphasis on meteorology. From that point on, I continued to dress in that fashion when I was on the Columbia campus, and I got an A in each of my courses. Damn it, I think I earned every one of those marks, but I'll never really know. Professors kept inviting me to their offices and asking how they could promote my interest in their field. I would just smile and tell them that their wonderful lectures and comments on my papers were enough, and I'd let them know if they could help in any other manner. I never returned to their offices."

Burns paused for a moment allowing Aliya to say, "I understand, and I'm sorry."

"I'm sure you do," she responded without sarcasm. "And I also can see that you were smart enough to match dress up with dress up, but I'm guessing that underneath you're a ponytail and no makeup girl most of the time. Am I right?"

Aliya laughed and nodded. Both turned to me. I was on my third sandwich. Why I blushed, I don't know, but I didn't have anything to add.

"You stayed in New York after graduation?" Aliya asked.

"No, New York was expensive, so I went back to Mom and Dad in Kansas City. My goal was to get myself into the National Weather Bureau headquarters there. But feminine wiles don't work if no one responds to your applications. I took a job at KCMO-TV writing the weather reports for the men who presented them on air.

"One day in January of 1957, Glen, the Weather Man, got sick and didn't show up for the six o'clock news. I took advantage of the panic that set in and volunteered that since I had the script in hand and knew how to present to the cameras, I could do it. The station manager reluctantly agreed. I went on without a hitch. That would have been that, since Glen showed up the next day, but viewers, mostly men and a few women, for various reasons, wrote in saying I was refreshing compared to Glen. I was given the 10:00 o'clock spot on Saturday and Sunday nights that no one wanted.

"After a year at KCMO, I wanted more, and my anger was rising. I wrote the weather scripts for stodgy Glen and myself, and all I had were the weekend night spots and occasional days when a man couldn't be found to substitute for Glen. But I did have film, so I left Kansas City and started working my way east over the next five years, all with pretty much the same results: write the scripts and take unwanted weekend appearances. St. Louis, Cleveland, Philadelphia, and then to WPIX here in New York. I now write scripts only for myself and sit in with real meteorologists to predict the weather. I have weekend spots that, given it's New York, lots of people watch, and I'm hopeful of getting prime time. But I'm getting older, and there are many attractive younger women, some with meteorology degrees, who are competing with me."

Burns stopped speaking. Her previously bright eyes dulled as she seemed to draw into herself but then reemerged angrily as she looked at me: "But not once did I actually give away my body for a job or a promotion. Not once, if you believe me or not!"

I held my ground and did not look away. "I do believe you," I said firmly.

Aliya drew Burns' attention away from me. "I also believe you, and I know my husband, and so does he. But might I ask, how is it you became involved with CPH?"

Burns settled down. "Yes, of course, that's really why you're here. My affair with the rabbi and my fury at the way he treated me. I'm also a suspect in Mrs. Flaum's murder, aren't I?"

I nodded, and Aliya replied, "Yes, at this point, you are. Please continue."

Burns looked past us and began. "After starting at WPIX, I took an account of myself. Here I was, over 30, making decent money, working toward my career goal, attractive on the outside, in and out of a few relationships, but still that girl who at Columbia had used her appearance to fight back. Now I desperately wanted a makeover within. My appearance had become too much a part of me to change, but I couldn't bear the shallowness inside me any longer."

Burns smiled.

"I met Burton at a dinner party hosted by a Barnard classmate. As usual, I was nicely attired even though most people were in their early 1960s dress-down. And Burton was tall and debonair, wearing a dinner jacket and an ascot. We were a striking couple. He was already a successful real estate developer, recently divorced with two children who were living with their mother. We hit it off right away, and he wooed me in the stock way of flowers, chocolates, jewelry, expensive restaurants, and romantic trips. But while those expressions were welcome, what drew me mostly was his tie to Judaism, and he passionately wanted to share it with me. As I told you, I was born Jewish but hadn't practiced in any way.

"In short, we were married in Manhattan at B'nai Jeshurun on the Upper West Side in June, 1966. I kept reading about and taking classes on Judaism, its rites, its history, its culture, its contributions to humanity, the importance of Israel. My inner self, I felt, was being remodeled nicely, except…"

Burns looked from Aliya to me and back to Aliya. "Except, I couldn't have children, which I wanted very much. Burton was sympathetic, said the right words, but I knew he already had children and it didn't matter as much to him. I didn't blame him, but in terms of my feelings, he was falling short for me."

"You're saying you started to fall out of love with your husband?" Aliya asked.

Burns tilted her head. "Dear, I'm not trying to be condescending, but you're young. When you're older, you'll understand that falling in and out of love is more complex than it now seems. I never said that I fell in love with Burton, did I?"

We both shook our heads as we looked at each other and back to Burns.

"I cared for Burton a good deal, and I still do, but I never fell in love with him. That's where Rabbi Flaum came in. Maybe it's the mid-western girl in me, but I never grew to like living in an apartment in the City. We moved to this house in Jamaica Estates, what Burton called 'an oasis in the middle of Gotham' when he first showed it to me. Just before we moved, we attended a dialogue presentation between the rabbi at Jeshurun and Rabbi Flaum who was speaking for modern Orthodoxy. Both of us were very impressed with Rabbi Flaum, his magnetic personality, the clarity and sensibility of his words, and his total dedication to our religion."

Here Burns blushed and said, "And I guess I would say I was smitten." She waited for us to respond, but both Aliya and I remained quiet.

Burns continued. "It was Burton's idea, and I readily agreed that we would leave B'nai Jeshurun and join CPH, even though it meant a violation of the Sabbath and some holidays in driving to the synagogue. If you have been to CPH on a Saturday, you must have noticed all the cars parked along Avenue I and 10th Street. Lots of people do it, and not once has the rabbi said anything about it.

"While I superficially interacted a few times with David, that is Rabbi Flaum, I mostly sat in the ladies section, watching him and listening to his sermons and lectures, his presence and words filling my heart and making me feel whole. I don't expect anyone to understand."

Was Burns making a statement, posing a question, or demanding rebuttal, that yes, certainly we understood? I wasn't sure and kept mum, but Aliya said: "I think there's a part of all of us known only to ourselves, perhaps not fully, but always removed from everyone else. But I think both Joel and I get what you're telling us."

Burns smiled. "Okay, then, I felt comfortable with Burton but had an aching sense I was missing something. My attraction to Rabbi Flaum came to a head about eighteen months ago. I couldn't stand myself as a hypocrite, just comfortable with my husband but in love with another man. And Rabbi Flaum, of all people, whom I knew only from a distance. I told Burton I wanted a divorce, offering him stock explanations, but not telling him about my attraction to our rabbi. Was I afraid he would hurt David? And I don't mean just physically. You see, Burton is powerful in our community and could have damaged David. Or did I just not want to come across as silly and flighty in expressing love for a man I hardly knew? I'm not sure."

Burns paused and surveyed us for a response. My expression remained neutral. I looked at Aliya who also did not flinch. Burns went on.

"Burton at first was incredulous, claiming I was going through a depressive phase and it would pass. Then when I kept insisting, he became angry and said that he would fight getting the divorce, both in a Jewish court of law and in the secular courts. I finally used my little girl, cajoling wiles and convinced him if he truly loved me, he would agree to the divorce. Not only did I succeed, but I also got Burton to use his connections to expedite the various divorce proceedings. Soon after, I was one of those divorced women."

Burns once again stopped and looked at us before continuing. "I then convinced myself that as a CPH congregant, I had a legitimate need for pastoral counseling. So I made an appointment to see the rabbi. For the first few sessions, he sat at his desk, and I sat across from him. Then we sat together on the couch, and then, one day—say about three months after our sessions began—right in the middle of someone saying something, we were kissing, and it was wonderful for a while. Then it became tawdry soap opera history made horrible by Batya's murder."

I said: "May I ask where you and the rabbi would meet?"

Aliya winced, which Burns noticed. "It's okay," she said to Aliya. "I realize it's your job to see me as a suspect and ask these indelicate questions."

Burns took a breath. "To answer your question, not once did we consummate our affair within the synagogue, not even that first time when we spontaneously kissed. Hotels in the City, yes, my home, yes, out-of-town when the rabbi attended conventions and I would join him, yes, but never in the synagogue."

I bobbed my head to indicate I believed her. At the same time, I wondered at her pride in not carrying on the full extent of the affair at the synagogue. I waited a moment for Aliya to ask a question or comment, but she remained quiet. I went on.

"How did you feel about Mrs. Flaum during your affair?"

"Easy, I was jealous. She had what I wanted without dressing up every day, without trying hard, without posing, with children of her own, while at the same time making life unhappy for her husband."

"Did the rabbi actually tell you his wife was making life difficult for him?" Aliya asked.

Burns' voice flared, "Honey, he sure did. We spent hours together with many of them listening to him tell me how troublesome and non-supportive Batya had become, how much I understood him, gave him energy, and made him feel vital again. Those words were, for a while, the framework of my inner remodeling. But honey, never overestimate the fragility of words. To be fully honest, yes, there were times I wished a bus would hit Batya, and David would be free to marry me."

Aliya asked softly: "That inside frame collapsed, didn't it, after Mrs. Flaum was murdered and still the rabbi wouldn't commit to you?"

Burns quickly replied. "Pretty much. But I had a sense even before the murder that he regretted our relationship, at least while he was still married. He wasn't often available for my calls, and when I would drop by, Mattie would make excuses about him being busy. When he would see me, we wound up arguing.

"But after Batya's death, all of his fine words, charm, religious offerings, magnetism, and assurance of my importance disintegrated, and I lost what I thought was beautifully growing in me. I became enraged. It felt as if I had fallen for one of those pretentious professors at Columbia, and I wanted revenge. Odd how one can hate someone while still being in love with him. But that's the way it was when I called Martha Brennan to give her my story. I had stewed and stewed, but there it is. Now I question if I did the right thing. Burton is gone for good; he won't be coming back, and I'm at a loss without having his loving support. He moved to an apartment in the City, and all this time he hasn't said a word about my staying here. But I'll leave. It's only fair."

Burns became quiet. Aliya asked: "Did Rabbi Flaum ever tell you directly that he would marry you if his wife was not in the way?"

Burns squirmed. "No, not exactly. I guess I convinced myself it was true."

"And by going public you wished to hurt him as much as you felt he hurt you?"

"Yes," Burns shrugged, and her eyes were moist. "But maybe it's for the best because now Mr. Wolf and the two of you are on the case and will find out who killed Batya and what role the rabbi may have played. Or is that too much of a rationalization?"

Aliya surprised me when she responded, "Yes, it probably is."

Burns flinched and said nothing. I decided to wade in. "Let's consider that the murder was not tied to a robbery. Do you have any idea who killed

Mrs. Flaum?

"No, I don't think so."

"You don't think so," Aliya retorted, "or you don't know?"

"Okay," she answered back firmly, "I don't know!"

"And then one more question, please," I said. "Did you have anything to do with the murder?"

Was it fear or anger or disdain I heard when she answered? "No, I... No!"

That concluded our interview. Barbara Burns walked us out and bid us a good evening.

* * * *

We walked away from the house onto Dalny and made a left on Midland Parkway where Aliya stopped me.

"I fell in love with you, Joel, okay. I wanted to make sure you knew."

"And so did I, okay?" I took her hand, and we continued walking toward Hillside. "What did you make of her?" I asked. "In some ways she wasn't what I expected."

"And what did you expect, Joel?"

"Oh, a shrew, a shallow person, maybe a gold digger, but she's really not like that at all. I didn't dislike her."

"But you didn't like her," Aliya prodded.

"No, I'm not sure exactly why. Maybe I was put off by the manipulative part of her to which she herself admitted. And of course for her going public about the affair when Rabbi Flaum may not have had anything to do with the murder."

Aliya dropped my hand and took my elbow. "But there was a vulnerable side to her, wasn't there? It reduced your dislike and made you consider the plight of an intelligent and attractive woman in a land controlled by men. And how she, out of rage, had to resort to duplicity to gain what was rightfully hers. I think at her core she's a decent person with an emptiness inside. Perhaps it's due to childlessness, but probably more, that she can't fill. When her self-romanticized relationship with Rabbi Flaum didn't work out, her rage hit a boiling point, and going public was the result of the explosion. As a man, I'm not sure you understand."

"Of course I understand!" I replied loudly.

We had just reached Hillside, and Aliya released my elbow. I wished she hadn't. "Good then, we'll leave it at that," she said.

The walk back to the subway on 179th was different from our leisurely stroll on Midland Parkway, even from when we had arrived a few hours earlier when Hillside churned with multitudes rushing in each direction, chattering above other voices, car horns, and transistor radios turned up high. Many had been shopping for the night's dinner and morning's breakfast. Everyone had looked ahead not to bump into others while at the same time avoiding eye contact.

Though just after 8:00 with a good deal of daylight left, I sensed that tension had set in as the clang of smaller stores shuttering with double bolted locks could be heard one upon another. Aliya and I were lifetime New Yorkers, trained in the evening to walk with peripheral vision finely tuned. We positioned ourselves away from buildings and doorways, and our minds focused on our destination. When we had been on Midland Parkway, we strolled relaxed and open to the surroundings. Now we hustled down Hillside, attuned and wary.

On the train ride home, we didn't talk much. Aliya put her head on my shoulder and closed her eyes. I thought back to our conversation. Did I really understand Barbara Burns? Perhaps not, I admitted as my irritation subsided. My mind raced trying to digest Barbara Burns' rage and drive for vengeance. I knew these factors often figured in a murder. I thought of Batya Flaum, lying in her home's foyer. Was there a connection between the two?

TUESDAY, JULY 8, 1975

After our meeting with Barbara Burns, we had arrived home a little after 9:00. We noticed the message indicator flashing on our tape answering machine. We were the first among our friends to have one. It was both a toy and a necessity since I worked late hours and my mother, alone with Grandfather, was nervous that she might not be able to reach us.

I pressed the playback button and heard my mother's agitated voice: "Joel, Aliya, please call when you return home, if it's before 9:00. I'm frightened. I just returned home from the store, and your Zaida showed me a threatening letter that came in the mail special delivery around 6:00. He says it's not to worry, but I am worried. If not tonight, please call in the morning as early as possible. Also, I know the three of you have appointments tomorrow, so please come by to pick up the car. I'll take the train into the City. Not only will it be hot for Zaida to trudge around, but also this way you'll always have an eye on him."

Since it was after 9:00, and I didn't want to risk disturbing my grandfather who went to bed early, I waited until morning at 7:00 to call. Grandfather answered.

"Are you alright?" I demanded?

"I am now eating my cheese Danish with a coffee. It is not to worry." He sounded perfectly relaxed. "I believe you are coming to the house for us to go together to my office for our meeting with Shoshannah Marcus and, after, her brother, Jonathan Flaum, yes?"

"Yes," I replied.

"Good, then when you come, I will show you the letter, and you too will not worry. And we shall arrive at my office early enough for you to convey to me your interview with Ms. Burns before Shoshannah arrives, yes?"

"Yes, of course," I replied and ended the conversation.

Aliya and I wolfed down some breakfast and rushed out. When we arrived, Grandfather, fully dressed, sat in his easy chair with a sheet of paper and an opened envelope. He was wearing thin plastic gloves, part of evidence-collecting kits he kept at home and at his office. My mother heard us and came out of her bedroom.

"Mom," I immediately said, "we'll drive you to the subway on the way to Grandfather's office. But first, can we look at the letter Zaida received?"

"Yes, Joel, it's the paper Zaida is holding. I really am frightened."

"We're here now, Mom, and Zaida doesn't seem too worried. We'll take a look."

Aliya and I walked over to Grandfather. He carefully adjusted the gloves and lifted the paper. He motioned Aliya and me to stand over his shoulder. He instructed us not to touch the paper "as it may become evidence to be given to Detective Carlucci." Just as in a B movie, letters cut from a magazine read: **DONT BOTHER THE RABBI HE DIDNT HAVE ANYTHING TO DO WITH THE MURDER.**

"Your mother believes it is meant as a direct threat to me and our efforts to investigate the case." Looking toward my mother, Grandfather added softly: "Malkeh, it is not. Do not be afraid for us. It is meant to provide us with information rather than intimidation."

Grandfather then showed us the envelope. We scanned it without touching it.

I said. "The envelope has your name and address typed and no return address. And I believe it has a Brooklyn postmark."

"You are correct, Yoeli." Grandfather held up the envelope closer to us. "Brooklyn and the Boro Park postal station. It is dated on yesterday, July 7, at 10:00 AM. And it is special delivery, as if the sender was determined that I receive it as soon as possible. Let us keep in mind that *The Daily News* story came out that morning."

"Boro Park and not Flatbush! And yesterday. Who do you think sent it, Zaida, and why not also type the note instead of the theatrics of cutting out letters from a magazine?"

I began reviewing the suspects in my mind.

"I believe I know who is the sender," Grandfather said.

"You know?" my mother blurted, moving closer. "Who? And you'll notify the police right away?"

"Sha, sha, sha, Malkeh," Grandfather cautioned. "It is Eli Schorr, the maintenance director at Congregation P'nai Hesed. I am quite sure. And I have already spoken to Detective Carlucci and asked him if we might retain what we received until the completion of the investigation. He agreed."

I asked. "I can guess why you suspect Eli Schorr, but how can you be sure?"

Grandfather let the paper settle on his lap. "Joel, Aliya, let us re-enter the world of this man that we visited just yesterday. Are the words in style and in a way, Yoeli, what you term 'theatrics,' not similar to how Mr. Schorr expressed himself? Therefore yes, that stylistic resemblance contributes to a strong suspicion. But more, the pasted letters themselves give him away. Do you remember what was written on the door to his dwelling at the synagogue?"

"Yes, his name and title," Aliya replied, "and beneath a warning not to come in, or something like that, without permission."

Grandfather smiled. "Yes, you have summarized what was placed on his door including his admonition, which is odd. Can he not lock the door to keep others out? I believe that posting such a warning exposes Mr. Schorr's state of mind. He wishes to demonstrate the power of his position. But what exactly did the admonition say, do you remember?"

Aliya and I looked at each other. We admitted not recalling the precise words.

"Then I shall tell you. Exactly it declared: **ENTRY ISNT ALLOWED WITHOUT PERMISSION**. And, even more precisely, '**ISNT**' is stenciled without an apostrophe, just as **DONT** and **DIDNT** are pasted onto this paper. It is always wondrous to me how suspects reveal themselves in the easiest of manners."

"So you think Eli is the murderer?" Aliya asked breathlessly.

"Sha, sha, sha, my child. At this point, all that I am saying with surety is that he gave himself away as to the person who sent this paper. I am not at all suggesting that he is involved in the murder. We have a good deal more investigating to perform. Shall we go so that my daughter is not late to her store due to worrying about my safety? And shall we take two folding chairs from our closet so that we have enough seats for our guests and for ourselves? We cannot impose on Mr. Khan since it is a business day."

* * * *

Grandfather had a twinkle in his eye as we left the house and got into my mother's car. I drove, Aliya in the front passenger seat, and my mother and grandfather in the back. As usual, Aliya and I knew that Grandfather didn't like talking about a case while we were driving, especially with my mother in the car. Following Aliya's suggestion, we decided to drop off my mother at Grandfather's office, a short walk to the train station. She would save time by taking the train from there into the City. I looked in the rearview mirror. My mother had entwined her hand with Grandfather's.

Aliya, even before we married, would at times hold Grandfather's hand. I thought back to the last time I had done so. I was standing at my father's grave. Grandfather had one arm wrapped around my weeping mother and one hand holding mine as I held back tears of sorrow and anger.

A car pulled out from a spot right in front of Grandfather's office. "Yes," I said loudly, experiencing a moment of New York serendipitous joy. Did it indicate we would have a good day? I parallel parked flawlessly. After giving my mother goodbye hugs, I opened the trunk and took out both chairs. Aliya insisted that she carry one. We followed Grandfather up the three flights to his office.

The office was hot and stuffy. I turned on the air conditioner full blast. As soon as Grandfather had hung up his hat and suit jacket, we seated ourselves, Aliya in the folding chair to the right and I in the one to the left of the guest chair.

Grandfather asked: "What was most salient about your visit to Ms. Burns?"

"Well," I led off, "are you familiar with Jamaica Estates?"

"Yes," Grandfather responded, "I have availed myself of a few walks in that lovely enclosure in the middle of our bustling metropolis. It reminds me of similar settings in European cities including my old Vienna. But is there a relationship between this locale and what Ms. Burns had to say?"

Aliya answered first. My mind was momentarily distracted marveling at the number of areas in New York with which Grandfather was familiar: Boro Park, Williamsburg, Washington Heights, and now Jamaica Estates in Queens. When had he been able to make all these visits?

"I'm not sure if Joel is thinking the same way, but for me, Zaida, there is a relationship. I had never been to Jamaica Estates before last night. When I saw the houses, the landscaping, the differences from what I'm used to in New York, I had expected Barbara Burns to fit my make of her surroundings. But I was wrong, and she wasn't at all what I expected. Seems I'm learning every day in the short time I've joined you two on this case."

Grandfather smiled at Aliya. "In what way was Ms. Burns different from your expectations?"

"I expected her to reflect opulence, superiority, disdain, distance, and bravado. Some of those are there on her surface, but, beneath, she is a very different person, one, as I was telling Joel, I could like if not for…"

Aliya paused and closed her eyes, as if trying to find the right words. "…if not for her anger and muddled sense of herself that I believe creates a rage and a distance from others. Ironically, I also sense that she expects others to fill a void inside her."

We spent the next few minutes recounting the personal history Burns gave us and her reactions to the direct questions we posed about Batya Flaum's murder.

Grandfather cupped his face in his hands. I wondered if by now, Aliya also recognized his Univac-like processing of what he had just heard.

"You will please tell me again her response to your question if she had any notion of who killed Mrs. Flaum, yes?"

"Yes," I took over. "Verbatim, at first she answered, 'I don't think so.'"

"And then you confronted her to respond unequivocally, and her response was, 'I don't know,' meaning she did not know if she might have a sense of the murderer or, she had no knowledge, absolutely?"

"I think the latter, Zaida," I replied, "but now that you bring it up, I think we're not one hundred percent sure. Right Aliya?"

Aliya nodded.

Grandfather went on. "And when you asked if she herself had any culpability in the murder, she answered…"

"As I remember, she said, 'no,' but I detected a momentary hesitation. Joel, what's your memory?"

"I recall clearly. She said 'no,' hesitated, and said 'no' more firmly."

"Also, did you ask her, or did she volunteer if she had shared her feelings about the relationship with anyone else besides Rabbi Flaum?"

"No, Zaida," I replied, "I guess we should have."

Grandfather waved his hand. "The opportunity was missed but not lost. Aliya, you will contact Ms. Burns and ask this important question?"

Aliya agreed quickly. "Yes, right now I'll dial Martha Brennan and ask her to contact Barbara Burns to see if it would be okay for me to call her. I have Brennan's number written down." Aliya plucked her notebook from her bag and picked up the phone.

* * * *

Aliya got through to Brennan quickly. "She's going to call Barbara and get back to me. I left both Zaida's number here and our home phone."

Aliya had just finished speaking when I heard the office door opening. I spotted a very thin young man with a gaunt face, about my height, entering with a taller Shoshannah Marcus, a half-step behind. I recognized Jonathan Flaum from Shoshi's wedding and a few social events. Both of Shoshi's hands wrapped around Jonathan's arm, half guiding and half pushing him into the room.

Still holding onto his arm, Shoshi offered: "Jonathan didn't feel comfortable coming alone. He also wanted to have more time to look for work. So he came with me. I hope it's alright."

Aliya and I looked at Grandfather who had just stood. He put out his hands in welcome: "It is nice to meet you, Jonathan. Joel, might you allow Jonathan to sit in your chair?"

I moved to stand behind Aliya. Shoshi sat in the middle guest chair, and Jonathan to her left in my vacated seat.

Seated, Jonathan grabbed the bottom of the metal chair, keeping his body rigid. His right eyelid pulsed in a steady tic. He had clean-shaven sunken cheeks and short hair. He wore a buttoned blue and red plaid dress shirt and a thin, solid-blue tie. His skinny black pants flared over dress shoes with an in vogue, one-inch heel. Not PWR acceptable, I considered, but appropriate dress for job-hunting in some fields.

His head was bare, unlike in previous occasions when I had seen him. No *kippah*.

Shoshi had on a cream colored blouse, full sleeved, over a blue denim midi-skirt. Her light brown hair was tied back and fell to her left shoulder. She wore no make-up, nothing to disguise the lines and redness of her eyes. Tall, with long legs, Shoshi always seemed uncomfortable wearing a skirt, crossing and uncrossing her legs. as if trying, and forgetting, to be decorous. This morning, the number of crossings increased. I sensed Shoshi's anxiety and regretted that I might be contributing to it.

Given her connection to Shoshi, I guessed that Aliya would not initiate the questioning. We had not discussed the interview approach with Grandfather. Should I take the lead? I was about to speak when Shoshi burst out.

"I want to say right off that my father's affair was reprehensible. It's not that I forgive him, but when it comes to my mother's murder, I am absolutely certain he had nothing to do with it!"

Grandfather had a way of drawing the attention of an agitated person toward him, immersing the person in a well of understanding and compassion. "He is your father, after all, and it is understandable, despite his errors, that you care for him deeply and cannot comprehend any guilt in the crime against your mother. Shoshannah, might I assure you that we did not ask you to come here today to convince you otherwise. We require your presence to clarify some questions that have come before us."

Jonathan began wiggling in his chair, still clutching its bottom. "I'm not saying I know he was involved in my mother's death, but if it came out that way, well, I wouldn't be shocked."

Shoshi turned toward her brother. "Jonathan, please, you don't mean it!"

"You mean I shouldn't say in front of others what I've said to you privately since the story of Abba's affair broke?"

"No, it's not that, it's…" Shoshi's voice faltered, and Grandfather took command.

"Shoshannah, Jonathan, if you will allow, might we guide the conversation with questions directed to each of you separately and with direct responses to our inquiries?"

Jonathan's tic was still there, but had slowed. Shoshi's leg crossings also moderated. They both nodded.

"Good, then," Grandfather said soothingly. "My first question is to Jonathan. Might you tell us why you believe your father is capable of culpability in your mother's death besides your father and son difficulties? Is there anything factual you might share with us?"

Jonathan drew back and stared down. He replied, almost in a whisper: "Ever since I can remember, I haven't felt comfortable with my father. Not the way you've been able, Shosh."

Shoshi wanted to speak, but Grandfather put a hand up and indicated to Jonathan to go on.

"I've always felt he doesn't like me, that he's disappointed in me, and frankly, that he wouldn't mind if I weren't around. The opposite of what I felt from Mom, who loved me for me, for whatever I did or didn't do. And that's the way I always felt."

Jonathan turned toward Shoshi. "And I also recognize it when he's not pleased with other people. Those last few years, I saw those same clouds hanging over Mom whenever Dad spoke to her, whenever he walked by her, whenever he walked away from her. I knew it would be alright with him if she wasn't around anymore. So no, I have nothing factual, no evidence, but that's why I think he could have been involved in her death."

"But that's not fair!" Shoshi raised her voice. "Just because you felt alienated, you can't just assume it was true for Ima and Abba!"

"Be that as it may, Shoshannah," Grandfather said, "but we will not invalidate any feelings as we speak today. If I may, another question, Jonathan. How many positions have you held since graduating from college?"

Jonathan frowned. "Three, four, I don't know. They just weren't right for me. Why do you want to know?"

Grandfather leaned back. "My inquiry is mere background to the call you received the evening before the murder to come for a job interview in Manhattan, yes?"

"Yes."

"At what time did you receive the call, please? And did the person give you a name? Was it a man or a woman?"

"Around 7:30. It was a man, and he didn't mention his name. He said he was calling from Telemetrics Computing and gave me an address on Madison Avenue and asked if I'd like to interview at 9:00 the next morning. I'm a computers person, so I jumped at the invitation even though I had never heard of the company. I figured someone gave them my name and number."

"And was there anything you remember about the voice?"

Jonathan thought for a moment. "Yes. He sounded robotic, slow and even, as if he was reading from a script."

I asked: "And what time did you leave the house in the morning?"

"Around 7:30. Walked over to the subway, but there was a delay. I was nervous I would be late. So I took a cab. Another one of my flubbed decisions. Traffic was terrible. Got to the address in the City around 8:50, but there was no Telemetrics Computing at the address I was given. I even checked several nearby buildings. I hated myself for probably writing down the wrong address and not taking a call back number. Around 10:00, I took the train back home where I found out…"

Jonathan swallowed hard, and the rapidity of his tics increased "…

what had happened to my mother."

I allowed Jonathan a moment's respite before I asked: "And when you left in the morning, your mother was alone?"

"No, my father was still there, but he was getting ready to leave for that breakfast club meeting at Kornblatt's. Oh yeah, the plumbing people were supposed to come around 8:00 to fix the leak in the upstairs bathroom."

"And last question from me. Was the safe in the living room open or closed when you left? Do you remember?"

Jonathan turned toward Shoshi and laughed lightly. "I don't remember exactly, but I'd say it must have been closed. You remember, Shosh, how Mom disliked having the painting open except when she had to go into the safe. What would she say—it showed 'an absence of decorum?'"

Shoshi returned a brief smile. "Yes, 'an absence of decorum,' that's what she called it. A bit of family humor."

No one spoke for a minute. Then Grandfather asked: "Aliya, is there a question you would like to pose to Jonathan?"

Aliya thought for a few seconds. "Just one. We're aware of the conflicts you had with your father and how you looked to your mother for refuge. But did you feel your mother protected you well enough? Were you ever angry that she wasn't doing enough?"

The rapidity of Jonathan's tics increased even more, one hardly distinguishable from the next. "Yes. Sometimes I hated her too for not doing more."

Again there was an uncomfortable pause. Grandfather extended his hand toward Shoshannah. "A few questions more for you, please. Your brother indicated that your mother experienced isolation in her relationship with your father. Did you also take notice of the same? Did she ever speak to you on this subject?"

"No, she never brought up the subject. There were times, especially in the last year before her death, I'd catch her looking sad, and I would ask if there was anything wrong. 'No,' she'd reply, 'I've got the store on my mind, that's all.' But Jonathan isn't wrong. Something had changed in her relationship with our father. I remember how easy and natural they were for many years, and then something changed. They interrupted each other more often. My father was away from home more often. There were more silences between them. And when they walked past each other, each would look away."

"But she said nothing to you directly about the relationship or its ramifications, yes?"

Again Shoshi paused. "Not directly, but one thing sticks in my mind. One Sunday in December before her murder, she came to our apartment after a Sisterhood meeting at the *shul* to babysit so I could do some Chanukah shopping. She looked confused, upset, and without any prompting said: 'I wonder if I've somehow offended at the *shul*.'

"When I asked why, she told me that Mattie, with whom she'd been very close for years, lately seemed uneasy with her. And in her own words, 'And Eli just walks by me without a return hello when I greet him.' Then Ima said, 'Oh well, I'm here now to spend some time with my two wonderful boys'"

Shoshi began to weep. Aliya clasped her hands together as if stifling her reflex to comfort her best friend. To my surprise, Jonathan let go of the bottom of his chair and leaned toward Shoshi. He took her hand and also began to cry: "Oh Shosh, don't. It's okay."

Grandfather waited a moment before he said: "Thank you Shoshannah and Jonathan. We know the anguish of losing a loved one to violence, and we know our asking for your recollections is very painful. With permission, just one more question: Did your mother ever speak to either of you about Mrs. Gelb?"

Jonathan released Shoshi's hand and again grabbed the chair edges. Shoshi dabbed her tears and sat up straight. When Jonathan shook his head, Shoshi glanced at him and slowly nodded.

With a cross and uncross of her legs, she said: "I imagine you're referring to Mrs. Gelb's thefts at the store. I came over unannounced one late afternoon not long before Ima's death, and she had been crying. She told me she had discovered that Marcia had been embezzling money from the store and, although Marcia promised to pay it back, Ima felt the partnership had to be dissolved. She felt sorry for Marcia but couldn't trust her anymore. That's all our mother needed, this trouble heaped upon whatever else was bothering her. Marcia had been her best friend for years. But it helped, she said, that Marcia wasn't being difficult about the decision."

Grandfather stood and bowed toward Shoshi and Jonathan. "We are most grateful to you for your coming to see us today. May your mother's memory of love and kindness be for a continuous blessing to you."

They rose, and this time Jonathan took hold of Shoshi's arm as they headed to the door. I slipped into the seat next to Aliya. She was pale and biting her lip.

Grandfather came around from his desk and stood before us. "All three of our professions have strong similarities, do they not? The work of a private detective, a clinical psychologist, and an attorney expose the souls of our clients to the light that, for the sake of justice and healing, we need to analyze and place in perspective. But as with those professionals who deal with radiation, that exposure often burns into their own bodies and psyches. To keep an equilibrium that will aid others, we must constantly rally our own strengths and self-understanding, self-forgiveness, and self-discipline, do we not?"

Aliya smiled. "You know what, Zaida, you are right. But let me turn the tables. Are you sure you don't want to stop being a private detective and join me in my clinical psychology practice after I graduate?"

Grandfather laughed, and I joined in. I could count on one hand the number of times Grandfather, even in the most humorous situations, laughed out loud. He returned to his desk, sat down, and, with the laughter subsided, said: "It is good to have merriment, but unfortunately our grim task is still before us. My children, shall we review the visit of the brother and sister?"

I said eagerly. "Let's look at what additional information we gained from the interview. For instance, based on what Jonathan told us, I think it's even more likely that the safe was unopened when the murder occurred."

Grandfather nodded. "And the meaning for us?"

"Again, whoever killed Mrs. Flaum knew where the safe was located and the combination. Either it was one of our main suspects or one of them gave it to the murderer."

Grandfather waved a finger. "Wait, wait, wait, Yoeli. Let us assume that your first premise is correct. But perhaps there was a way for the murderer, if not one of our main suspects, to have obtained the combination. No?"

"You're right," I answered and changed direction. "Then there's Jonathan whom I don't know very well. Boy, he can make anyone nervous. I know we shouldn't let our emotions dictate to critical analyses, but I feel sorry for him. He seems smart enough, but losing job after job in such a short period of time certainly can unsettle anyone. It's strange that nothing worked for him.``

"Not so strange, Yoeli. Not if we consider that wherever the young man goes, he takes himself with him. Yes?"

Grandfather had to be correct. Despite his brains and technical training, Jonathan displayed nervous mannerisms: his eye tic, his hands grasping the sides of the chair seat. He made people uncomfortable.

The facts suggested that he couldn't have killed his mother by himself. I took in a breath as a thought hit me. "What if," I said slowly, "in a moment of anger and helplessness, he hired someone to kill his mother? In his mind, he might have felt that she failed him. Maybe he gave out the safe combination and shared the money or simply let it be the payment."

"It's possible," Aliya said, "but I don't think Jonathan could last a day with that on his conscience. He would completely unravel."

Aliya rose and started to pace slowly. She stopped in front of the air conditioner, adjusted some dials, and turned to us. "But can we now conclude categorically based on our interview that Shoshi had nothing to do with the murder?"

I looked at Zaida, and he back at me, before he replied: "'Categorically,' Aliya, is a dangerous word when we have not fully concluded the case and identified the murderer. But since you are the beloved wife of my grandson, I will say that at this point I do not believe your very good friend had any involvement in her mother's death."

I looked at my watch. A painful hour and fifteen minutes had gone by, and we were due at Mrs. Caviglia's house in under three hours. Since Mrs. Caviglia's house was not far from my old childhood home, I thought we might take Grandfather back to East 7th and make sure he had some lunch.

"Zaida," I said firmly, "if there's nothing more to say about this morning's interview, I think we should drive back to our house, have some lunch, rest, and prepare for our visit to Mrs. Caviglia. Make sense?"

I looked to Aliya for support. She nodded.

"Not fully, Yoeli," Grandfather replied. "We still have some additional business to perform this morning. We have come to a point in our critical analyses where we know a good deal, but when we must also ask the question of what do we not know?"

Grandfather picked up a pen and gently drummed on his desk. "We are confident that Mrs. Flaum was not killed by a random robber, yes? We surmise that she was killed by someone who knew or was given the combination to the safe, yes? We have some confidence that the two children were not involved in their mother's murder, yes?"

Aliya and I both exclaimed, "Yes!"

Grandfather continued. "It is clear that Rabbi Flaum, Ms. Burns, and Mrs. Gelb did not wield the murder weapon by themselves, yes? But did they pay or persuade another to murder for them?"

"Yes," Aliya said, "'pay' I get, but 'persuade'—what does that mean? What could have persuaded someone to kill Mrs. Flaum besides money?"

"Ah, a very good question, Aliya. If we accept that it may have occurred, it is something we do not yet know."

Once in a while as a young child I would get lost trying to follow my grandfather's thoughts. I would sometimes get angry, feeling inadequate and placing the blame on him. But as I grew older, I learned either to ask for clarification or to try harder to understand.

My reverie didn't last long as Grandfather said: "Yes, Joel, it is a good suggestion for us to stop at our home to reinvigorate ourselves prior to our visit to Mrs. Caviglia. But before we leave, let us consider what investigative matters and materials are left for our review."

Grandfather was about to answer when the phone rang. It was Martha Brennan. Grandfather handed the phone to Aliya.

"Yes, I have a pen and paper, Ms. Brennan, please go ahead." I could see Aliya writing numbers in her phone book. "Yes, got it. And she's okay with my calling her—? Great, thank you for your help."

Aliya handed the phone back to Grandfather and relayed what we understood. Brennan had asked Burns if Brennan could give her number to Aliya, and Burns agreed.

Grandfather said. "You will call Ms. Burns to inquire if she shared her emotions with anyone besides Rabbi Flaum, Yes?"

"I will when we get back to the house," Aliya replied. "And I'd like to make the call in private to set up a girl-to-girl atmosphere to establish the mood for our conversation."

Was it my gender genes, gender training, law school instruction, or PWR male-centric interactions? I would not have thought a moment about setting up a "mood" for myself in a phone conversation. Perhaps I needed to understand more and try harder.

But not Grandfather, who said admiringly: "Very good and understandable, my child. When we are at the house, you will make your call in private."

I was going to say, "What else, Zaida?" when the phone rang. It was Detective Carlucci. Grandfather spoke with him in a warm voice for a few minutes. Afterwards, he relayed the information Carlucci had given him. Phone records for the Flaum home and bank records of Rabbi Flaum, Barbara Burns, and Marcia Gelb—whom Zaida had added to the list in a call to the detective the previous day—were ready to be picked up at the 61st Precinct. Since we had my mother's car for the day, I volunteered to drive over and pick up the documents after our visit to Mrs. Caviglia.

Aliya said, "I'll go with you Joel. And now we'll return to the house, Zaida, so we can get a little rest and time for reflection, right?"

"Yes, my shayne kopp," Grandfather replied, the Yiddish phrase for *beautiful one*. Grandfather often used that term for me when I was a child, leaving me pleased but at times not quite sure why I merited such adoration.

* * * *

Traffic snarled the BQE heading home. We arrived at 12:30. Aliya immediately excused herself to call Barbara Burns. I prepared sandwiches in the kitchen. Aliya returned within a few minutes.

"Barbara was home. She vehemently denies telling anyone else about her affair with Rabbi Flaum."

At the table, we didn't discuss the case. As soon as we began eating, Grandfather offered his view that the mediocrity of both the Mets and Yankees that summer may have been due to both teams having to play at Shea, since Yankee Stadium was being renovated.

"The Shea Stadium suffers from a weariness that reflects in the out-ofkilter performance of the players. Might my assessment of the situation be accurate?"

To say my grandfather's sense of humor could be droll would be an understatement. We groaned but continued our baseball exchange. Aliya insisted that her beloved Yankees were being treated as aliens by Mets management. I countered that the Yankees playing at Shea ripped up the field and made it harder for the Mets to feel at home.

"It seems," Grandfather said, "my assessment a few minutes ago did not merit the derision it received. You also are indicating that the stadium suffers from weariness."

By the time we finished eating and arguing, it was 1:20. Grandfather said: "Joel, I will not compromise your promise to your mother to protect my health. Therefore, I will not insist we walk in the heat of this day to Mrs. Caviglia's home. Might we drive north on 10th Street and park right before Avenue K, at which point we will not be seen by anyone who may be looking out from the home? We will sit for a few minutes observing 10th Street from Avenue K toward Avenue J, yes?"

"Okay," I answered gladly.

We made our short way to 10th before it hit K. Parked, I ran the Buick's air conditioner while we sat silently. We could see the Flaum house just past Avenue K on the right and Mrs. Caviglia's home at a diagonal across the street. Grandfather had asked to sit in the front seat. As soon as I had pulled over, he unbuckled his seat belt, cupped his face in his hands, leaned forward, and stared ahead for the next fifteen minutes.

At 1:55, he broke the silence. "Nuh, shall we exit the vehicle? I am sure Mrs. Caviglia is awaiting us."

My watch said exactly 2:00 as we mounted the steps to the house. Halfway to the top, the door swung open and a diminutive woman with a bun of black hair with silver streaks gazed down at us.

"Hello," she said warmly, "I am Mrs. Roberto Caviglia. Please come in."

She had to be in her mid-seventies, Grandfather's age, but her olive skin showed few creases. The amber cat-eyes glass frames she wore ornamented a twinkle in her eyes, similar to ones I'd see in Grandfather's. Her full-sleeved, dark brown dress of satiny material came down below the knees, ending in brown nylon stockings and sensible shoes.

After entering a small foyer, Mrs. Caviglia directed us to the left toward a bright kitchen that bowed out to the street through a large, uncurtained bay window. Before entering, I paused and took a quick look at a living room on the right. Above a screened fireplace hung a large, black plaque embossed with a crucifix. I looked away as I always do when viewing a crucifix, not because it alienates or threatens me, but rather because the graphic suffering of a human tortured by other humans sears me.

The kitchen gleamed from its yellow linoleum floor to seashell white walls and ceiling. The pure white stove and refrigerator matched the enameled steel cabinets which showed no sign of a chip, dent, or rusting. The bay window sat atop a wooden ledge, also painted seashell white with wooden drawers beneath. Five throw pillows with white on one side and yellow the other lay neatly on the ledge. Various pots and pans that looked as if they were newly purchased hung on a scullery rack over a spotless sink.

A rectangular black-framed cloth with stitched writing hung over the sink to the right. It read:

> *This is the day*
> THAT THE **LORD** HAS MADE;
> **LET US** rejoice **AND** be glad **IN IT**.

Mrs. Caviglia had set the kitchen table with four flowered paper cups and plates along with plastic utensils which marked the four seating places. A steaming glass teapot sat in the center next to a napkin holder with a yellow baby chick design. Lipton tea bags filled one small glass bowl, individual packets of sugar in another, along with a jar of Maxwell House instant coffee along side. Encouraged by Mrs. Caviglia to sit where we wished, Grandfather took the chair which allowed a view of the street across to the Flaum house.

Mrs. Caviglia took the seat opposite Grandfather and smiled at him. "I wasn't sure of your religious needs, but Batya, may her soul be at rest, taught me that some Jewish people cannot eat at a house that does not observe the kosher rules. So I made hot water for tea and coffee as I would when Batya visited."

"That is very gracious of you," Grandfather replied, taking off his fedora and placing it on his lap but keeping his kippah on. "Plain tea and sugar is sufficient for me and, I believe, for my colleagues whom I would like to introduce. My grandson Joel and his wife of one year, Aliya Blum."

Mrs. Caviglia turned to Aliya. "When you were little, I met you a few times at the Flaum house and when you played on the street with Shoshannah. Do you remember me?"

"I do, I do, Mrs. Caviglia! I just didn't connect you to living in this house."

Grandfather's gaze drifted to his right, and he pointed to the motto on the wall. "It is from Psalm 118, is it not, Mrs. Caviglia?"

"Yes, Mr. Wolf. I see you are familiar with the Psalms."

"Yes, I have some familiarity," Grandfather replied.

"Some familiarity!" I laughed inside. Grandfather was ordained a rabbi in the old country before the War, and although he became a philosophy professor, he knew scripture and often quoted from them as I was growing up.

Mrs. Caviglia looked admiringly at Grandfather and leaned toward him. "You do remember correctly. It is my favorite Psalm, and for most of my life, I have read it as I have started each day."

"A very good habit," Grandfather said. "There are many of the Jewish faith who begin our days in a similar fashion."

Grandfather poured himself some hot water over a tea bag. Aliya and I followed. Mrs. Caviglia folded her hands in her lap and kept her attention on Grandfather.

After a few sips, Grandfather asked: "Mrs. Caviglia, did Batya Flaum visit you often?"

Mrs. Caviglia's eyes brightened. "I wouldn't say 'often,' but from time to time, especially after my husband Roberto passed away eight years ago. My daughter is in New Jersey and son in Florida. Batya said it was nothing more than neighborly to see how I was doing, and that she liked talking with me. Her visits were less frequent after she opened her store, but still kind and always welcome."

"When was the last time she visited?" I asked.

She smiled and turned to me: "I know exactly. It was December 30, the Friday afternoon right before New Year, around 3:00 after she had come back from the store. She had baked cookies and wanted me to have some."

"How did she seem?"

"A bit subdued for Batya, as I remember. She said she was exhausted from the Chanukah business at the store and was looking forward to a restful Sabbath."

"Did she ever talk about her family?" Aliya asked.

"Yes, often. I think that Shoshannah was the apple of her eye. They were so much alike. You know, Shoshannah would also visit me and has come over a few times even after her mother's death. I love when she brings her two boys."

Mrs. Caviglia stopped talking. I waited a moment: "And about Rabbi Flaum, did she ever bring him up?"

"Yes, especially in the early years after they moved across the street, and the rabbi took up his duties at the synagogue. She was proud of him, telling me about his programs and awards. But not much in the last few years. It's what happens to many women after several years of marriage when the youthful magic ends and everyday routine sets in. It happened with me and Roberto, requiescat in pace, but I loved him dearly until the heart attack took him from us."

Grandfather knew what to say. "We are sorry for your loss, regardless of how long ago it took place. I believe you remain comforted by his memory?"

"I do," she replied with a strong voice. "Your wife, Mr. Wolf, is she still with us?"

Grandfather looked at me. "She is not. This young man's wonderful grandmother died during the Holocaust in Europe."

Mrs. Caviglia's expression hardened. "You mean she was killed by those murderous beasts who, I am not ashamed to pray to my Lord, should continue to burn in hell."

She paused. "But you have come here to ask me questions about another brutal event, Batya's murder. How can I be of assistance?"

Grandfather turned back to Mrs. Caviglia. "Perhaps you can share with us what you probably have already told the authorities? We have read the police report that summarized what you observed on the morning of the murder, but we would like to hear your own words."

Grandfather pointed to the bay window. "To begin, you happened to look out the window on the morning of February 21 of this year?"

"Mr. Wolf," she said, "it just didn't happen that I was looking out the window. I am the neighborhood snoop. Since Roberto's death, it helps me to pass the day to look out at life on my street. Not, please understand, to judge anyone but to be part of a community since I am alone so often."

Mrs. Caviglia pointed to the small TV on the counter. "On weekday mornings, I combine my street watching with the *Today* show between 7:00 and 9:00. I enjoy Barbara Walters very much. I cannot say that I was giving what was occurring on the street my best attention, but I do remember that around 8:00 the Chansky men came to the Flaum house. The Flaum boy, Jonathan, left the house maybe a half hour earlier and the rabbi, I think, a few minutes before the plumbers arrived."

"You are familiar with the Chansky plumbing business? They are also your plumbers?"

"No, I use the Marcacci boys. Their old man Jimmy was a friend of Roberto. But I know the Flaums have used Chansky for years, and I clearly saw their truck with the company's markings."

I asked. "And you saw the Chansky people leave?"

"Yes, a little after 9:00. The *Today* show had wrapped up, and Channel 4 had just gone to local news to which I do not give my complete attention, since I have 1010 WINS on for most of the day for that. Yes, it must have been a little after 9:00."

"And then," Grandfather asked, "you saw no one else entering the Flaum home until Mrs. Gelb arrived?"

"Well, I did see Mrs. Gelb arrive just about 10:00 when the local news had ended. Then the sirens. But before that, just a few minutes after the

Chansky truck left, one of the plumbers came back to the house. He must have forgotten something because he didn't stay long. Came out and headed in the same direction that he came from."

I restrained a gasp. Nowhere did the police report mention a Chansky plumber returning to the house. Grandfather put his right palm on the table and lifted his fingers, a signal I knew from my youth that meant *don't say anything right now*.

Grandfather broke the silence. "And you are sure it was a Chansky plumber?"

"Oh yes, Mr. Wolf, his overalls had the company name on the back, and he was belted with plumbing tools."

Grandfather followed up gently. "But could you tell which one of the Chanskys?"

She thought for a moment and slowly shook her head. "I don't think so. I wasn't watching carefully when they first entered the house. I don't even know how many there were. This one had a dark woolen cap pulled over his head to his eyes. I'm not sure I would ever recognize his face. But he was stocky, that's one thing I remember. And for sure, the back of his overalls indicated he was with Chansky."

"And again, Mrs. Caviglia, in which direction did the man go after he left the house?" Grandfather asked.

"Toward Avenue J. where I imagine the truck was waiting for him to return."

Perhaps Aliya did not know Grandfather's palm down, fingers up signal, but regardless, someone had to ask: "And may we know, Mrs. Caviglia," Aliya asked hesitantly, "if you mentioned it to the police. The police report does not indicate the return of a Chansky employee."

Mrs. Caviglia shrugged her shoulders. "Well, perhaps not. They didn't ask any follow up, I guess."

She shook her head. "I should have mentioned it to the police. But..." she sighed, "it may be difficult for you to understand. Nicola Sacco was my uncle."

Sacco—how did I know that name? It took me a few seconds to put it together. She had to be referring to the infamous Sacco and Vanzetti case. In the 1920s, anti-foreigner fever swept the nation after the Russian Revolution. Sacco and Vanzetti, two immigrant anarchists, were arrested for robbery and murder, tried, and executed, despite questions about the evidence and testimony. But what had that to do with Mrs. Caviglia's withholding information?

Mrs. Caviglia continued. "Following my uncle's wrongful execution, Roberto and I, just married, left Massachusetts and came to Brooklyn. Here, Roberto opened a shoe repair business. We did well, but both of us, with other Sacco and Vanzetti family members, kept working to clear their names. I don't know if you understand what happens when a loved one wrongfully suffers at the hands of the authorities. Even though police are needed and, for the most part, work for the good, you never fully trust them. You share information with the authorities only to satisfy their questions asked and nothing more."

Mrs. Caviglia's eyes became moist. "Maybe I was wrong not to have mentioned the return of the Chansky plumber to the house. But I didn't do it on purpose."

"Mrs. Caviglia," Aliya asked softly, "didn't it make any difference that Inspector Carlucci, who is Italian, has been leading the investigation?"

"You mean, my dear," and she smiled at Aliya, "because he's one of our own? There are many times where being among one's own people is a wonderful experience, but other times it makes no difference. After all, Mussolini, may he burn in hell, was one of our people, too, but Roberto and I would fight him to the death."

"I understand," Grandfather said.

She turned to him. "Am I in trouble? Will I now get an unwelcome visit from Detective Carlucci?"

The missing child investigation that Grandfather and I had worked in Williamsburg two years earlier came to mind. I recalled the attitude I carried into the case: smugness about my version of Judaism being much more appropriate in the modern world; of the contempt for the supposed insular and alienated state of the ultra-religious Jews who lived there in the midst of greater Brooklyn; and my lack of understanding as to why they harbored strong pockets of resistance to working with the police. So Grandfather's reply did not surprise me.

"I think not, Mrs. Caviglia. While we will share this information with the detective, we will also tell him that you have now freely added it to the investigation. Your attitude in relation to the authorities is not uncommon. Our own people in Williamsburg, Crown Heights, or Boro Park, who suffered first through pogroms and then the Holocaust, experience much difficulty in speaking to the police who for too long sought harm, and not benefit, for them in those places of persecution. Please do not feel badly about yourself."

Mrs. Caviglia looked grateful. "Thank you, Mr. Wolf. You are kind."

We took a few minutes to finish our teas and, at Grandfather's motion, rose to leave.

At the same time, Mrs. Caviglia also got up. "Mr. Wolf, do you like opera?"

"I do," Grandfather replied. "The young Mr. Pavarotti is very esteemed by my ears. My daughter and I were fortunate to be present at the Metropolitan Opera House a few years ago to hear his magnificent performance in *La Fille du Regiment*."

"Good," she said, leading us to the door. "I would not take it badly if you called on me some time to share some tea and Verdi."

Grandfather nodded and smiled.

* * * *

Walking to the car, Aliya kept glancing at me as if to say, "Can we talk? I don't believe what I just heard from Mrs. Caviglia." But I motioned that we should be still, knowing that Grandfather wanted silence. I was certain that he had returned to the day of Batya Flaum's murder, rearranging timeframe, interactions, emotions, and individuals' actions to incorporate the new information.

We didn't have to wait long. Now seated in the backseat, Grandfather announced: "I know it was your plan to transport me to the house and for you to proceed to the 61st Precinct to obtain the phone and bank records, but please drive us back to my office which is the optimal location for our digesting of what we just learned, yes?"

"If you think it best, yes," I said.

Grandfather continued: "In addition, I would like to give you the Polaroid camera and film to take some pictures tomorrow morning."

He leaned forward and smiled at Aliya. "As I had once explained to Joel, the Polaroid is a great advance in the technology that supports our private investigative profession in how much time it saves us. Where I wish you to take the photos, I will explain when we are in the office."

Grandfather laughed softly. "And in this manner, I will not succumb to the lure of the easy chair calling to me."

We also laughed. I put the car in gear, heading back to Ocean Parkway, which I took all the way to Atlantic Avenue, then to Grandfather's office. I avoided the BQE so as not to give jolts to Grandfather's body which might distract him from the world into which I knew he was entering.

With no spaces available in front of his office, I dropped Grandfather and Aliya off and drove a few blocks to a parking garage. When I rejoined them and sat in a folding chair next to Aliya, the air conditioner already ran full blast. The Polaroid camera and film sat on his desk. Grandfather had returned to our world.

"So, my children," he began, "please tell me please what you learned from our visit to Mrs. Caviglia."

"The main thing for me," Aliya said quickly, "is that one of the plumbers came back to the house and probably was the last person there before Mrs. Gelb found the body. So, the strongest suspicion now lies on the Chanskys, or at least on one of them."

I had also been thinking similarly, but something muddied this conclusion for me: "The only thing is that Mrs. Caviglia said that the Chansky guy didn't stay long, which might mean he killed her quickly, but how did he know about the safe behind the hanging picture? Did he force Mrs. Flaum, while still in the foyer, in such a short time, to tell him that there was a safe with money inside? Forced her to open it or give him the combination? Also, Carlucci seemed to have done a thorough job checking out the Chanskys' story and going over their shop forensically. Things are not adding up for me."

Aliya touched my arm. "I see what you're thinking, Joel. It's possible that the person did forget something and was in and out of the house quickly. Perhaps Mrs. Caviglia missed someone else going in and out after, I don't know. I sort of understand about Mrs. Caviglia's not telling the police about the return of the plumber, but the police record doesn't indicate that the Chanskys mentioned it either. Where I was sure just a while ago that we were on to something big, I'm still confused."

Grandfather leaned back. "Aliya, do not underestimate the value of this new piece of information and do not feel deflated. There come points in an investigation where a dead end darkness looms before the investigator. What is required is to find that bit of light for the critical thinking to make its way. Why did the plumbers not mention one of them returning to the house? How many plumbers were at the scene? Two? Perhaps three? Who were they, and if one of them did so, which one went back to the house? Are all of the plumbers complicit? All of these questions must be resolved, yes?"

"Zaida," I said, "why do you say 'if one of them.' From what Mrs. Caviglia reported, don't we know for sure that one certainly did? She clearly saw the man in a Chansky uniform."

Grandfather put up a hand. "Might we ascertain for ourselves the accuracy of Mrs. Caviglia's claim? Here is my request to you. Tomorrow morning you will please go to the Chanskys shop on the New Utrecht Avenue and the 62nd Street and take pictures of their shop, trucks, every uniform they possess, and front and back pictures of each employee, good?"

Aliya and I agreed.

"Here is why, with an apology upon my lips, I ask this critical task of you. Yesterday I spoke to Mr. Isaac Chansky, the elder Chansky, and asked him if there was a need to do so, might we visit his place of business? He readily agreed but with one caveat. We might do so either at 6:30 in the morning before they left for their service appointments or after 7:00 in the evening when they returned. Tomorrow, I would like you to choose the first option as determining the reason and importance of the person returning to the house is now paramount in our investigation. We do not want to let a whole day to lapse. Am I to be forgiven?"

Aliya said, "Of course, Zaida, who needs a long night's sleep when you're on the case!"

"Good, then it is settled. Here, with your permission, is how we will proceed. Since you will be passing our house on the way to the 61st Precinct, might you take me home? After you pick up the materials from the station, you will come back to return your mother's car and share the reports with me. Given her kindness, might we make dinner for her? We will not discuss the case anymore today. Then you will return to your apartment to gain some needed rest before you venture out early in the morning to the Chansky shop. I will let them know you are coming. Also, I will be at my office at 9:00 where you will please join me with the pictures. We will then review our next steps."

* * * *

I took the camera and film and went to retrieve the car.

On the way home, down Ocean Parkway with rush hour traffic not yet upon us, we all began to relax. My attention drifted for a moment as I relived my best childhood memories of riding the Parkway with my father and mother.

Aliya turned to face Grandfather in the back and said: "This isn't exactly a case-related question, but do you remember the Sacco and Vanzetti trial? Were they wrongly executed?"

Grandfather answered. "I remember it quite well. Their arrest in 1920 and their execution in 1927 overlapped with the Leopold and Loeb tragedy in 1924. For us in Vienna, despite my birth city's claim to culture and learning, the United States was the 'Golden Land.' We could not comprehend how Leopold and Loeb, two wealthy Jewish young men, well-educated, and living in a haven of safety, could commit the murder of an innocent young boy. For vanity, for excess, for the literal execution of a philosophy?

"The Sacco and Vanzetti prosecution and their subsequent electrocutions further unsettled many of us. I joined several rallies protesting not so much their innocence as I wasn't sure if they were guilty or innocent, but rather against the stirred up, frenzied hatred against their political views, of their foreign identities, and of their refusal to be passive in response. Though a horrible period in American history, I am glad our country, for the most part, righted itself as opposed to what I already, in 1927, was sensing in my Austria and of course in Germany."

Grandfather paused. I glanced in the rear-view mirror at his grim face. "I am sorry, Aliya, if I assumed a pedantic voice. I believe I reverted back to my previous profession."

"It's okay, Zaida," Aliya responded. "I think I need to do some historical catching up on Sacco and Vanzetti and Leopold and Loeb."

* * * *

The rest of the day rushed by. It was already 4:30 by the time we dropped Grandfather off and proceeded to the 61st to pick up the bank and phone records. Carlucci was at the Sergeant's Desk when we arrived.

He acknowledged us with: "Mr. Wolf, he's something else. He called me. How we missed getting from the neighbor lady that one of the plumbers came back to the house, I don't know."

When we said nothing in response, Carlucci half turned toward Aliya and said, "Nice to see you, young lady. You still on the case?"

Aliya later told me that she could have punched him at that moment, but she responded calmly: "Yes, Detective, I am and will be until it's solved. We are here for the records."

Carlucci seemed indifferent to Aliya's retort. "Louie," he barked at the officer behind the desk, "give me those two envelopes I left with you."

The sergeant handed him two large envelopes, one marked "phone" and the other "bank." Carlucci was about to hand them to me when Aliya reached out and took them.

"Thank you Detective," she said, taking my arm. "Have a nice evening."

* * * *

With traffic heavy, we didn't arrive back to the house until 6:00. Since Tuesday was a slow day at the store, my mother would be home at 7:30. Plenty of time to make dinner, but Aliya and I took the lazy way out and headed for Kornblatt's where we picked up some soup, deli, and breads. My mother walked in right at 7:30, looking pleased at the fully laid dinner table.

Everyone claimed tiredness while eating, and we did not discuss the case. My mother did not ask, and instead talked about events at the store. Although she did not use the term "blood diamonds" which came along a few years later, she described how difficult it was to obtain stones not tainted by exploitation, human degradation, and violence. She tried her best to locate ethically mined diamonds but was increasingly frustrated in her search. Anecdotes about customers' idiosyncrasies lightened the mood.

After quickly cleaning up, we headed to the subway to take the train home. It took us an hour. Exhausted, we plopped into bed. Even though we planned to take a cab to the Chansky shop, we set the alarm for 5:00. Before falling asleep, we pillow-talked briefly.

"Joel," Aliya whispered curling toward me, "it seemed Mrs. Caviglia took a liking to your grandfather."

"Yes, indeed, I think she did."

"I think he parried her advances very adroitly, don't you think?"

I enfolded Aliya more closely. "Yes," I jested. "And even if it weren't a matter of Mrs. Caviglia being of a different religion, I do believe he's already keeping company with Mrs. Wachter whom he met during the dorm murder case. He's no two-timer."

Aliya poked me in the ribs, a pain I still enjoy to this day.

WEDNESDAY, JULY 9, 1975

With a grumble, I reacted to the alarm and reached for Aliya. Nothing but air.

I smelled coffee brewing and stumbled to the kitchen. Aliya, already dressed, pecked me on the cheek, then led me to a kitchen chair: "I woke up an hour ago and couldn't fall back to sleep thinking about the case. I didn't want to bother you by tossing around."

I had slept like a log. Aliya placed a mug of coffee with milk, the way I liked it, on the table.

"Thanks. I'll gulp this down, throw on some clothes, and back to Brooklyn we go."

I very much wanted to wear shorts, a tee, and sandals, but I thought better of it. I was, after all, representing The Frank Wolf Detective Agency. I put on a button-down, short-sleeved shirt and lightweight slacks, matching Aliya's neat, casual dress approach.

The cab dropped us off on 62nd Street in Brooklyn, a half block from the New Utrecht subway stop. We were in Boro Park, but in a more industrial area than Grandfather and I had visited along 13th Avenue while working the Stein case.

The Chansky business squeezed between a Merit and a Phillips 66 gas station. Even at this early hour, the whining starts and stops of air guns removing and applying tire bolts reverberated from both stations. The heavy smell of gasoline soaked the air. *Chansky Community Store,* etched into freshly painted wood, hung from chain links above a glass door. A paper sign on the inside read *CLOSED*. Metal grills protected both the door and the glass window to our left. We passed a small truck marked *Chansky Plumbing & Heating* parked along the curb. Another Chansky truck sat in a driveway on the left.

I rang a large doorbell button embedded in a paint-flaking, white wooden frame that encased a glass door. A short, gray-haired man neared, peered out, smiled, and waved us in.

"You are the young people Mr. Wolf said would come to the shop to see me and my son," the man began in an Eastern European accent. "I am Isaac Chansky, and my son Asher is in the back. Come with me to meet him."

On the front of his overalls was embroidered, *Chansky Plumbing & Heating* over a caricatured representation of a plumber racing forward with a wrench held high. The back, clearly etched in red, also showed *Chansky Plumbing & Heating*.

"Nice to meet you," I said, introducing myself and Aliya. "My grandfather told you that we would be taking some pictures? May I start in this showroom?"

Chansky agreed readily. I hoped I didn't sound condescending when I said "showroom" since it was more a semblance of one. Yes, various items displayed for sale: toilets, sinks, wrenches, pipes, couplings and fittings, two water heaters, a tub, and cements and adhesives. But just a few were in their original packaging. Instead, a hand-written price was taped to each item.

Remarkably low prices, even for secondhand. After my father passed away, I took responsibility for home repairs and knew what these things cost. Before I started snapping photos, I said: "I should shop here. Looks like you offer good deals."

"You are always welcome. My wife is here in the shop from 9:00 to 5:00, Monday through Thursday and until 3:00 on Friday. We try to serve the community, the way this country took care of us after the War."

Chansky scratched his head with his left hand, and his sleeve slipped up showing tattooed numbers on the outer side of the forearm. I understood his sentiments and also noted he was a left-hander. If Batya Flaum had been attacked from the front, the murderer would have hit Batya Flaum on the right side of her head, not on the left, in keeping with the swing of a left-hander.

"There are many in need in this and other neighborhoods, new immigrants like the Puerto Ricans, Dominicans, and some of our fellow Jews. They cannot afford to pay for plumbers to come to their homes, so they try to do their own work. We make parts available, at cost, and I call back many in the evening to give them instructions. But please, take the pictures you need and ask us questions which I think we already answered to the police."

I took a few shots of the showroom including an antique wooden NCR cash register on a glass counter. The counter's exposed shelves displayed buckets of screws, nails, washers, and toilet flappers, marked with prices from a penny to a quarter. I imagined Mrs. Chansky sitting on the stool positioned behind the counter. After the picture developed, Aliya carefully placed each of the Polaroid photos in a labeled envelope.

Chansky waited patiently for me to be done. He then indicated a back door out of the showroom. We followed him through to a large space that served as a warehouse and garage. The service truck parked in the driveway when we first arrived now stood in this space. Isaac introduced us to his son Asher who continued to load supplies. He stopped, shook hands, and excused himself to continue his work. He was in his late 20's, perhaps an inch or two taller than his father, stocky with a weightlifter's build, large hands, curly dark hair, and a few days of scruffy beard. He wore the same uniform as his father, along with a tool belt.

"Before we hold you up, do you mind if we take a few pictures of you?" I asked. "Your father probably mentioned that as part of the investigation of the Flaum murder, some new information has come our way, and we are here to take pictures of Chansky plumbers, trucks, and shop areas, and ask a few questions."

"Knock yourself out," Asher replied, coming to stand in front of me. Then to his father: "Remember Dad, we have a job at the Schwartz house scheduled for 8:00 in Brighton Beach."

It was 6:50. "Yes, I know," his father replied. "We will come on time."

Looking proudly at his son, Isaac added: "Asher, when he was a child, was not a book reader like his younger brother and sister. He liked to discover how things work, to take things apart and put them back together. When he was five, he would get up early and come with me on my jobs, watching, always watching, what I did. By ten, he could tell by himself what to do and take care of simple jobs. And he pushes always to be on time. He is a fanatic about what he calls 'customer service.' He is a good boy."

Unsmiling, Asher cooperated as I took three frontal pictures to see if his facial expressions would change, and one of the back that captured the uniform design. Done, Asher silently went back to loading the truck while I repeated the photo process with his father. I circled the truck and took shots of the sides and back where displays of *Chansky Plumbing & Heating* appeared.

"We don't want to delay you, Mr. Chansky," I said. "We'll ask you a few questions and be on our way. First, are there other overalls or uniforms a Chansky plumber might wear when out on a job?"

"A Chansky plumber? You mean Asher or me? Yes, our overalls take on many stains. My wife is always washing."

He pointed to a rack near the door. "There are all our other work overalls. Rosa washed them last evening."

I wandered over and took a few pictures of the rack. When I returned, I asked: "And the truck, parked along the curb, is it the same as this one?"

"Yes, a year older. We use both trucks when we are sure just one plumber is necessary on a job. In this way, Asher and I can go separately."

"And when you went to the Flaum house on the morning of the murder, you thought it would be a two-person job?"

Isaac thought for a moment. "Like I remember, we were not sure from what Mrs. Flaum told us when she called if it should be a one or two person job. We did not want to take a chance of needing to come back. And, of course, it was our rabbi's home, so both of us came."

"And there was no third plumber with you that day?" Aliya asked.

"Third plumber! Again, no, never, there is always just Asher and me. We even take our vacations the same time."

"Then which of you," I asked, "went back to the Flaum house within minutes after you left?"

Isaac's eyes widened. "Went back to the Flaum house! We did not go back. Not Asher or me. We drove straight to our next appointment—in Sheepshead Bay, if I remember right."

I took a few seconds to think how I should frame my next question: "What if a witness saw someone from Chansky Plumbing & Heating returning to the house minutes after the truck left, staying a very short while, and then heading back on East 10th toward Avenue J, probably where your truck was parked?"

Isaac sputtered, and I sensed fear and anger. "Truck was parked! We did not park our truck! I believe you accuse us of the murder! Is this like Europe again where false witnesses are found to lie about someone when the real criminal cannot be found or the authorities do not want to find the truth! This is America. Such things should not happen here. I tell you not Asher or me returned to the house."

Asher came rushing over. "What's going on, Dad?"

Isaac took a deep breath. "Nothing, Asher, it is okay. I am just answering some questions. Go back to loading for the Schwartz job. We will leave in a few minutes."

I put up my hands feeling defensive. "No, no," I said after Asher had gone back to the truck. "We are not at all suggesting that you or your son murdered Mrs. Flaum. No, not at all."

Aliya came forward and lightly touched Isaac's arm. "Mr. Chansky, we are not saying what the witness reported is accurate. But please understand, we had to follow up. Please accept our apologies if we upset you."

If the Chanskys had anything to do with the killing, Aliya's statement may have been much too conciliatory. For now, I thought, no harm done. We would process Chansky's reaction with Grandfather and see what he thinks.

"Yes, I am greatly upset, young lady," Chansky retorted, waving us to depart through the driveway. "If you are honestly in search of the truth and find it, please call me and say that your suspicions were wrong. Will you do that for us?"

"We will," Aliya answered as we hurriedly walked out of the Chansky shop. "We promise."

* * * *

After I quickly took photos of the Chansky truck parked at the curb, we walked briskly to the New Utrecht station. We took the D to Atlantic Avenue, switched to the 3 to Boro Hall, and walked for two minutes to Grandfather's office. We arrived a little after 8:15. Grandfather was already at his desk with the bank and phone records spread before him. The previous day, Aliya and I had done a quick perusal, and we didn't see anything that stood out. But then again, we didn't possess Grandfather's eyes. He greeted us warmly and held out two paper bags.

"Your wonderful mother has wrought her miraculous goodness again. She packed you egg sandwiches. She was afraid you might have departed on your mission this morning without satisfactory nutrition."

"We're starving," Aliya exclaimed for both of us. "But we're also hungry to let you know about our visit to the Chanskys and review with you the phone and bank records. Did you see anything interesting? Nothing significant struck Joel and me."

A smile spread over my grandfather's face. He loved plays on words. We also smiled, but we became serious as Grandfather swept his hands over the papers and said, "Nuh, is there not something here of great significance?"

We looked at each other. If I hadn't been very tired last night, I would have pushed myself to review the records more carefully. We stared at Grandfather like two school children who hadn't completed their homework assignments.

"Let us begin with a most salient item in the phone records. Jonathan did not fabricate the existence of a call to him the evening previous to his mother's murder requesting him to come to an interview in Manhattan. From where did the call come? From Manhattan? From a Chansky phone? Mrs. Gelb's? From Barbara Burns? From the synagogue? From a phone booth near the synagogue? From a phone booth in Flatbush? From where?"

Aliya and I sat in embarrassed silence. Grandfather handed me a sheet labeled Jonathan Flaum phone records. It was dated February 20, 1975, and had an entry circled 7:32 PM. The call originated from a phone booth on the corner of 13th Avenue and 55th Street in Boro Park. I then handed it to Aliya. There were no other items.

"Wow, Boro Park," I said. "The anonymous letter also came from somewhere in Boro Park. Not one of our suspects lives there. Whoever made the call…"

"Whoever made the call," Aliya said, "wanted to hide his or her identity."

"Or," I added, "it was from a hired accomplice."

"All possibilities," Grandfather said, "but let us not make an absolute assumption that the accomplice was, as you stated, 'hired,' yes?"

Of course, I thought. Two people may have been working together without one hiring the other.

"What else of importance did you note in the phone records?" Grandfather asked.

"Didn't Barbara Burns make almost daily calls to the synagogue in the two weeks before the murder?" I asked. "Do I remember correctly, Zaida?"

"You do, Yoeli, good. Do you remember anything special about the calls?"

Nothing came to me. Aliya shook her head.

Grandfather handed another paper to Aliya who looked it over and gave it to me. It was Barbara Burns' call record.

"All the calls are short," I said, "not one over two minutes."

"Which might suggest what, my children?"

"That she wasn't getting through to Rabbi Flaum. Which was probably making her angrier and angrier as those weeks went by," Aliya replied.

"Angry enough to plan Mrs. Flaum's murder!" I said.

Grandfather shook his head. "Nuh, nuh, Joel, perhaps. Now it is just an important conjecture, but not more than a conjecture. Is there anything else in the phone records you would like to discuss?"

Though a bit afraid to hear what we might have missed, I asked: "What else is interesting, Zaida?"

Grandfather answered: "To my eyes, there is nothing more of interest from the phone records."

"And the bank records?" Aliya asked.

"Yes, the bank records. What are your observations?"

"Well," I gave it a shot, "Jonathan's didn't have much activity. Marcia Gelb's were erratic, with up and down jumps in deposits and withdrawals. For Rabbi Flaum, it looks like weekly salary deposits of the same amount. And Barbara Burns, salary deposits and withdrawals each week on a Thursday morning. Probably to do shopping for the Sabbath and weekend."

"A reasonable assumption," Grandfather responded, picking up another paper. "Do you remember the amounts of the withdrawals?"

Aliya answered. "I think $200 each time. Am I right?"

Grandfather gave the paper to Aliya who looked and said, "Oh, I see." She then handed it to me.

"Zaida," I said, perusing the report, "for several weeks prior and two weeks after, her withdrawals were each for $200. But on February 20, the day before the murder, she withdrew $300. Are you saying that's significant? Might she just have simply needed another $100 that day?"

"Yes, certainly it is possible," Grandfather answered "For now let us file the anomaly as a consideration within the totality of our critical analyses. Let us move on to hearing about your visit to the Chansky business, yes?"

Aliya retrieved the Polaroids from her handbag and handed them to Grandfather. He looked at each one carefully while I summarized our visit.

"And you say that Mr. Chansky insisted that there is never another plumber that works with them?" Grandfather inquired.

"Right, Zaida," I replied.

"And the son Asher is short and stocky, yes?"

"Yes. He fits the description that Mrs. Caviglia gave us of the plumber who returned to the house."

"And Mr. Chansky was very upset by the implication of their involvement in the murder?"

I felt embarrassed thinking of my exchange with Isaac Chansky. I was wrong to question him in a prosecutorial manner. Zaida would have handled it differently. I made a note to learn from this experience and answered: "He vehemently denies Mrs. Caviglia's claim that one of them returned to the house."

"And perhaps one more question, my children. You saw no company markings indicating *Chansky Plumbing & Heating* that were different from the presentations on their uniforms and trucks?"

Aliya took this one. "No, I also looked at the pictures carefully on the train coming over here. The writings and logos were exactly the same."

Grandfather drummed his fingers on the desk. He looked up: "Then we have our tasks for today before us. You will please return to Mrs. Caviglia this morning after I call her to ascertain that she will be home. Please take the pictures with you. To Mrs. Caviglia you will show the pictures of the Chansky men, front and back, and inquire if the business identification of *Chansky Plumbing & Heating* is what she saw on the man that returned to the house. You are able to do so for us?"

We nodded, and I asked. "And you, Zaida, you're not coming with us? I'm sure Mrs. Caviglia would love to see you."

Grandfather did not rise to my bait, and Aliya gave me a sideways glance.

"No, Joel," Grandfather replied neutrally, "I shall make my way to the 13th Avenue and do some perambulations. You know I have a great liking for the 13th Avenue, and I may find some bargains there. We will meet back here at 2:00, yes?"

"Zaida, you want to walk around 13th Avenue?" I said. "Today? In this heat? To look for some bargains?"

"Sha, sha, sha, Joel," Grandfather answered. "I will explain when we return and also show you any bargains I may have found."

Grandfather looked up Mrs. Caviglia's phone number in his small, well-worn address book and dialed. After a short conversation, we heard him say, "Yes, I too am sorry I will not be able to come personally today, and as you kindly say, perhaps some other time. Joel and Aliya will be at your residence in just a little over an hour. Thank you again."

Off Aliya and I went leaving Grandfather sitting quietly, miles away within himself.

* * * *

We took the Q Train to the Avenue J station. We may have known this neighborhood since we were children, but in the last few days, we had gained even more familiarity with each candy store, pizza joint, gas station, dry cleaner, supermarket, storefront law office, butchers, clothing shop, the Midwood Theater and, of course, *Bezalel Judaica Gifts*. I still considered Mrs. Gelb a suspect, even if I couldn't see her having delivered the fatal blow.

We turned south on East 10th. The temperature display on the Apple Savings Bank on 14th and J indicated a high of 95 for the day. I thought about my grandfather trekking around Boro Park in this heat.

Two men were unloading a refrigerator from a large P. C. Richard & Son appliances truck with its motto, *Keep Sunshine in Your Heart* emblazoned on the side. A car marked, **A. G. Koslowe, Electrician**, ignored 'no double parking' signs, its back seat loaded to the roof with equipment and its trunk open and spilling out electrical devices and tools. As we approached Mrs. Caviglia's home, I assumed she was watching from the bay window.

If she was watching, Mrs. Caviglia didn't show it by opening the door for us before we rang, as she had the day before. But Aliya's ring summoned her quickly. Mrs. Caviglia beckoned us in.

"I understood from Mr. Wolf that he could not come himself today. I hope he is well. How can I help you?"

"He's fine. He had to attend to another matter," I replied as we followed her into the kitchen and took the same seats as before. Only the napkin holder now sat on the table. "As Mr. Wolf, I believe, explained over the phone, we're here to show you some pictures and ask you some questions based on what you see."

Mrs. Caviglia nodded.

Aliya dove into her bag and extracted the envelope with the Polaroids. She shuffled through them, selecting the pictures of the Chanskys and their trucks. We had discussed on the train our strategy on how we would present the pictures. Aliya started with the truck, laying three shots before Mrs. Caviglia.

"Can you please confirm," I asked, "that the plumbers' truck you saw on the morning of the murder looked like this one?"

"Of course it does," Mrs. Caviglia replied with a frown. "I told the police, and I told you yesterday that it was a Chansky truck. And the police didn't need me to tell them that. Everyone knows the Chanskys were there that morning."

"Yes, of course," I said, trying to reclaim ground. "Aliya, could you please show Mrs. Caviglia pictures of the plumbers."

Aliya placed the photos on the table, and I pointed first to pictures of Isaac Chansky. "Do you know this man?"

"Yes," she replied with less testiness. "That's old man Chansky. I have seen him from time to time in the neighborhood, and Roberto knew him personally. Said he was a nice guy, good to people of all sorts around here."

"And this man?" I asked, pushing forward photos of Asher Chansky.

Mrs. Caviglia took a few seconds. "That's the Chansky kid who works with his father. I don't know his name, but I hear from my nephew Jimmy who's also a plumber that the boy is very good. Jimmy says he sometimes calls him to get his advice on a difficult repair."

I took back Asher's pictures. "Do you think either of the two might have been the man who returned to the house?"

Mrs. Caviglia knitted her brow. "Could be the boy based on his build, but I couldn't say for sure. The man had a woolen cap on."

I proceeded to lay out the Polaroids of the Chansky overalls, two each of fronts and backs. "Mrs. Caviglia, are these the same uniforms the plumbers wore the day of Mrs. Flaum's murder?"

Mrs. Caviglia picked up each of the pictures and looked at them carefully. She repeated the inspection before answering: "I can tell you for sure that the men who went in the house wore overalls with the same as the fronts as in these pictures. Their coats were unzipped. I could see their fronts. But I couldn't see their backs."

"But you could see the back of the plumber who returned to the house?" Aliya jumped in.

"Yes," Mrs. Caviglia answered slowly, obviously bewildered. "But he was dressed differently. He wore a pullover sweatshirt with the Chansky name on the back. Or it was another Chansky plumber?"

Aliya and I looked at each other. I thought she must be as confused as I was. I fumbled for two pictures, one of the back of the Chanskys' overalls and the other of the truck's side panel. I placed them in front of Mrs. Caviglia.

"Do you see how *Chansky Plumbing & Heating* is displayed on the back of their overalls and truck?"

Mrs. Caviglia nodded.

"And is that what you saw on the back of the sweatshirt the man was wearing who returned to the house?"

"No, not at all," she answered vehemently.

Aliya and I glanced at each other. "Then please, why did you think he was a Chansky plumber?" I asked.

"Because it said so!"

Aliya rose, fished in her bag, and took out her notepad and a pen. She opened the pad to a blank page and placed the pad on the table. "Could you please write what you saw on the man's back."

Mrs. Caviglia took the pen and slowly wrote separate, capitalized cursive letters. After carefully bolding each letter, she held up the pad to us. We gaped:

C P H

"You see," Mrs. Caviglia said proudly, "just what I told you. CPH! Chansky Plumbing & Heating!"

* * * *

We thanked Mrs. Caviglia for her time and promised we would convey her regards to my grandfather. We didn't say a word about what she had written. Our goodbyes were hurried. I hoped that she hadn't noticed.

On the street, Aliya started to speak, but I gave her Grandfather's palm down, fingers slightly raised symbol. She understood. I set a leisurely pace. Once I was sure that we were out of Mrs. Caviglia's sight, I exhaled deeply, took Aliya's elbow, and stopped.

I said: "I was afraid if we started talking earlier we'd look excited. If Mrs. Caviglia was watching us, she'd wonder what she had said and try to call Zaida right away."

"It's okay." Aliya put a hand on my shoulder. "Keeping it in for two minutes hasn't killed me. But wow, are you thinking what I am?"

"That it wasn't one of the Chansky plumbers, that CPH stands for something much closer to home, that CPH is Congregation P'nai Hesed, that Mrs. Flaum's killer gave himself away, that given Mrs. Caviglia's description of the man, that he was wearing a tool belt, we might guess who it was." I ran out of breath.

"And you're guessing Eli Schorr, am I right?"

"I'm guessing Eli Schorr, yes!"

Despite the muggy, hot day, a chill shot through me. Someone from the synagogue was a vicious murderer. And for what? The money? Perhaps. But Eli appeared perfectly content living in his "pad" at the synagogue. He was probably paid a decent wage for being the "Maintenance Director."

And would he have known the combination to the safe? Or did someone hire Eli to kill Mrs. Flaum? If so, I shuddered. Was it the rabbi?

We started walking, and I shared my agitation with Aliya.

"Yes," she said, "those thoughts are rattling me too." She tightly gripped my arm. "Joel, I'm angry and scared. A man who could be Mrs. Flaum's murderer is in the synagogue. Other people may be in danger. I'm picturing a person, with whom I had civil interaction just a few days ago, smashing Mrs. Flaum's head. I see her lying in a pool of blood. I want to call Carlucci and insist he pick up this brute before he harms someone else. But, but Joel, do you remember what you told me after the Williamsburg kidnapping case?"

When I hesitated, Aliya continued.

"You told me that although your grandfather was fairly certain who had kidnapped the boy, he didn't want the police openly involved as it would tarnish the suspect's reputation if he was wrong? Zaida didn't want to take even the smallest of chances. What if we're wrong about Eli Schorr? We shouldn't call Carlucci right away, should we? For instance, the Chanskys might also have a sweatshirt with *CPH* on its back that they didn't show us."

"You're right, we won't call Carlucci. We can't rule out the Chanskys. But I have an idea. We're due at Zaida's office at 2:00. It's almost 11:00. We'll eat some lunch and review everything we learned in the last few days including Mrs. Caviglia's revelation. When we see Zaida, we'll ask him what he thinks. At home, I'll also call the Chansky shop. Mrs. Chansky is probably there. If she does all the business' laundry, she'll know if there is a *CPH* branded sweatshirt."

"And she'll tell you the truth? She might also cover up her family's involvement."

"She may lie, but I just don't think so."

* * * *

At the house, Aliya said she would find something for lunch. I sat down and dialed the Chansky business. Mrs. Chansky, in a heavy Eastern European accent, answered with a cheery "hello." Once she knew the reason for the call, would the warmth disappear?

I introduced myself and asked if the business had any sweatshirts with CPH on the back?

She first responded with "Vos", the Yiddish for "What?" and then stated that a "Chansky plumber never wears such a sweatshirt." I thanked her and hung up.

Then I had another idea. I called the Congregation P'nai Hesed office. Mattie Hirsch picked up. "Does the *shul* have any sweatshirts with a CPH identifier on the back?" I asked.

She did not ask why. "Yes, we do. The *shul's* teenagers like to wear them when the weather is cool. If you'd like one, they will be on sale in the gift shop before Chanukah."

"And do *shul* staff members ever wear them?"

"Yes. S*hul* maintenance people are given sweatshirts because they often need to work outdoors in the winter, and coats get in their way."

"One more question, please Mrs. Hirsch. Are the letters italicized?"

"Why yes, they are."

I thanked Mrs. Hirsch, asked that she keep this conversation between us, and politely hurried off the phone. I filled Aliya in.

"Supports our suspicion, doesn't it, Joel?" Aliya said.

"Yes, but again, let's see what Zaida thinks."

Just in case he had returned early to his office, I tried Grandfather. No answer.

* * * *

During lunch, Aliya and I went over the same ground repeatedly, more and more convinced that Eli Schorr had killed Batya Flaum. Lunch over, we tried Grandfather again. Still no answer. Even though Grandfather had said to meet at 2:00 and it was only 12:45, where was he? He hadn't said where he was going except that he would walk around 13th Avenue and possibly find bargains. During the Stein murder investigation, when he had made a similar statement about finding "bargains" on 13th Avenue, I had been miffed at what I took as a cavalier statement. As it turned out, he had discovered "bargains," but much more that led to the case being solved.

This time there also had to be something more in Boro Park. We were sure Eli Schorr had sent the threatening letter to Grandfather from there. That Grandfather might get himself into some danger kept nagging at me. Until I saw him back at the office, I would worry. Though early to head to the subway for the ride to Boro Hall, I asked:

"Aliya, can we leave right away for Zaida's office? I'll feel better when we find him there."

Aliya grabbed her bag. We headed out.

* * * *

We bounded up the stairs to my grandfather's office. As we entered the third-floor hallway, I noticed the office light on. I tapped Aliya to slow down. We went in and saw Grandfather sitting behind his desk with the bank reports we had reviewed earlier before him. While the air conditioner blew strongly, sweat still dotted his forehead. He must not have arrived much earlier. I also noticed two shopping bags on the floor, one marked

Jacobson Custom Wear, and the other, with celery leaves peeking out, **Esposito Fruits & Vegetables — Brooklyn's Freshest**.

"Hello, my children." Grandfather smiled and looked at his watch. "It is 1:45, and you have rejoined me. Your early return is most welcome."

"And you Zaida," I said pointing to the bags, "I see you found bargains on 13th Avenue. Will you need us to help you bring them home?"

"I do not, thank you, for they are quite light. You must be quite curious to ascertain what is in the bag from the haberdashery store, no? I am pleased to tell you, Yoeli, that after many years of advisement, I have listened to you and purchased, because of their bargain prices, two new white dress shirts. You are pleased, yes?"

I would have continued bantering but Aliya spoke. "Shouldn't we tell Zaida right away what we discovered from our visit to Mrs. Caviglia? Isn't time now of the essence in arresting a possible murderer?"

"Aliya, my child," Grandfather responded, "I observe some matter is causing you dismay. Please, what is it you wish to tell me?"

Aliya recounted what Mrs. Caviglia had divulged about the *CPH* on the back of the sweatshirt worn by the supposed plumber who had returned briefly to the Flaum house. She related my call to Mrs. Chansky and the woman's denial that any such sweatshirt existed. She added what Mrs. Hirsch had said about a CPH sweatshirt.

She concluded with: "Zaida, do you think it's time we contact Detective Carlucci and ask that Eli Schorr be arrested?"

We waited for Grandfather's response as he lightly finger-drummed on his desk. Finally, Grandfather shook his head and said: "Ay, ay, ay, my children, tragedy piles other tragedy upon itself. I must congratulate you for your excellent detective work."

Grandfather addressed me. "Joel, your initiative in contacting Mrs. Chansky to disconfirm the existence of CPH on the plumbers' apparel and Mrs. Hirsch to confirm such an existence on a *shul* garment was exemplary. But one consideration comes to mind — might CPH be an acronym for still another entity besides Chansky Plumbing & Heating or Congregation P'nai Hesed?"

"You're right, Zaida," I said. "How could we not have thought of that?"

Grandfather waved a hand: "It is fine, my children. You see, in addition to bargains, I discovered in my Boro Park perambulations evidence most incriminating to Mr. Schorr in the murder of Batya Flaum. Do you remember what framed poster was hanging on the wall in Mr. Schorr's quarters at the *shul*?"

"A poster of an Orthodox-looking guy with all sorts of illegal drugs and the name of an addiction center?" I said tentatively.

"**Refuah Addiction Center**, I believe. Am I right?" Aliya added.

"Yes, you are correct," Grandfather replied. "Do you remember the address of this center?"

Aliya and I shook our heads.

"Then I will tell you. The center is situated in a small storefront on the 13th Avenue by the 52nd Street. I entered the premises which had a table, several chairs, and two metal filing cabinets. A thin man in a long beard, large kippah, white shirt, and *tzitzit* at his waist sat behind the table. A *tefillin* bag lay on the table along with sheets of printed paper. On two walls there was the exact same poster as we saw in Mr. Schorr's room on one, and on another wall a similarly horrifying poster of a young adult in an addiction state.

"I believe the man in the office, by the shape of the hat placed on top of a file cabinet, is a Hasid of a group with which I am familiar. The man seemed surprised to see me, but he arose and greeted me cordially. I explained, speaking in Yiddish, who I was and that I was investigating the murder of Batya Flaum. I asked him if he was acquainted with Eli Schorr. At first he insisted that he could not divulge the names of anyone who has an association with the center. But I persuaded him to cooperate by saying he could talk to me or be asked to come down for interrogation to the 61st Precinct along with police visits to his group's headquarters.

"He squirmed, but I had convinced him. He confirmed that Mr. Schorr had been coming to the center, at first as a client, but later as 'a volunteer and supporter.' I inquired if being a supporter included financial contributions, and he answered affirmatively.

"'Then might you possess a record of his contributions?' I asked. After I assured him that I was not interested in his legal obligation to report donations, particularly of the cash nature, he went to a back room and brought out a large ledger book tabbed alphabetically and turned to the Ss and said, 'I will trust to your word. Look as you wish.'"

"And what did you find?" I asked.

"Ah Joel, the following. The page, or I should say pages, were filled with entries from top to bottom going into the past for approximately seven years, the time Mr. Schorr began his work at the congregation. Cash donations regularly for ten, sometimes 20 dollars, except…" and Grandfather halted for a moment, looking grave, "…except for an entry on Sunday, February 23, 1975, for $815. Does that sum recall anything for you?"

"Isn't that the amount that was stolen from the Flaum home during the murder?"

"Not precisely," Grandfather responded. "The amount was $715, a discrepancy of $100. Does anything come to your minds concerning $100?"

Aliya said excitedly. "The extra amount Barbara Burns withdrew from the bank a few days before the murder! She must have given Eli that money to kill Mrs. Flaum. She may even have given him the combination to the safe which she had somehow obtained as an inducement. Barbara Burns paid Eli Schorr to commit the murder!"

I fell silent, letting Aliya's indictment sink in. To me, she was right on the mark. Grandfather, who had been drumming momentarily, opened his hands to us.

"It is your belief that the case is solved, that we will call Detective Carlucci, that he will arrest Mr. Schorr and Ms. Burns, that they will admit to the crime, and that Rabbi Flaum, except for his dalliance, will come out guiltless?"

Before we could reply, Grandfather turned to Aliya: "I will convey forthrightly that I have come to a point in our investigation that I am convinced that Eli Schorr murdered Mrs. Flaum. But tell me please, Aliya, you spent time with Ms. Burns. You believe you understand her. You stated that you liked her. Envisage Ms. Burns now before you and gaze upon her. Do you think she conspired with Mr. Schorr to kill Mrs. Flaum? Do you think she said to him directly, 'Here is a $100 and the combination to the safe. Go, commit the murder?'"

"Zaida, I... No, something's wrong. I can't envision that sort of an exchange. But I feel sure the extra $100 figured into what Eli donated to the center and that somehow Barbara is tied to the murder."

"I agree," Grandfather replied. "We must delve further into what being tied to the murder involves, must we not?"

"Yes Zaida," I said, "and we do not have enough to hold Schorr. After all, even to get an indictment, we have to expect his lawyer will point out that Mrs. Caviglia is elderly, that she can't identify Schorr in a lineup, and as you said, that CPH could stand for something else. And at trial, a defense attorney will ask the jury to consider that Chansky Plumbing & Heating could be lying about not having such a sweatshirt. I know the evidence seems stronger than the defense, but there might be enough shadow of doubt for a jury not to convict him."

Grandfather beamed. "I see our law school tuition has resulted in a very fine attorney. You are correct. We need an admission from Mr. Schorr that he was the killer. Then we may determine the connection with anyone else to the crime."

"And just how and why will Schorr admit to the murder?" I snapped.

"Ah, Yoeli, I hope I am not exhibiting misguided hubris, but I believe I comprehend the sad psychology of Mr. Schorr and the destructive forces that played within his mind to wish Mrs. Flaum dead. And those forces will lead to his admission. We will see if I am correct tomorrow."

"Tomorrow!" Aliya exclaimed. "What is happening tomorrow?"

"Ah my child, it is not just what is happening tomorrow. It is also what is happening tonight. You see, after I left the addiction center, I stopped at a phone booth and called Detective Carlucci. I informed him of what I discovered and suggested that Eli Schorr, as a suspect in the murder of Batya Flaum, be taken into custody in the evening after all functions at the synagogue end. Detective Carlucci agreed, and Mr. Schorr will be held overnight for questioning in the morning. Also, the detective has kindly allowed me to do the interrogation. What you reported confirms for me that I have acted correctly.

"I also requested from the detective that unless the ledger at the addiction center is needed as evidence, that he turn an eye away from it and the unreported cash nature of the donations. The detective said, this in his own words: 'If you crack this case and Schorr confesses, then I won't bother about the ledger. I know you got to protect your own.'"

"Then why don't the police pick him up in the morning? Why hold him overnight?" I asked.

"Ah, again an excellent question, Joel. It is my assessment of Mr. Schorr that he is a person who found comfort and stability at the *shul*, living in its environs, working there, knowing everyone's business as if he were central to the *shul's* existence. It is a life experience lacking in him prior to coming to the *shul*. Adrift, he had become an addict, homeless at times, alienated from family, in jail for petty offenses. To achieve my objective of obtaining the truth, including if anyone else was tied to the crime, he must be separated overnight from the *shul* to be made uncomfortable, unnerved, and even aggressive. He will not sleep well under custody. Demons from his past will capture his mind driving him to be less guarded and confrontational when I question him. It is what I like least about my profession, but it must be done."

"I think I understand," Aliya remarked, "but here's what I'm wondering. Isn't that rather brazen, or I might even call it stupid, calling attention to his place of employment by wearing a CPH sweatshirt? What don't I understand?"

"My child, your reaction that is based on rationality expresses your expectation of how a person should behave when the person's soul, heart, and mind are operating within a lighted existence. Like an eclipse of the sun, or in criminal instances such as with Leopold and Loeb, or the kidnapper of Yosele Rosenstock in Williamsburg, or the killers of Ori Gold in his dormitory room, when some form of darkness casts a shadow and darkens one's being, one stumbles into bad decisions, distorted assumptions, impulsive behaviors, and an arrogant sense of invulnerability. It may be that such individuals suffer darkness emanating from within themselves from the time of birth, or from upbringing, or from poorly chosen interactions with others. Unfortunately, such darkness never disappears totally. It lurks like a virus gone underground, the host its victim, who at times is spurred to injure others."

"And it's possible, Aliya," I added, "that this darkness blinded him to the risk of being seen with the CPH identifier or that he thought with his face unexposed, such an identifier would not be sufficient to convict him."

"Yes, Yoeli," Grandfather said, "that is why I will attempt to obtain a confession from him and how others may have been involved."

Grandfather paused. "Also Aliya, I know you are in possession of Martha Brennan's phone number, yes?"

"Martha Brennan! Yes, I have it written down in my case notebook. But why?"

"For two reasons, my child. Did we not promise as consideration for her assistance with Ms. Burns, we would give her an advantage in reporting on this story? Before you and Joel return to your apartment to take up important rest before we meet tomorrow at 9:00 at the 61st Precinct, you will call Martha Brennan and advise her that Eli Schorr will be taken into custody tonight at the *shul* under suspicion in the murder of Batya Flaum. I am sure Ms. Brennan will have a photographer at the *shul* and at the precinct house. It will be a big story in tomorrow morning's edition of *The Daily News*. I requested from Detective Carlucci that he find a way for Mr. Schorr to see it before we arrive. The good detective replied, 'Just leave it to me.' Seeing himself arrested in the newspaper will be the final unsettling stroke which, I am sorry, must be inflicted on Mr. Schorr."

Aliya jumped up and took out the notebook. "I'll do it right now." She picked up the phone and dialed.

THURSDAY, JULY 10, 1975

Light peeked through curtains around 6:00. Aliya hadn't slept much. Neither had I. We both had the looming confrontation with Eli Schorr on our minds. I hoped that Grandfather would not insist that he be alone in the interview room with Schorr. I simply wouldn't allow it. No way Grandfather would convince me — it was too dangerous even if it only took a few seconds for us to rush in from the observation room.

We were dressed by 6:30. We supplemented our coffees with dry corn flakes and milk. We knew it would be a tough day. At 7:00, my mother called.

"Joel," she started tensely, "I will be taking Zaida to the 61st Precinct this morning. I'm guessing it has something to do with the arrest of that man in the Batya Flaum murder. Zaida went out at 6:00 and brought home a *Daily News*. The front page screams *Synagogue Janitor held in Killing of Rabbi's Wife,* along with a picture of the man being led into the precinct house. Joel, you'll keep an eye on Zaida. Please promise me. I'm worried if he will be in the presence of a murderer."

"Well," I responded, "where could Zaida be more safe than at a police station?"

"Joel..." my mother said. I immediately sensed her irritation. I had good intentions — I had wanted to alleviate my mother's concerns. But my brash approach was thoughtless. I was wrong and wanted to make amends:

"Mom, I understand. Aliya and I are also worried. I promise I'll look out for Zaida and not let him get hurt. We'll call after we leave the station."

"Thank you, Joel."

As a law school student at the Brooklyn DA's office, I had spent time at various Brooklyn police stations. I knew we might be passing by holding cells. How would Aliya respond to what she would see and hear? I advised her to appear as she usually did with no or little makeup, hair pulled back, a top at least elbow length, slacks, and shoes without heels. Aliya agreed.

Before getting on the subway, we picked up a *Daily News*. On the train, we read Brennan's story. There it was on page one—the blaring headline and picture just as my mother had described it.

"He looks dazed," Aliya said, pointing to a picture of Eli Schorr being taken into the precinct with an officer at his side. "Maybe a light bulb flash exaggerated the look on his face?"

"Or Zaida had it right predicting how we would react to being arrested."

Besides Schorr's being taken in, Martha Brennan really hadn't much else to report. She described Schorr's appearance, his age, troubled background before coming to the synagogue, and his current position.

"Grandfather must be absolutely certain of Schorr's guilt and that he would confess," I said. "Otherwise, as we discussed, whether Schorr is guilty or not, his reputation would be compromised, and an innocent man might lose his job at the *shul*."

Aliya added. "And Grandfather would be devastated if that occurred."

We got off the train at 8:30. As we approached, Aliya motioned toward the station.

"Is my agitation coloring what I see, or is there a lot more activity going on than when we came previously?"

I looked. Police and civilians rushed up and down the red steps leading to the precinct doors. Voices, angry, threatening, complaining, crying, or trembling, filled the air.

"No, it's not you, Aliya. The 61st has a lot of business today."

A long line led to the *Desk Sergeant* enclosure where, this time, two officers triaged the traffic. Visitors occupied every single cubicle. Some leaned close to the officer and whispered, some shouted and thumped furniture, and some sat limply and cried. To the right of the enclosure, I spotted Grandfather with Detective Carlucci. They were chatting amiably.

Carlucci waved to us. I heard him say, "Well, Mr. Wolf, it seems your *famiglia* have also arrived early. Should we go down to the interview room, and then I'll have an officer bring Schorr?"

"Good morning, Joel, good morning, Aliya," Grandfather's voice betrayed not a bit of discomposure or worry. "I hope you are well rested. We have an arduous task before us this morning."

Holding up the newspaper, I inquired: "Has Schorr seen the story yet?"

"I imagine he has," Carlucci responded. "He wasn't taken to the holding pen in the basement, but instead he was placed in an isolation cell near the interview rooms. I gave orders that he get *The Daily News* and be told that all prisoners in this precinct get to see a paper in the morning. Which, of course, is pure malarkey. But he wouldn't know that, would he?"

Carlucci concluded with a short laugh and looked at Grandfather. "Well, folks, shall we go down and get going?"

Grandfather put up his hand. "Yes, in a moment, but first, a brief discussion of how we shall proceed. I will interview Mr. Schorr without your presence, yes, Detective Carlucci?"

Carlucci nodded. Before I could speak out, Grandfather continued: "And you, Joel, will be in the interview room with me, and you will please sit on the same side of the table as I, toward the back facing the entrance and to my left, yes?"

I could care less on what side of the table I sat as long as I was also in the interview room. "Yes," I answered. "And Aliya?"

"Ah," Grandfather turned toward her. "You will please join Detective Carlucci in the observation room."

Once Aliya agreed, Carlucci bounced forward. "Ok, kiddos, let's get this party going."

We followed Carlucci down stairs to the basement level. A chill spread over me, exactly as it had when I passed jail cells as a law school student. I noticed Aliya grew pale as we slowly passed black steel bars on the right and left. She kept her eyes fixed straight ahead.

On the left were persons arrested on lesser charges, among them drunk drivers, vagrants, vandals, family support deadbeats, pickpockets, shop-lifters, narcotics users, and domestic violence offenders. Around 20 men crowded into a rectangular area no larger than 200 square feet with two toilets partially enclosed by ringed curtains. All had on street clothes. Half of them smoked cigarettes, choking the air. Grandfather cleared his throat once, making an effort not to cough. A few benches lined the walls, and light peeked in from a small window above the center wall. While most of the prisoners stood milling, I saw one snoring on a bench, one staring glassy eyed up at a ceiling bulb, and another sitting and weeping. I heard multiple languages.

I whispered. "Most of them will be arraigned within 24 hours and set free or released on a small bail."

Aliya whispered back, looking straight ahead. "Who are those men in the bars to the right?"

I glanced back to the cell on my right. It was much smaller than the one on the left. I saw six men, also in street clothes. Five of them maintained distance from each other and, whether seated on benches or standing, staked out their spaces by glaring or with balled-up fists. They glowered as we passed. But one gray-templed man in glasses and wearing a suit jacket sat on a cot and cowered, turning his eyes to us as if he was pleading for help.

I answered quickly. "They've been arrested on more serious charges such as murder, robbery, burglary, and grand larceny."

Several of the men on the left called out asking if we were lawyers come for Santos, or Martinelli, or Davis, or Donovan, or Fineman.

"Hey, old man," one screamed toward Grandfather, "I don't care if you look ancient. If you're a lawyer, I want you."

Another demanded, "Hey, look at me, I'm in here. I ain't done nothin'. Get me out."

Whistles and coarse comments were directed at Aliya. Two uniformed police officers standing by snarled at the men to "Shut it down!"

A cement wall separated the men's cell on the left from the women's cell. That area, also smaller, held about a dozen women, most, from their appearances, pulled in for prostitution.

I whispered again. "They'll be back on the street by nightfall."

One young woman rocked back and forth on a cot, probably going through withdrawal. After arraignment, the addicts, both the men and women, would be sent to the detox unit at the Brooklyn Hospital Center on Dekalb Street. Many, I thought, would be back at the 61st a month later.

One woman let out a cat call aimed at me. I ignored her.

Interview and observation rooms began after the women's cell. Wooden benches lined the walls. Carlucci pointed down the hall and said: "At the end are two isolation cells. Schorr is in one of them."

Carlucci stopped us at a door labeled **Interview Room 2**. An unmarked room followed which I knew to be a darkened observation area. Aliya and Carlucci would watch while Grandfather and I were with Eli Schorr. Carlucci opened the door to the interview room and motioned for Grandfather and me to go in. He flicked on the lights illuminating the room brightly so anyone in the darkened observation room could see clearly.

"Honey," Carlucci addressed Aliya, pointing to the observation room door. "Go on in and take a seat. I'll join you after Schorr is delivered."

Carlucci chuckled to himself. "We got him wearing a jail outfit since you wanted him to feel special. We just happened to have a few Department of Corrections duds lying around."

Aliya turned and entered the observation room.

Grandfather and I went into the interview room and closed the door. It had a rectangular metal table and four chairs. Grandfather took a seat on the far side of the table on the right facing the door. As instructed, I took the chair next to him on his left. A two-way mirror covered most of the wall to our right. I glanced at it and gave a quick wave to Aliya even though I couldn't see her. Grandfather put his hand to his mouth and whispered "no."

We didn't speak for the two minutes we waited. Finally, a uniformed officer along with Carlucci led Eli Schorr into the room. Schorr, in an orange jumpsuit with **DOC** printed in large letters on the back, had his hands cuffed in front of him. His ruffled hair and sweaty beard contrasted dramatically with the last time I saw him at the synagogue. Then he had jauntily shown us around as if he were a major domo.

His eyes looked manic. His head moved in all directions, seeming to seek an escape outlet.

"I'm not going back to prison, I didn't do anything," he screamed repeatedly. His head swiveled with each outburst.

Grandfather stood, and I followed. His firm voice subdued Schorr's shouts: "Mr. Schorr, please, whether you did something or not, let us pursue that question in a more calm fashion, yes? And whether you shall go to prison, that will be a natural outcome of our discussion."

Grandfather pointed to the chair across from him. "If you will be seated, we will begin, yes?"

Addressing Carlucci, Grandfather added. "And Detective, might you take off the handcuffs from Mr. Schorr so that he may be more comfortable as we talk?"

"You're sure?" Carlucci looked unhappy. "The guy is showing signs of violence."

What was Zaida thinking? I hoped some police protocol would prevent taking the cuffs off Schorr. I tensed and prepared for the possibility of violence

"I am sure, Detective. After all," and Grandfather pointed to the two-way mirror, "Mr. Schorr certainly understands that he is being observed from the nearby room and any necessary intervention is just seconds away. In addition, my associate Joel will also provide protection. Yes, Joel?"

I said strongly, "Yes, I'm here with you."

Carlucci motioned to the officer to remove Eli's cuffs. Eli rubbed his wrists and took his seat, muttering about not wanting to go back to jail. Carlucci and the officer left the room.

Calming, Eli adjusted his focus from Grandfather to me and back to Grandfather. After a short while, his eyes halted on Grandfather.

"Mr. Schorr," Grandfather began, leaning back, "I know it was you who sent me the unsigned paper admonishing me not to investigate Rabbi Flaum in the murder of his wife, was it not?"

Schorr squirmed, gave me a quick look as if asking for assistance, and turned back to Grandfather. "So what! Is sending a letter that told the truth about something a crime? It's not a crime, it's not a crime. It proves nothing!"

Grandfather remained calm. "It does prove one thing, Mr. Schorr, and that is you are a loyal friend of Rabbi Flaum and wish to shield him from implication in this case. Am I correct?"

Eli grinned. "I am, and I do! I am, and I do. He had nothing to do with the murder."

"But how can you be so sure?" I demanded. "Eli, it's as if you know exactly who killed Mrs. Flaum."

Eli answered rapidly. "I don't know, I don't know. I just know it wasn't the *Rav*."

Grandfather leaned forward and spoke firmly. "But you are not telling the truth, Mr. Schorr, are you, which is that you murdered Mrs. Flaum."

Eli, smirking, grabbed the table. "I didn't do it, and you can't prove that

I did, and I'm not going back to jail."

Grandfather opened his hands toward Eli. "But I think we can prove that you murdered your *shul's* rebbetzin. Let us start with the obvious."

Grandfather paused: "You have been arrested on the suspicion of the murder because a witness saw an individual with a CPH on the back of his garment entering and leaving the Flaum house at the exact time of the murder. You are often clothed during the workday in such a garment, are you not?"

Eli laughed. "Yeah, I love the *shul,* and I'm proud to wear its colors showing CPH. That's not going to send me back to jail. We sell those sweatshirts around Chanukah time. Lots of people buy them. That doesn't prove anything, nothing!"

Grandfather continued calmly: "Mr. Schorr, I do believe that you are proud to be a defender and promoter of your beloved synagogue and its rabbi, and that when you embarked on your misbegotten mission of ridding the *shul* and Rabbi Flaum of an enemy, you *bekiven,* purposefully, even in the midst of winter, wore your work clothes with **CPH** exposed on the back and with your head hooded. It was as if you were rushing to battle with your insignia proudly showing, what you call your 'colors.' You calculated if you were not seen, then good, but if you were seen and your face was shrouded, then you could claim, as you have done so, that there are many such sweatshirts or even that the CPH can also refer to Chansky Plumbing & Heating. Might I be correct, Mr. Schorr?"

Eli gave Grandfather an admiring look but continued his denial. "You can make up what you want, but I didn't kill her, and I'm not going back to jail. Besides what you make up, you have no evidence. I didn't kill her, and I'm not going back to jail!"

"But we do have such evidence, Mr. Schorr. You killed Mrs. Flaum by striking her on the head with one of your wrenches or hammers, did you not? And we will find the residue of blood on one of those tools and match them to Mrs. Flaum's blood through the scientific marvel of serological testing, whose advancements are now available to police."

A smirk, bigger than before, returned to Schorr's face. "Well that may be if you had that tool, but even if I had done it, which I didn't, around the time of the murder, or maybe after, I don't remember exactly, it was time for me to get new tools. I got rid of the old ones and filled my work belt with new ones."

Eli sat back for the first time and relaxed as if he had achieved a victory. It didn't last long.

"But that is where you are mistaken, Mr. Schorr," Grandfather said. "Did you dispose of your work belt? You see if you had also disposed of your belt, then certainly demonstrating your guilt would be more difficult.

But if you had not, then the belt that the police took from your room last night and sent for forensic testing will reveal even the slightest amount of blood that will be analyzed for a match to Mrs. Flaum's blood."

My mind reeled. Could the blood testing to which Grandfather referred really be done? I had been working securities at PWR for the past year, away from criminal law. Did the police really take Eli's work belt? Was it really at some lab? I had seen Grandfather bluff the truth in a previous case. Was he doing the same now with Eli Schorr?

"The police have my work belt!" Schorr gritted out, leaning forward. His white-knuckled hands grabbed onto the table. He glared at my grandfather. "The police have my work belt!" he repeated.

I recognized the look, the posture, the pent-up fury about to be unleashed. I had seen it often as a kid, playing with my friends around East 7th and Avenue P in what we called "our parks." Boys from off Kings Highway and "their parks" would descend and challenge us to a three-on-three basketball game or touch football. They were mostly bigger, but we usually held our own. And when we did, the other kids recognized our athletic abilities and left with at least some grudging respect.

Most of the time.

Once in a while, one or more of the others would take a loss as a personal insult, a threat to identity, and the right to dominate over surely less athletic kids. They would plant their feet firmly into asphalt, knot their fists, glare threats, and throw out expletives. Anticipating what was coming became second nature. If the other kids were a great deal bigger, I can say, unashamedly, that we would run. We were always faster. If we sized them up as not having markedly superior strength, we would hold our ground, awaiting the rush that always came. There would be a few minutes of scuffle ended by a nearby police officer or adults who broke things up. Sometimes I suffered a cut lip or scrape, but nothing more.

Sitting across from Eli Schorr, I knew what was about to happen. I shot up a split second before Eli lunged at Grandfather. I threw myself across the table. I landed on Eli's outstretched hands and then grabbed him around his shoulders, pushing him back. How the table didn't collapse, I don't know. Carlucci rushed in and helped secure Eli. As I eased myself off the table. I saw Aliya in the doorway.

"The police have my belt, the police have my belt!" Eli whined over and over, trying to stand.

Carlucci held Eli's shoulders from behind. "Hey, what do you think you were about to do?" He shoved Eli forward, slamming his body into the table, his head grazing the top. "If nothing else, I'm going to have you charged with attempted assault."

Carlucci released his hold and addressed me. "Nice instincts, kid. Want to join the force? Can't offer you nearly what you're making at that fancy law firm of yours, but I think you'd rise quickly in the ranks."

Of all the time for me to blush, but I did. I gave Carlucci a perfunctory smile and shook my head. I looked for Aliya in the doorway, but she was gone. I guessed she had returned to the interview room.

"Want me to stay here?" Carlucci asked Grandfather.

"Detective," Grandfather replied, "your concern is greatly appreciated, but I believe the venom that Mr. Schorr had been suppressing has been expelled to no one's harm besides his own. Mr. Schorr will now safely continue with the interview. Mr. Schorr, yes?"

Eli lifted his head slightly and nodded.

"Okay, then," Carlucci said. "I'm leaving, but I'll be watching the whole time, you understand, Schorr?"

Eli again nodded. He had stopped his whining and sat up once Carlucci left the room. "I can't go back to jail," he uttered just once.

I remained on edge, keeping a careful eye on Eli. Grandfather's voice was steely strong. "Mr. Schorr, you certainly will be going to jail for the murder of Mrs. Flaum as your work belt will indict you, so may I ask that you tell us completely in your words why you killed Mrs. Flaum? An admission may be of help to you."

Eli sagged in the chair, shoulders and head slumped toward the table.

"It's just that I always wanted to do good and always messed up. When I got my position and home at the *shul*, I felt, finally, finally, I was safe from the world around me and even from myself. Don't you understand, I couldn't just watch one of our most wonderful *shuls* and the world's most wonderful *rav* be threatened and suffer and not do anything about it. Don't you see I had to act for the *shul*, for him!"

"How are Rabbi Flaum's troubles necessarily the synagogue's troubles?" I asked.

Eli glanced at me. "How are they the same, how are they the same? Don't you get it, the *Rav* is the *shul*, its heart and soul, and lungs, and brain, and everything else!"

How could this cult of personality and hero worship take over Eli's mind and lead to murder?

"Mr. Schorr," Grandfather asked, his voice softer, "might you please answer yes or no. Did you murder Mrs. Flaum?"

Eli picked up his head and sat ramrod straight. "Yes, of course. I did. I had to. I had to."

"Because you had to save the *Rav* and CPH!" I said, disgusted.

Grandfather said gently: "Mr. Schorr, you felt as if Rabbi Flaum saved your life, gave you a home, a place to succeed, and is it possible that you experienced not just gratitude but also fright for yourself as your whole world was being threatened?"

Eli nodded and smiled, which amazed me. How could he feel good confessing to a brutal murder? He was excited, but not agitated as when we had started the interview.

Looking pleased, Eli continued. "After the *Rav* took me in, I clearly understood what David, the King, must have felt in Psalms when he said, 'From the depths I called You, O Lord.' Do you know how many times in my life I had called and called and no answer, until, until the *Rav* heard me and saved me. I owe him my life and my faith and my protection."

Eli stopped for a moment. "If I was a woman, I would have slept with the *Rav* had he asked me."

He shuddered and went on. "And I even think if he had asked me to commit, to commit one of those unnatural acts, I probably would have agreed."

Grandfather said sadly. "When you slaughtered Mrs. Flaum, you felt no qualms and later no regrets about your actions?"

Eli did not hesitate. "No, not really, and I don't care if you don't get it or think I'm a nut. I don't care." He glowered. "You know, after I struck her from the front the first time and she fell back on the floor, blood spilling from her head, she was still conscious and looked at me and said in Yiddish, 'Eli, Eli, why, why? What have I done to you?' And I said nothing back but thought, 'you've created so much trouble for the *Rav*, for the *shul*, and for me. What else can I do than make the trouble go away.' I hit her again and again so she wouldn't talk anymore."

Was Grandfather as stunned as I, hearing how easily Eli rationalized the murder? Could Eli really be wondering how anyone could think he didn't deserve a prison sentence?

Grandfather's voice held no emotion. "Then you planned your actions carefully in advance, am I correct? If so, and I will surmise, you took into your account the following. You were aware that the Chansky plumbers were to arrive at 8:00, yes?"

Eli smiled. "Yep, it was on the *Rav's* calendar. I always looked at his calendar to see where I could be helpful."

"And of course, you knew that Rabbi Flaum would leave for his Friday morning Bracha Breakfast group by 7:50, yes? And that would leave Jonathan to take into consideration. You put in a call to him the evening before and drew him out of the house that morning with an offer for employment you knew he would find enticing, again yes?"

Eli smiled again and nodded.

Grandfather continued. "And you wanted to plant a red herring for the police by making it appear the murder was part of a robbery. You certainly were aware that on Fridays the *Rebbetzin* and Mrs. Gelb had their weekly deposits in the house before they went to the bank around 10:00, yes?"

Eli answered, "Sure, sure."

"And somehow you had obtained the combination to the safe. May I inquire how you had done so?"

Eli answered. "I got a good memory for some things. When Mrs. Flaum began her business a few years back, I overheard a conversation she had with the *Rav* in the hallway in front of his office. She said she was going to put in a safe in the wall of the living room behind that large picture because she wanted to keep cash locked away until the very last minute before taking it to the bank."

I was furious, sensing that Eli was swelling with pride. "But you had the combination. How?"

Eli jerked his head toward me. "Oh, easy. After the safe was installed, Mrs. Flaum left the *Rav* a note with the combination on his desk. Every evening I look through the stuff on his desk while I tidy up. I wrote down the combination for the future, you know, just in case."

"Just in case!" I wanted to scream. At that moment, I hated Eli passionately, rage coiling inside. I was ready to lunge at him. I probably wouldn't have done so, but Grandfather's asking another question made sure.

"Mr. Schorr, I will surmise that you were aware of the narrow window of opportunity you possessed for executing your plan. You must have been watching the house for the moment that the Chansky plumbers left, yes?"

"Yep, I started watching around 7:30 from down 10th Street just to make sure the Flaum kid left and also the *Rav*. At 9:00, the Chanskys were still there. I was going to give myself until 9:30 in case the Gelb lady came early. But those plumbers left a little after 9:00, and as soon as I saw them driving away, I said to myself, 'Okay, God doesn't seem to want to stop me, so do it.'"

"Thank you, Mr. Schorr, for your openness and details," Grandfather said wearily, "but what of the Chanskys who you were trying to implicate for the crime? Did you not experience a moment's hesitation that innocent people may have been wrongly imprisoned?"

Eli grimaced. "Oh I did, I did, I felt bad thinking about it, and I would have sent a note, like I sent you, to the cops saying they got the wrong people. But even if that didn't work, putting the welfare of the *Rav* and the *shul* ahead of the Chanskys made sense to me."

Schorr looked at us before saying: "And you know I gave every penny from that safe to charity."

We sat in silence for about five minutes. Not every penny, I thought. Eli went back to rocking and muttering about not going back to jail. Grandfather folded his hands and leaned back, deep in thought. I seethed with hatred for Eli and deliberated whether the death penalty—last imposed in

New York in 1963-might be appropriate in this situation.

I waited for Grandfather to ask whether Rabbi Flaum, Barbara Burns, or both, or perhaps anyone else had any connection to the crime? Was Grandfather waiting for me to ask? Something told me to leave it alone. If I didn't ask, Grandfather certainly would.

But he didn't. Instead, Grandfather put his hand out toward the mirror and said: "Detective, our interview with Mr. Schorr is completed for today. He has fully confessed to the murder of Batya Flaum. Please come in."

The door opened and Carlucci entered along with a uniformed officer. The officer yanked Eli up and put the cuffs back on him as Carlucci informed Eli that he was being charged with the murder of Mrs. Flaum and read him his rights. Once done, Carlucci told the officer to take Eli back to his cell.

Aliya, ashen, came in. She remained standing and asked: "Zaida, what did you mean when you said the interview with Schorr 'is completed for today?' He's confessed. Is there more?"

Grandfather motioned for Aliya and Carlucci to sit. Aliya took the seat in front of me and Carlucci sat where Eli had been. Until Grandfather spoke, my eyes met Aliya's repeatedly. Hers showed a mix of sorrow, anger, and confusion.

"Aliya, you ask a most important question," Grandfather replied. "No, our work is not done. We know that Mr. Schorr dealt the fatal blows, but had Rabbi Flaum or Barbara Burns induced him in any way? I do not believe anyone else had complicity. Toward that end, Detective Carlucci, would you insist that the rabbi and Ms. Burns come in tomorrow morning and participate in two separate interviews with Mr. Schorr present. It would be most helpful if we could see Rabbi Flaum and Mr. Schorr together at 9:00 and Ms. Burns and Mr. Schorr immediately after. Would that be possible, Detective?"

"I don't see why not," Carlucci responded, "unless one or both of them went out on the lam."

Grandfather stood. "Very good, thank you Detective. We will see you tomorrow, yes?"

"Uh-huh," Carlucci replied. "But by the way, you know we haven't impounded Schorr's work belt to send to the lab. We will though, but I don't know if the lab boys can or will find anything."

"Yes, I know Detective," Grandfather answered. I'm sure I caught Grandfather's hallmark twinkle in his eyes.

"Well you're one smart cookie, Mr. Wolf. One smart cookie. Tell you what, since you helped us nail this weird guy, how about if one of my boys drives you home? I know you got dropped off this morning."

Grandfather did not object.

"We'll go back with you Zaida," I volunteered. "Then we'll take a train to our apartment." Aliya quickly seconded my suggestion.

Descending the precinct steps, Aliya linked arms with Grandfather, and we proceeded at his pace. A patrol car pulled up, and Officer Coleman opened the door to the back seat. Although the least comfortable position, Grandfather asked that he sit in the middle. Grandfather gave each of us a muted smile. I knew he would retreat into himself for the duration of the ride.

* * * *

Back in the house, Grandfather headed for his easy chair. As he lowered himself and placed his feet on the footstool, he let out a sigh, half weariness and half anguish, along with a hushed, "*Oy, meine kinder.*"

"Zaida, would you care for a Sanka?" Aliya asked.

"Yes, thank you." Grandfather answered. "And since it is just 11:00 and not yet time for the midday meal, also a cheese Danish from the refrigerator, if it is not too much trouble."

While Aliya tended to Grandfather's request, I sat down on the couch opposite him. We waited for Aliya to return before saying anything more about the case.

As she sat down next to me, I noticed that the ashen look that she showed at the precinct was still there. I took her hand and squeezed it.

"It has been very difficult for you, am I correct Aliya?" Grandfather asked, leaning toward her.

I knew Aliya never liked being singled out as weaker than others.

"I'm sure less than for you, Zaida, and probably no more than for Joel."

But then her words erupted. "That man is a monster. How could he do that to Mrs. Flaum! The images of her lying bludgeoned to death on the floor are in my mind day and night. Only a monster could have done that. I've been advocating against the death penalty, but my view on the subject is now very much shaken."

I felt similarly but said nothing. I figured Aliya and I would talk on our way home.

We sat in silence for a few minutes until Grandfather said: "What Mr. Schorr did was a monstrous act, but I struggle with identifying him as a 'monster.' Why so, my children? And I speak only for myself with no intention to convince. Yes, I grant that what the Nazis did, may their names be blotted out forever, made them into monsters. I would be employing sophistry to quibble otherwise. Perhaps it is a matter of scale, but in all the cases I have worked since entering my profession, I have dealt with darkness that permeates to varying degrees the human condition.

"Clearly Mrs. Flaum is the victim, her life extinguished by Mr. Schorr.

But what of Mr. Schorr? Our tradition teaches that each one of us has been created in God's image. If so, how can Mr. Schorr have behaved as he did? I have asked myself similar questions since my youth, but especially during and after the War. My only answer is that we are given the blessing of being born in the image of the divine, but then it is up to us to limit the recession from the divine that easily occurs. Just look at Adam and Eve in the Garden of Eden. Within minutes, the erosion, through threat, duplicity, evasion, and jealousy, took place to drive the two into the reality that is our human lot. Therefore, it is for us as individuals and as a community of human beings to understand that such erosions occur and contain it as best we can.

"Why did Mr. Schorr kill? Were the eroding forces within him at birth? Perhaps. If so, what assistance was he given to contain them? From parents? From teachers? From judges? From the prison system? From addiction services? Remember what Mr. Schorr said, that he had called out from the depths many times only to be failed until Rabbi Flaum heard him, brought him into the synagogue, and reversed the erosion until the rabbi's own departure from the divine set off the decline again. I am not suggesting pity for Mr. Schorr, nor exoneration in any form, for he must be punished severely. That will be for the judicial process to determine. But we must understand fully how these crimes happen, to anticipate, to intervene, and, if too late, to seek justice."

I jumped in. "And seeking justice includes knowing precisely who else may have been involved in the murder, right?"

Grandfather nodded. "Yes, and we will have a very difficult day tomorrow. Full accountability must be established. I will ask your mother, Joel, for one more kindness. To take me to the precinct again. You both will meet me at the precinct in the morning, yes? For now I will ponder within myself what approach to take during the interviews."

Aliya and I came over and hugged Grandfather, kissing his forehead.

"Ah, thank you for your affection," Grandfather said after slowly releasing us, "but there is one more action I will ask you to take before departing. Aliya, please once again call Ms. Brennan and let her know of Mr. Schorr's impending arraignment for the murder of Mrs. Flaum. After all, we do have to keep up our part of the bargain, do we not? And also please let her know that the rabbi and Ms. Burns will be at the station tomorrow morning for, might you call it, 'interviews'. Please do not divulge why they are being interviewed."

Aliya went straight to the phone. As she made her call, I made sure that Grandfather could easily retrieve the lunch my mother had prepared.

When she returned, Aliya said: "I also made two more calls. As I promised, I called the Chansky shop to let Mr. Chansky know that the real murderer has been caught. Mr. Chansky was out on a job, but his wife, who burst into tears, thanked me and said she would tell him as soon as he came back. I also called Mother to let her know we are all safe. She had been waiting on pins and needles to hear."

* * * *

On the train to our apartment, Aliya and I discussed the chores that we needed to do with our "free" time that day which included trying to get a little more sleep. Aliya said that she must call Shoshi to see how she was doing and would not mention her father's interview tomorrow.

At one point, she took my arm and said: "That was really brave of you to jump in front of Schorr before he got to your grandfather. I'm really proud of you."

I took Aliya's chin into my hand and replied: "I acted only because I was sure you'd be into the interview room within seconds to help me."

She freed her chin and punched me on the shoulder. "Well, you know I was on my way."

We laughed and continued our discussion of chores. Even a momentary release from the week's tension felt good.

* * * *

Once home, Aliya called Shoshi.

"Eli? Why, why!" I could hear Shoshi's shriek even with Aliya holding the receiver to her ear. Did we ourselves understand fully?

Aliya continued her conversation. I fell asleep on the couch thinking she would be just a few minutes. But when Aliya woke me, two hours had passed.

"Maybe the chores could wait till tomorrow?" I mumbled hopefully, rubbing my eyes.

Aliya laughed and kissed me. "Sure."

We lazed the afternoon away reading *The Times* and catching up on the previous week's edition of *Newsweek*. We had a frozen pizza in the freezer which, with some salad, served as our dinner. Afterwards, we switched back and forth from Cronkite to Chancellor and Brinkley for the news. At 8:00, since shows were in summer reruns, we went back to catching up on our reading. Almost 9:00, Aliya was exhausted. She fell asleep just as we were deciding if we'd watch the *CBS Thursday Night Movie*.

Aliya slept well enough until 6:00. I, not too well, as I kept reliving the moment when Schorr lunged for Grandfather.

FRIDAY, JULY 11, 1975

We picked up a *Daily News* on the way back to the 61st Precinct. It sensationalized Eli Schorr's arraignment. File photos of a manic-looking Schorr, a subdued Rabbi Flaum, and a glamorous Barbara Burns took up the front page below the headline, **JANITOR TO BE ARRAIGNED FOR KILLING RABBI'S WIFE.** The inside story rehashed what had been previously written with no mention of anyone else's complicity.

On the train, we exchanged guesses as to whether the rabbi and Burns would show up. How would Grandfather handle the interviews? Would the rabbi and Burns see each other? Would each be interviewed separately? Would Schorr really be in the room during both interviews?

A half block from the precinct, Aliya grabbed my arm and pointed ahead.

"Isn't that your mother's car parked across the street from the entrance? Why is she still here? Even if she leaves this minute, she'll still be late getting to the store."

I took Aliya's hand. "Let's hurry."

I could see my mother in the driver's seat and Grandfather in the passenger seat gazing toward the precinct. When Grandfather saw us, he signaled to get into the back seat quickly.

We did so, and I asked: "What's going on, Zaida? Is everything okay?"

"Yes, all is well up to this point," Grandfather answered. "Your mother, who has graciously agreed to become a member of our investigative team, and I are on a stakeout. We are keen to observe how Rabbi Flaum and Ms. Burns appear as they enter the station."

"Well," my mother chimed in, "good morning to you both. And let's just say I am glad to agree to what I have been asked to do, which is to wait here while your grandfather, and now probably you two, make your observations."

"Good morning. They haven't arrived yet?" Aliya asked.

"Partially so, my child," Grandfather replied. "Rabbi Flaum entered a few minutes ago. As he climbed the steps, his head down, he appeared to me shrunken and stooped. Yesterday, I had asked Detective Carlucci to place the rabbi when he arrived at the bench in front of our interview room."

Grandfather paused, maintaining his sights on the precinct. "Ms. Burns had not, at least until this moment, arrived." He looked out and pointed. "But that is she, yes, about to climb the steps?"

Aliya half turned. "Yes, that's Barbara Burns."

Burns had on a knee-length, half-sleeved, red tunic dress with a black collar, mesh stockings, and two-inch heels. She wore sunglasses and held her head high as she climbed the steps.

"When she comes to the Sergeant's Desk," Grandfather explained, "she will be taken to a room away from where the interviews will occur. I do not wish for the rabbi and Ms. Burns to have any contact with each other until we have completed questioning him."

Grandfather opened the door. "Let us exit the vehicle so that my very understanding daughter need not be any more late to her work."

Aliya and I climbed out of the car quickly. My mother gave us her expected admonition to be careful and drove off.

We crossed the street, but before ascending the steps, Grandfather stopped us.

"It is important that you are aware of how we will proceed. Mr. Schorr will be in the room when we interview the rabbi and then again when we interview Ms. Burns. Joel, you will attend Rabbi Flaum's interview with me and sit exactly where you sat yesterday. The rabbi will be seated in front of me, and Mr. Schorr in front of you, yes?"

"Yes, and the same for the Burns interview?"

"No, Joel. For the interview with Ms. Burns, you will trade places with Aliya. You will be in the observation room, and she will sit near me and Ms. Burns where the rabbi had been situated, yes Aliya?"

"But what if Schorr gets violent again like yesterday, and I'm not there?" I objected.

Grandfather tried to calm me down. "Joel, do not be afraid. Mr. Schorr will be on his best behavior in Ms. Burns' presence. And you are comfortable, Aliya?"

I thought Aliya would simply reply "I am." But instead, she said, "I may not be, but I wish to do it. Thank you, Zaida."

I shook my head. "Okay, and I'll be watching carefully."

Just inside the station, Carlucci approached us. "They're both here," he said looking at Grandfather, "and I put them just like you asked. The rabbi is sitting on the bench in front of the interview room, and I stashed the Burns lady in an empty office until you're ready for her.

"Boy, that lady's a looker," he concluded with an impish glance at Aliya.

We again made our way past the gauntlet of shouted entreaties, expletives, and wolf whistles. Aliya had chosen loose fitting slacks, a long-sleeved cotton blouse, and flat sandals. Again, she had not put on makeup and wore her hair in a ponytail. After showering, I had been too tired to worry about my attire. I defaulted to clothes already out, the previous day's shirt and pants. As for Grandfather, he had added a vest to his suit, tie, and white shirt. At least the temperature was predicted not to go over 80 for the day.

Rabbi Flaum came into view. He sat on the bench, hunched forward with his Homburg hat on his lap and a large knitted kippah on his head. He wore a wrinkled brown suit, olive dress shirt, and bronze tie. One side of his collar jutted up. Stubble spotted his face. What a difference from his appearance just a few days ago! When he saw us, he slowly rose and extended a hand toward Grandfather.

"*Sholom Aleichem*, Mr. Wolf." He barely acknowledged Aliya and me and totally disregarded Carlucci. "I see that your worthy reputation has preceded you. You have solved my wife's murder case, and I thank you despite the pain it causes me to know that it is Eli who is implicated."

"Yes, I am sure you are in pain," Grandfather answered.

The rabbi shook his head several times. "Ay, ay, that it is Eli, that after seven years of rehabilitation, he should not only slide back, but slide back so horrendously as to murder my wife! And I can't help feel it is my fault, since I took him into the *shul*. I surmise that you have a full confession from him and why he did such a thing. Was it for the money?"

"Rabbi Flaum," Grandfather replied, an edge to his voice, "Mr. Schorr has indeed confessed, but as to a full understanding of what contributed to his act, that analysis is not complete and may reside further in our discussion with you this morning."

The rabbi shuffled his feet. "But how might I help anymore? I shared with you everything I know when we spoke at your office."

"That may or may not be, Rabbi Flaum," Grandfather answered. "But would you not be interested in hearing from Mr. Schorr himself his own explanation for why he murdered Mrs. Flaum? Might it not spur some additional thoughts and feelings that you may possess?"

"I will be seeing Eli? He will be in the same room with me for the interview?"

"Yes, that will be so," Grandfather replied. "Detective Carlucci, will you please bring Mr. Schorr to us?"

"No problem." Carlucci motioned to a nearby uniformed officer. "Make yourself comfortable, gentlemen, and we'll bring him in right quick." Carlucci turned to Aliya. "You gonna be with me in the observation room again, honey?"

"For a while," Aliya replied. "Just for a while."

We entered the interview room and took up the positions Grandfather had requested earlier. In his office just a few days before, Grandfather had treated Rabbi Flaum amiably, even with some deference. Now Grandfather sat with tightened lips and eyes riveted on the rabbi. Neither one made an effort at conversation.

Rabbi Flaum bent forward. He never turned to look fully, but every few seconds he would flick his head to the door on the left through which Eli would arrive. Beads of sweat oozed on his forehead, and a drop slowly made its way down his cheek. He did not wipe it away.

I, too, was perspiring, although not nearly as much as Rabbi Flaum. What would we discover when we had both Eli and the rabbi in the room together? How would each behave? Would there be a violent eruption from Eli? Would we find that a rabbi revered by so many could actually have induced Eli to murder Batya Flaum?

With no knock, the door opened. The rabbi flinched. Carlucci entered first, followed by Eli and a uniformed policeman.

"Cuffs off again, Mr. Wolf?"

"Yes, Detective," Grandfather replied. "If you will please, and let us have Mr. Schorr sit in the chair available." Grandfather pointed to the right of Rabbi Flaum.

As the cuffs were being removed, Eli blurted: "Rebbe, Rebbe, I just did what I thought you wanted me to do, and now I will have to go to jail. I don't want to go to jail!"

Carlucci pushed Eli toward his designated seat. "Okay, the rabbi hears you, but pipe down for a minute and let Mr. Wolf ask some questions." Carlucci motioned the officer to leave. He followed, closing the door behind him.

Eli turned his chair and moved it toward Rabbi Flaum.

"Don't try anything," I snarled, rising.

Eli looked at me as if I were the criminal. "Try anything, try anything! What would I try? I would never hurt my rebbe, never hurt my rebbe. I have always only wanted to help him."

"Mr. Schorr," Grandfather directed, "if you will please return to your place, we will be able to proceed in a more orderly fashion, yes?"

Eli scraped his chair back toward the table and faced me. I sat down.

Grandfather did not hesitate: "Mr. Schorr, would you please repeat what you conveyed to us yesterday as to why you murdered Mrs. Flaum."

I thought Eli would turn away from the rabbi as he responded. Instead, he did a 45-degree pivot toward him and extended his hands as if in prayer.

"Why, Rebbe, why? I think you get it and even approve. You helped me when I needed it. I saw that you and the *shul* were in distress. I thought it was my turn, thought it was my turn to help you. You remember, you remember when we sat one night talking like two old friends and drinking schnapps, and you told me, 'Where there is no *sholem bais* in the home, there is no peace elsewhere' Do you remember? And I saw how happy Barbara Burns made you. For a while, you were getting back to your old self, so I did right by what you needed, what you wanted, didn't I? And I will go back to jail, but I did right, did right, didn't I?"

By the time Eli had finished, he faced Rabbi Flaum, his hands still outstretched. He gave no indication of violence, but I stayed vigilant. The rabbi leaned away, breathing hard. He looked from Eli to Grandfather, then spoke.

"Eli, Eli, you mistook me, certainly you must realize you mistook me!" The rabbi stopped for a moment. "I did consider you a friend, and even a confidant, for it is difficult for someone in my position to have close friends. But even if I did have some marital issues at home, when I referred to peace in the home, I also was referring to the conflict of lay leadership at CPH. Although I had entered into a liaison with Barbara, which I deeply regret, I am sure Batya and I would have worked out our differences. How could you have thought that I wanted my dear wife murdered!"

Rabbi Flaum ended out of breath, tears streaming and mixing with sweat. He took out a handkerchief from his suit pocket and mopped his face. Eli sat up and dissolved into tears: "I wanted to help you so much, so much."

The rabbi looked at Grandfather. But Grandfather remained stone-faced and turned toward Eli.

"Mr. Schorr, please tell us. Did Rabbi Flaum ever ask you directly to murder his wife?"

Eli did not hesitate. "No, not what you call directly, no, he didn't have to. I was sure he wanted me to take care of it."

"Take care of it, take care of it," Rabbi Flaum shouted, spittle joining sweat and tears around his mouth. "How could you think so? Why didn't you ask me if that's what I wanted? I would have told you directly that, heaven forbid, I did not want such a thing."

And then to Grandfather. "You see, Mr. Wolf, what a horrible misunderstanding occurred, and if I, even in a little way, contributed, I can never forgive myself."

At this point, I expected softening from Grandfather. But no. "Misunderstanding or perhaps lack of understanding combined with lapse of responsibility, was it not so, Rabbi Flaum?"

The rabbi, who may have expected at least a modicum of forgiveness, flinched. "What are you saying, Mr. Wolf?"

"I am saying that while your behavior will not lead to a legal indictment, there is much for you to consider as to your contribution to Eli's crime. When we were children first exposed to the Talmud, I expect we both started with the same tractate, no?"

Grandfather turned to me. "Joel, since you are much closer in age than the rabbi or I to our first exposure to the Talmud, would you please tell us what you recall?"

I answered immediately. "*Bava Kamma*—the *First Gate*—the tractate that discusses damages and accountabilities."

"Yes, exactly Joel," Grandfather beamed before returning to his steely expression. "And it was for me as a child. And for you Rabbi Flaum?"

The rabbi nodded, and Grandfather turned back to me. "Joel, would you remember upon which biblical text the opening of the tractate revolves and what animal it employs to make its point about damages and personal responsibility for the damages?"

"Well, the second question is easy — an ox? And I think the biblical passage is somewhere in Exodus, but where exactly, I don't recall."

"And do you remember, Rabbi Flaum?"

I looked at the rabbi to see if he would flare with resentment for being treated on my level. He didn't. He answered curtly: "Exodus, Chapter 21, in the portion dealing with *mishpatim*—ordinances."

"Yes, thank you Rabbi, exactly. Ordinances, laws that apply and regulate our behaviors. There are two verses I would like to summarize. The first deals with an ox that does not have a habit of goring. If that ox kills a human being, the ox's owner is not held liable. But, and I say but, Rabbi Flaum, if the ox does have a history of goring and then kills a human being, the owner is held culpable as if he himself had performed the killing."

Grandfather halted for Rabbi Flaum to speak. But the rabbi remained silent.

Grandfather put out his hand toward Eli. "I am not saying that Mr. Schorr is an animal, nothing more than an ox. No, not at all. But we know in our tradition that what we learn from concrete descriptors in our teachings is extrapolated to more general human behavior."

Grandfather turned back to the rabbi. "So Rabbi Flaum, when you took Eli into CPH and under your wing, while admirable, you knew of his weaknesses and proclivities for acting criminally, devolving into addiction, needing attention, and exhibiting bad judgment. Did he then not fall into the second category of the ox having a history of goring, showing various warning signs, and demanding oversight? Were you not then, in extrapolation, the ox's owner? Was Eli not then your vulnerable ward whose predictable rashness and lack of judgment you failed to anticipate or harness through your own thoughtless words and actions? Did you not then have an influence on your wife's murder?"

Eli jumped up, and I quickly followed. But he remained still as he bellowed at Grandfather: "What's he talking about, Rebbe? You didn't kill Mrs. Flaum, I did. You're not going to jail, you're not going to jail."

Grandfather motioned Eli to sit. "Sha, sha, sha, Mr. Schorr, and please be seated. I believe you did not understand me fully. Rabbi Flaum will not go to jail."

The rabbi's tears had stopped. "Yes, Eli, please sit. Mr. Wolf is correct. I do not believe I will be going to a physical jail. I will, however, be encased in self-imprisonment for the rest of my life. And while you go through your trial, sentencing, and prison time, while I am able, I will try to support you. I will try to be a much better rebbe than I have been. I am sorry, I am very sorry."

Eli sat. "I don't understand, Rebbe, why what I did was so wrong? I very much wanted to help. You'll always be my rebbe, always be my rebbe."

Grandfather's demeanor relaxed. "I too am sorry Rabbi Flaum, for you, for your family, and for your *shul*. After one more interview, my work and the work of my associates will be over."

The rabbi slumped forward, elbows on table, and his head in his hands. It was both pitiful and farcical. My previous esteem for him had eroded greatly.

In a croaking voice, he continued: "I have at this moment decided to resign immediately from CPH. Although it is not the ending I had hoped for, you, Mr. Wolf, and your associates are to be congratulated. You indeed discovered who killed Batya and the contributing factors surrounding her murder.

"As for me, there is much studying to do along with reflection. I will need to try to reestablish my life and what I may still be able to contribute somewhere else than CPH. That we will see. But I also must repair my relationship with my children, especially Jonathan."

"And you will do us a favor, Rabbi Flaum?" Grandfather ordered as much as asked. "You will quickly contact your children. Aliya, as Shoshannah's life-long friend, will assuredly wish to report to her what has occurred during this interview. I will ask Aliya not to convey what had transpired beyond the elementary facts, as you yourself wish to tell it."

The rabbi regained his composure. "Yes, and I thank you for giving me that courtesy."

Slowly, the rabbi stood. "I take it the interview is over. I may leave?"

"Yes," Grandfather answered. "Mr. Schorr will remain for a while longer, and Joel will escort you out of the room. Goodbye, Rabbi Flaum."

I walked around and opened the door for the rabbi. He stumbled out.

* * * *

Aliya stood by Barbara Burns who was seated on the hallway bench. I gathered that Carlucci had just brought her, perhaps a bit prematurely, from where she had been "stashed." Rabbi Flaum blanched when he saw her: "Barbara, you're here. I did not know you would be here. What is it they want from you?"

"And hello and how are you, David," Burns answered. "I imagine because we're both suspects in the murder of your wife."

"But Eli has admitted his guilt. Why would they now wish to speak with you?"

"David, I imagine for the same reason they wanted to bring you in."

"Barbara, I…" the rabbi stammered. He did not finish his sentence before he moved slowly down the hallway.

"Give me 30 seconds," I said to Aliya as I turned toward the observation room, "for me to get situated and then, you two please go into the interview room."

I entered the room, closed the door, nodded to Carlucci, and took a seat. Grandfather introduced himself to Burns and motioned her toward the chair vacated by the rabbi. Burns at first hesitated when she saw Eli, but then, as she seated herself, she glanced at him with a slight smile. He reddened, glanced at her several times, looking down at the table.

Aliya took my seat. Eli ignored Aliya's presence, even after she reintroduced herself by saying, "Hello, Eli, you may remember me from the tour you gave us at CPH."

Burns' face was heavily made up, her hair pinned back, revealing silver earring studs. Was she again retreating behind the mask she had used as protection for years? She had wanted to rid herself of it through her relationship with Rabbi Flaum. I felt slightly sorry for her.

Grandfather began. "Ms. Burns, I am sure you are wondering why you were asked to come this morning. Simply, it is to determine if you had any complicity in the murder of Batya Flaum to which Mr. Schorr has admitted guilt."

Before Burns could respond, Eli shouted. "Complicity, complicity, she didn't have anything to do with it. It was all my doing, all my doing."

Grandfather spoke in an authoritative voice as if he were reining in a child in the midst of a tantrum. "Sha, sha, sha, please Mr. Schorr. It is possible in the next few minutes you will be asked a question, and then you can speak, but for now we would like to address questions to Ms. Burns, without any interruptions. Will that be possible?"

Eli threw a look of helplessness at Burns: "I guess so, but, but…" His voice petered out as he turned his head away.

"Eli, it's alright," said Burns. "I can take care of myself and have nothing to hide. I appreciate that you want to protect me. The truth is that I did not conspire with you to murder the Rebbe's wife."

"Good, then," Grandfather took over. "We will ask you a few questions, Ms. Burns. Since you have nothing to hide, then we will assume your responses will be truthful."

Grandfather swung his head toward Aliya. "And most of the questions will be asked by my associate, Ms. Blum."

Aliya looked at Grandfather but did not falter. She later confided in me that Grandfather had not told her that she would do the questioning.

"Barbara," Aliya began, "when Joel and I saw you at your house, you openly shared with us how and why you entered your relationship with Rabbi Flaum, your emotional highs and frustrations, and that you even fantasized how things could be simpler if Mrs. Flaum was not in the picture."

When Burns nodded, Aliya went on. "I'll ask you again as I did previously on the phone. Did you ever share your feelings with anyone else?"

Burns did not hesitate. "Anyone else? Who would I share them with? My ex-husband? Girlfriends to whom I'd run with my emotional distress to elicit some rote poor baby?"

Eli swiveled toward Burns and bit his lip, glaring.

"Mr. Schorr," Grandfather intervened, "if you have something to say, now would be an appropriate moment."

Eli turned away again and shook his head.

Aliya continued. "Then Barbara, let me ask you directly. Did you ever discuss your involvement with the rabbi, your emotions, your thoughts about Mrs. Flaum being in the way…with Eli?"

Burns fidgeted. "Well, yes, I did. On a few occasions."

Burns turned toward Eli. "I didn't mean to imply, Eli, that I thought you were a nobody when Aliya asked me the question. It's just that I was thinking about people outside of CPH. You were a big part of the *shul* and concerned about me and the rabbi. Well, you just never came to mind."

"Sort of like my being part of the furniture, part of the furniture," Eli barked.

"No Eli, don't say that, not at all, it's just that… It's just that, well you must know I don't think about you in that way."

"If I may then follow up?" Aliya pressed. "Barbara, how many times did you confide in Eli before Mrs. Flaum's murder?"

Burns thought for a moment. "Maybe five or so."

"Maybe more like ten," Eli snapped.

Aliya ignored Eli's correction. "Barbara, did you speak to Eli on Thursday, February 20, the day before the murder?"

"Thursday, February 20," Burns stammered. "I'm not sure. I may have. Did we talk that day, Eli?"

"We did," Eli answered firmly, "in the Family Room near the Rebbe's office where we always talked."

"And Barbara," Aliya asked, "was it your habit early on Thursday mornings to withdraw cash from the bank?"

"Yes, I would," Burns answered promptly. "It was my cash for the week's shopping."

"Would you withdraw a similar amount each week, and, if so, what was that amount?"

"Yes, $200 each week. Why?"

Aliya eyed Burns closely. "But on February 20, you withdrew $300, and then went back to $200 the subsequent Thursdays. That's what your bank statement shows. Barbara, why did you withdraw an extra $100 on February 20?"

"You saw my bank statement?" Burns looked from Grandfather to Aliya, but not at Eli. "Why, I'm not sure I remember, I must have needed another $100 for something."

"Mr. Schorr," Grandfather asked, "did Ms. Burns ever give you money during your conversations?"

Would Eli try to wiggle around the question? He didn't. "Yes, she gave me a $100 bill on that Thursday at the end of our talk. A $100 bill."

"So Barbara," Aliya asked, "do you now remember why you took out an additional $100? To give to Eli?"

Burns looked around the room. I thought she was searching for someone to help her. She touched her hair. Her hand trembled. Finally, she looked at Aliya: "Yes, I do now remember. I wanted to give it to Eli."

"For what purpose, Barbara?"

Burns' head sank forward. She glanced at Grandfather and then at Aliya: "I just wanted to thank him for his friendship and understanding, that's all."

"That's all!" Grandfather said. "Mr. Schorr, might you remember the words Ms. Burns used when she gave you the $100?"

"I do, I do," Eli answered slowly. "She was angry, just like all the times before. She told me what a great friend I was and how she, the Rav, and the whole *shul* would be happier if Mrs. Flaum wasn't around causing trouble and getting in the way."

Eli reddened again and turned toward Burns. "Then you said, 'Eli, you're very sweet, you understand so much,' and gave me the $100 bill as a symbol of your affection for me. That's what you said, 'as a symbol of my affection for you.'"

Burns shot up from her seat: "But you couldn't possibly have thought that I was giving you the money to kill Batya Flaum! You couldn't possibly have thought that!"

Eli began to weep. "But I did think you were giving me a sign that you wanted me to get rid of her."

"Ms. Burns," Grandfather ordered, "you will please sit down."

Burns sat, and Grandfather asked: "Mr. Schorr, did Ms. Burns ever explicitly ask you to murder Batya Flaum?"

"Explicitly, explicitly," Eli repeated softly. "You mean did she say 'kill her'? No, but she didn't have to. I thought we were the kind of friends that knew each other's minds. And the $100 was proof."

Grandfather sighed deeply. "Then, I will say, Ms. Burns, our interview is complete. Thank you for your time."

Burns stood and lifted her head. "Then I'm free to go? You understand that I had nothing to do with the murder?"

"That you had nothing to do with the murder," Grandfather replied, "is questionable. But I believe, unless Detective Carlucci thinks otherwise, our legal system will not address it. But at some period during your lifetime, I believe you will wrestle with that question."

I waited for an outburst from Eli proclaiming Burns' innocence as he had for Rabbi Flaum. But he remained silent, staring at the floor.

Carlucci left the observation room as soon as Grandfather had finished speaking to Burns. He called for a uniform to join him, and we all entered the interview room.

"Okay, lady," he said to Burns, "you can go. Like Mr. Wolf said, there's nothing I heard that we can hold you on."

"Thank you, Detective," Burns replied, "I am leaving." And turning toward Eli, she called: "I'm going to help you, Eli. I know some good attorneys. Someone will be in touch, I promise."

Eli said nothing. The uniform handcuffed him and led him away, followed by Carlucci. I wanted to give Aliya a hug but thought better of it. At that moment, she was my colleague and not my wife.

Aliya got up, and we started toward the door when we looked back and saw Grandfather still seated.

"Are you okay, Zaida?" I asked.

Grandfather rose slowly. "I recall, Yoeli, that at the conclusion of our Stein murder investigation, I may have appeared morose. You said something to the effect of 'I feel bad for you.' At that time, I may have also appeared dismissive. I may have wanted to protect my grandson from the harsher realities of life. I stated that satisfaction with having achieved justice does not necessarily conjoin with happiness, as often the victim and victimizer, each engender sadness. I told you that for a private investigator, deception, criminality, and death all lurk on the path to seeking that justice. In other words, just a part of the business.

"But your sensitivity was and is well placed. And while I very much believe what I said about the path to justice, it is time for me to treat you as the wonderful adult you have grown to be along with your life partner you fortunately married."

Grandfather sighed. "Yes, I feel much pain."

Aliya placed a hand on my shoulder. Grandfather gathered us toward him and said: "A police car that will take us back to our house awaits us. Detective Carlucci has once again graciously offered us this gesture of his appreciation. You will join me, yes? Then perhaps over lunch I may share some of my reflections on this case."

We agreed and walked slowly with Grandfather. None of us paid any attention to the shouts from those behind the bars. At the front of the precinct, an officer tipped his hat and ushered us into the back seat of a black, unmarked vehicle. This time I took the middle position. As expected, we did not speak as we rode 20 minutes through minor traffic.

* * * *

Home, Grandfather went right to his easy chair. "Please afford me a little time to myself for some contemplation. It is now 10:35, and might we join for lunch at 12:00, yes?"

Aliya and I had the same idea. We headed to my room and plopped on the bed. It had been a long week. I didn't remember being so tired at the conclusion of the three previous cases. Was it because this time I was more as a partner in the sleuthing process as opposed to just following Grandfather's directions? Was it because the case involved the family of Aliya's best friend? Was it because of Aliya's involvement? And, I had participated in dismantling the reputation of an iconic figure in the New York Jewish communities and beyond.

I embraced Aliya. "I'm really sorry," I said.

"For what?"

"For being jerk-like that first day when you said we had to postpone our vacation plans to help Shoshi."

"Oh Joel," Aliya responded, embracing me even more tightly. "You were wrong in that moment, but you're not a jerk. You know why?"

"Why?" I laughed with relief.

"Because, as I told you at the beginning of the case, you're not like many guys I had known. One reason I married you is you'll mess up from time to time, but you have the ability and decency to reflect and do the right thing instead of self-righteously sticking to a rigid position. There are many reasons we fall in love with someone, and that's at the top of the list for me."

"Thank you," I answered. "It's been very hard on you, hasn't it?"

Aliya sighed. "Yes, probably the hardest days of my life. But I feel I've grown. When I first saw the picture of Mrs. Flaum lying battered on the floor, it made me sick. As I keep saying, it will stay with me for the rest of my life.

"As it should. Without feeling sorry for myself, I think that awful sight will remind me to stay vigilant-for myself, for you, for our future children-because evil does exist in everyday life. We live in a world of complicated people and calamitous events. In even the best of novels, we're always a step removed from those things. And I feel I've grown professionally and learned so much in how to look at human emotion, human motivation, and human actions."

Aliya laughed. "And you know what, Joel? Maybe they all work together in what Zaida calls 'critical analyses.'"

I smiled. "I was looking for the reason my grandfather really liked you right from the beginning. Now I know exactly why."

We kissed and held each other for another half hour. Then, Aliya asked what we should do about lunch. While my mother probably had left something for Grandfather, she hadn't known we would be here. Another sprint by me over to Kornblatt's was the answer.

I made it there and back in a record 45 minutes. Aliya and Grandfather sat at the kitchen table, having a light conversation. Grandfather nursed a Swee-Touch-Nee tea. I had bought egg salad on rye for Aliya and me with cream sodas, and tuna on toasted wheat bread for Grandfather.

Grandfather ate even more slowly than usual. After 30 minutes, he pushed away his half-eaten sandwich, took his tea in both hands, and nodded first toward Aliya, then toward me.

"My children, yes, coming to the end of a case and drawing understanding from it and then moving forward are always difficult, but we must do so. May I ask, what was the central question of our inquiry as we began the case?"

"Who killed Batya Flaum?" I answered quickly.

"And so you are correct, Joel. Now at the conclusion of our inquiry, what is the central question?"

Aliya and I looked at each other. I nodded at her, and she responded: "Even though Eli swung the murder weapon, still, the central question is who else can be considered complicit? Meaning how do we take into account the roles Rabbi Flaum or Barbara Burns played in the murder being conceived and then executed?"

"Yes, my children, that central question remains and will always trouble us. Do you recall my pedantic treatment of Rabbi Flaum earlier this morning when I brought up the goring ox?"

I nodded.

"Might our teachers, right from the Talmud's beginnings, have provided us with both a concrete example of how damages occur in society and a metaphoric extrapolation as to how the ox exists within each of us? That is that we all possess a productive instinct along with a counter drive toward the destructive. And if we are unable to manage destructive presences in our own selves, then others, society, must establish fences, constraints, rules, and laws for proper behavior?"

"You mean," I interjected, "the idea of the drive toward good and the drive toward evil that as very young children we are told inhabits all of us and presents a life struggle? And now you're extending it into the interpersonal and societal?"

"Yes, Yoeli," Grandfather replied. "We know Mr. Schorr from childhood could not handle his inner battles and succumbed both to his inner and external goring. We know, as I mentioned, that as soon as Rabbi Flaum brought him into his community, the rabbi had a personal responsibility to help Mr. Schorr control the ox within him. But, because the rabbi could not control his own ox, he not only failed in his duties to Mr. Schorr but, over schnapps and self-indulgent commiseration sessions, placed what we might call a 'red flag' in front of Mr. Schorr's ox with Mrs. Flaum the object of his rage and rationalization for murder."

"And Barbara Burns?" Aliya asked.

"Ah, Ms. Burns. A very sad case of her own, yes? We can easily understand the oppressive plight that she has experienced as a woman in our society and the desperate means she adopted to manipulate her beauty and external sexuality to gain comfort. Acting destructively is often not clearly understood by the actors themselves. When Ms. Burns found comfort and power in luring Mr. Schorr into affection for her and watching his alienation and dislike of Mrs. Flaum, did something, in what Dr. Freud called her 'unbewusste,' her unconscious, propel her to bare her soul to Mr. Schorr and withdraw an extra $100 to give him, thus establishing complicity in the murder? Yes, I believe it did, but unfortunately not from a legal perspective. The woman, with all regal outward bearing, is tortured. I do not know how she will deal with this additional goring. Sadly, I surmise, she will again turn to some external source of comfort."

Aliya and I exchanged glum looks. We sat for a few moments in silence before Grandfather reached over and placed each of his hands on one of our own. I felt echoes of my childhood when something bothered me and he would call me over and cup my face in his hands.

"Unfortunately, my children, it is in this fashion that our cases always end. And perhaps for this reason, we are in our chosen professions because there is no other way but to proceed with a knowledge that there is much ox-watching to be done and justice to be pursued, yes?"

Grandfather smiled. "If you will allow me a moment's levity, perhaps a husband and wife team is just what the next generation of the detective business needs, much like Nick and Nora Charles of the revered Dashiell Hammett's *The Thin Man*."

We both laughed, even if it was an old joke.

Grandfather released our hands, settled back, and drew back his plate. "Tonight begins the Sabbath, and your mother and I will celebrate a joyous dinner, begin our relaxation and positive reflection, and rejuvenate. For a new case may soon be on me."

And, with that twinkle in his eyes: "Perhaps on all of us, together again. I think it is best you return to your own home for the Sabbath and find your own paths for reflection, rest and rejuvenation, yes?"

Together, we answered, "yes."

SUNDAY, JULY 13, 1975

Heading home on the train from Brooklyn that previous Friday afternoon, we had decided to heed Grandfather's advice about using the Sabbath for our rejuvenation and added our own initiative. We had decided to make something from the remaining few days of our originally planned vacation by taking a modified trip north. We would rent a car and leave Sunday to visit the state capital in Albany, then drive to Lake George and Saratoga for a few days. Down to Cooperstown and the Baseball Hall of Fame on Friday, staying over in Cooperstown to Sunday when we would return home.

We had pretty much nailed down our plans and started to make arrangements when my mother called. She sounded elated, but I wrote it off as her usual reaction to my grandfather's completing a case. I shared our travel plans with her, but she asked, no, she pretty much insisted, that we delay leaving for a day and come over for dinner Sunday night.

"Joel, after a very difficult week, it will be good for the family to be together. We could make it an early dinner, say 5:00, which will give you and Aliya time to return home early and complete packing? And I will have a friend come over too. Perhaps I am being selfish, but I would like it if you could."

"Mom, you see... Well, alright," I answered. "If it's okay with Aliya, we'll come."

Aliya readily agreed.

We arrived on Sunday around 2:00. Aliya went immediately to assist my mother with dinner preparation. Though I offered to help, they politely suggested I keep Grandfather company in the living room.

"I think Aliya and I will use the time to catch up, and I know how much you and Zaida love watching baseball together," my mother said, escorting me out of the kitchen.

Grandfather had on the Mets game. We watched the Mets lose, swept that weekend in a four-game series by the Cincinnati Big Red Machine which would go on to win the World Series that year. We spent most of the game lauding the skills of Pete Rose, Johnny Bench, Joe Morgan, and others. Toward the game's conclusion, Grandfather commented:

"But you know whom I admire most on this magnificent team? It is Mr. Anderson, who has the outstanding managerial capacity to lead such an immense assemblage of talent and not squander any of it."

The game ended around 4:00. Grandfather and I drifted into casual conversation. We didn't talk about the Flaum case. The doorbell rang, and I looked at my watch. 4:55.

"I'll get it," I announced jumping up.

I opened the door expecting to see a lady friend of my mother. Instead, I faced a man, about my height, balding, with a knit kippah on his head, wearing glasses. He was dressed in a button-down shirt, tie, sports jacket and light summer slacks. I glanced around to see if anyone else was with him.

After a moment, he extended his hand and said, "Hi, you might remember me from CPH? I'm Martin Ross, a friend of your mother."

"A friend of… Oh, oh. Pleased to see you again."

I strained to smile. Then I shook his hand and motioned him into our house.

Milton Keynes UK
Ingram Content Group UK Ltd.
UKHW042335081024
449373UK00006B/56